House of Secrets

Book Six of the Vital Secrets Series

D.F. Hart

with

K.W. Branzell

2 Of Harts Publishing

*I feel supremely blessed to have an awesome group of ARC readers –
my 'Hart's Heroes'.*

Among these folks are Don B, Leslie M, and Siobhan A.

*I am forever grateful for your passion, your excitement, your feedback,
and your support. You guys make this already fun journey even more
amazing for me.*

This is for you.

*With Affection,
D.F. Hart*

Prologue
Six years earlier...

"WHAT DO YOU THINK, PASTOR?"

Evangelist Remiel Lighte stood at the edge of a tiny little body of water a few miles south and east of a tiny little town in Jack County, Texas.

"How many acres is this again?"

"Just over two hundred. And it includes twenty acres' worth of this lake, since the land boundaries are *there*," his companion pointed, "and *there*, and they extend across the water."

Remiel closed his eyes and steepled his hands in front of his chest, a gesture that he had relied on for years to settle his nerves and open his mind to divine guidance.

Yes, he thought to himself as peace washed over him. *This feels like home. This location is perfect for my ministry.*

He opened his eyes and smiled as he turned to the old man standing beside him.

"Brother Abel," Remiel murmured, placing a hand lovingly on the man's shoulder, "I appreciate and accept your generous praise offering."

Chapter One

"You're getting pretty good at this," Nathan told Bella as he watched her maneuver herself up and off the chair, using her two-wheeled walker to help keep her steady.

It had been a long hard seven months since her accident, but Bella Thomas had finally received medical clearance to ditch the wheelchair – for short distances, at least – and do some actual walking outside of her scheduled physical therapy regimen.

"Yep. But the end goal is to be able to walk across the stage under my own power at graduation in three months. So just be ready, because in no time at all I will be back to my old self again, and when I am, *you* owe me dinner and dancing," she announced.

"Whoa, whoa. I never mentioned dinner," her husband teased, and she playfully swatted his arm.

"It's a given," she retorted with a mock pout as she shuffled her way over to the whistling kettle on the stovetop.

"So, what's on your list to conquer today?" Bella asked as she poured hot water over the teabag in her favorite mug, then leaned against the counter to wait while her drink steeped to the proper strength.

"Well, Jamesin's trial starts today. Sadly, I am barred from attending," Nathan answered with a grim look as he cleaned off Charlie's face and hands, then lifted the highchair's tray to free his son.

"Nothing would make me happier than listening to all the evidence against him being read into the record, but the Director thinks it's best if I keep my distance."

Bella tilted her head and gazed at him, remembering his uncharacteristic outburst of violence toward a sinister serial killer that had almost cost her family everything, including her husband's freedom.

"I think that's a wise idea," she murmured.

"Yeah, me too," he said on a heavy sigh. "But Steve sent me some files that I can be working on to distract myself. Besides, Lizzie's going, and she can be my eyes and ears since I don't get to see that psycho's downfall for myself."

And there is another thing I am grateful for, Bella thought to herself. *That he and Lizzie patched things up. They make an excellent team and there is no one I trust more to watch out for Nathan.*

Nathan asking Charlie, "You ready to go play at daycare, buddy?" and Charlie's emphatic *"go!"* brought Bella out of her reverie, and she laughed.

"I take it that's a yes. Have fun today, Charlie."

Nathan scooped him up and carried him over to his mother for a big kiss before Nathan kissed her as well.

"I love you, Bella. See you this afternoon."

"I love you too. I'll be right here waiting," Bella answered with a grin.

"Bye, Mommy!" Charlie whooped as Nathan carried him out, and Bella chuckled when Nathan's conversation with the toddler floated back to her as the two loves of her life headed toward the front door.

"Okay, buddy. Let's get you strapped in, and we will get on the road. Are you driving, or am I?"

"I just remembered that I've got a client meeting tonight over dinner," Donny said, his voice and face filled with a silent apology. "Mike and Grace are in town from Vail and want to get together."

"It's all right, since I have no idea what time I'll be home anyway," Lizzie assured him as she looked through her side of the closet for a suitable blouse to wear to work. "Among other things, the Jamesin trial starts today."

"Oh. Well, if you don't get too caught up, maybe you can meet us? I've reserved a table for four at Reata. Seven o'clock."

Lizzie's ears perked up.

"Reata? I will try my best to be on time."

She walked past him while shrugging into her blouse, and Donny chuckled before he reached out and caught her around the waist to turn her to face him.

"Oh, so since it's Reata, you're in?"

"Yep," Lizzie fired back, her eyes sparkling with mirth.

"I see how you are," Donny teased as he buttoned up her blouse for her. "It's all about the food, not me."

"That is so not true... it's not *all* about the food," she said, and hummed appreciation in her throat when he leaned down and kissed her. "And if you keep doing that, I am going to be late."

"Hey, I'm behaving myself very well for a newlywed, thank you. Exhibit A – your shirt got *less* revealing with my help, instead of ending up on the floor."

"I know, and I appreciate it – and I will make it up to you later."

"I'm gonna hold you to that, my very Special Agent Zimmerman."

Four hundred and ten miles south, in Corpus Christi, Texas, investigative reporter Susan Lawford was completely dumbfounded at the sudden turn the unscheduled morning meeting with her boss's boss had taken.

"What do you mean, 'indefinitely'?" she asked, her eyes wide with surprise.

"Exactly what it sounds like," Roger, the smarmy seventy-something owner and editor-in-chief of underground newspaper *The Watcher* said smugly. "While your... *relationship* with Mr. Andersen is not strictly against company policy, it does fall into a bit of a gray area, and I need some time to mull it over. So, I'm placing you on paid leave until further notice."

Susan closed her eyes and inhaled sharply through her nose, trying desperately to rein in her temper.

Who I date is none of your business, old man, she seethed in her head. *Besides, didn't your bubble-brained wife number three start out in the secretarial pool here? You have* zero room *to talk.*

"I'm the best investigative reporter you have, and you know it. Sidelining me won't do a thing except help you miss a lot of good stories."

"Matter of opinion," the owner said dismissively, waving his hand at her. "And irrelevant. What's important is the integrity of this paper."

Susan only barely managed to restrain herself from rolling her eyes and emitting a snort of derision.

That's rich. He wouldn't know integrity if it jumped up and bit him squarely on the...

And, railing about this is not helping, she chided herself. *Nod and smile, get out of here, and go home and polish up your resume. It's time to move on from this dump.*

"Whatever. *Sir,*" Susan ground out through gritted teeth, then stood and stomped out of his office to gather up her things from her cubicle and flee.

"You going to court today?"

"I am," Annie confirmed. "I'm supposed to leave with Lizzie in about five minutes. You?"

"I had planned to, but Nathan's asked me to hang out here," Ben, her teammate and boyfriend, responded with a shrug. "Steve sent down some profiles to work on."

"Huh. Well, I guess I will see you back here at some point today, then."

The conversation faltered into silence.

What is up with you lately? Annie almost asked but stopped herself. For two weeks solid, Ben had been giving off a strange vibe that she just could not decipher.

Can't force it. Whatever is going on with him is his to deal with, I guess. If he wants to share, he will tell me.

"Okay, so, see you later," she said abruptly, and left the break-room, relieved to see Lizzie waiting for her at her desk.

"You ready?"

"I am. Let's roll."

The two women rode the elevator down to the parking garage in silence. It was not until they climbed into Lizzie's vehicle that Lizzie broke the oppressive quiet.

"So, everything good with you two?" Lizzie asked Annie as they put on their seat belts.

"Truthfully? I have no idea. He's been acting super strange lately," Annie confessed, then turned pink. "I mean, I probably shouldn't even be talking to you about this, but you asked me."

"True, I did," Lizzie admitted cheerfully as she started her SUV for the short drive to the federal courthouse. "Because I can almost cut the tension between you two with a knife lately, and it concerns me, to be honest. Last thing we need as a team are distractions. That could get somebody hurt."

"I know that," Annie retorted a little sharply, then hunched her shoulders when Lizzie's eyebrow rose.

"Sorry. It's just... I am all over the place lately, and I have no idea what is running through that thick skull of his, and yeah, I worry about whatever this is putting us and the rest of the team at risk. And I have no idea how to fix it other than transfer off the team."

"Do you *want* to leave?"

"No. No, I don't. I like being a part of this team and I don't want to start over again somewhere else."

"Okay, then," Lizzie told her calmly. "Then you two are going to *have* to work on whatever is going on between you and get it solved."

Lizzie and Annie patiently made their way through the security checkpoint and took seats on the last row inside the courtroom.

"Lucky we got here early," Annie remarked quietly. "At this rate, it will be standing room only in here."

"Especially if the media is allowed in," Lizzie agreed. "That crowd outside was *huge*."

"It was. Glad I don't have to deal with them."

Lizzie's cell phone buzzed on her hip, and she retrieved it long enough to skim the message from Tank.

Tucker Cole Lydealea, nine pounds, four ounces, born at seven-eighteen this morning, the text read, and was accompanied by a picture of two tired but elated new parents with their baby boy.

She grinned and fired off a quick reply.

Tank, that's awesome! Congrats! I am in court right now but will call you later. Love you guys! – Zim.

As Lizzie put her phone away, Annie glanced around the gallery, then nudged her co-worker.

"See that man over there? Brown suit and glasses?"

"Yes. Who is he?"

"Mark Steward," Annie said sadly. "Elaine's husband and Timmy's dad. I'll remember the day Ben and I interviewed him for the rest of my life. It was heartbreaking."

The proceedings got underway promptly at ten a.m. as scheduled, starting with the jury being seated and the appearance of the defendant. The judge took his position on the bench and court was called to order.

Next came the list of indictments. With fifty-nine separate counts levied against Jamesin, noting the indictments for the official record took upwards of ten minutes.

One by one, the victims' names were read. Lizzie felt her own eyes misting up in response to the soft sobs of mothers and fathers whose children's lives had been cut short echoing through the large, eerily silent room. Her gaze drifted back to the bereft-looking man in the brown suit just in time to see tears coursing steadily down his cheeks as he stared straight ahead.

She closed her eyes and swallowed hard against the lump that formed in her throat when the memory of how the monster on trial had stumbled across Charlie rushed to the front of her consciousness.

Once the indictments were finished, the judge solemnly cleared his throat, then called for opening statements, and the lead prosecutor rose to make his first impression on the jury.

Susan had just gotten back to her apartment when her cell phone rang.

"Are you all right? I heard about what happened," she heard Trevor's voice, warm and concerned, say across the line.

"I'm fine, except we work for a crusty old hypocritical dickwad," she hissed as she set the box of her belongings down on her dinette table with an extremely satisfying thud. "Let me guess. *You* didn't get put on indefinite leave."

"I did, actually - but only after Carlos in Human Resources pointed out to Roger that treating us differently was illegal," Trevor confirmed. "So, there you go. Want some company? I happen to know for a fact that both our schedules just got cleared for the foreseeable future. I can pick up some pizza and beer on the way over, and we can work on our resumes together."

"Sounds like a plan, because my time at *The Watcher* is done, I can promise you that. I am not staying in an environment where my personal life is on trial. We didn't break any rules or company policies, and we are two consenting adults. If Roger has a problem with us dating, it is *his* problem, not mine."

"Just so you know, I'm not planning on staying there, either, for the exact same reasons. And I feel the same way you do, and we'll get through it together. Now, you want the usual?"

"Sure. See you in a bit."

Susan hung up and headed to the shower. When she returned to the kitchen fifteen minutes later, she noticed she had missed a call, so she opened her voicemail app and pressed 'play'.

Hey sis. Call me when you get a chance. I've got some awesome news!

Grinning at how happy Sophie sounded, Susan dialed and waited.

"Hey, you, what's up?'

"I have a gig!"

"That's awesome! Tell me about it."

"Well, there's this company in North Texas that's been looking for a videographer, and they reached out. They have seen some of my work on YouTube and they want me to do a project for them as a trial run. If it works out, I will have a full-time job. I'm leaving in the morning."

"Wow, that's fast," Susan mentioned as the hair on the back of her neck began to stand on end.

Something is not right here, she thought to herself. *Should I mention it?*

But as she listened to Sophie gush with excitement, her nerves settled. The younger half-sister that she had only discovered she had in the last year was brimming with confidence, something that Susan knew Sophie had been struggling with for several months.

You are just being overprotective. This will be good for her. Be supportive.

They talked for another twenty minutes, until Sophie said, "Guess I'd better spend the rest of today getting organized and packed so I can make my flight on time in the morning."

"You're flying? But you hate to fly."

"Yeah," Sophie sighed. "I do. But it is a five-hour drive one way. Besides, they are paying for the plane ticket, so I am only out a little of my time if it doesn't pan out. Anyway - I am booked on the seven-fifteen flight from Houston to Dallas, and you know I am *not* a morning person, so, I'd better square everything away now."

Susan chuckled.

"I remember. Be safe, and text me when you land, okay?"

"You got it. Love you, big sis."

"Love you too, little sis."

Susan held the phone to her ear a moment longer after Sophie had disconnected.

"It will be fine. Just fine," she murmured to herself. "Stop worrying. She is twenty-four and she's got an excellent head on her shoulders. She's got this."

Sighing, she plugged her phone into its charger.

***

By the time court adjourned for the day, the two FBI agents had reached their limits.

"That was *brutal*," Annie sighed with sadness when she and Lizzie walked out of the building. "*So* much raw grief in that room. I felt it weighing me down like a lead blanket."

Lizzie could only nod in response, her emotions too close to the surface to articulate cleanly.

I don't know if I can deal with sitting through this every day, Lizzie realized. *All those kids...*

"You okay?" Annie asked.

"That was... rough," Lizzie conceded as she turned to her teammate, "and to be honest, I was just questioning whether or not I can stand to be in there for the entire trial."

"You and me both, sister, you and me both."

Lizzie dropped Annie off at the office, then headed home.

On the way, she called her old partner, and began to feel the cloud lift from her soul the moment Tank's voice surrounded her through her car's speakers.

"Hey Zim!" Tank said softly. "I gotta be quiet, Tucker and Renee are both sleeping right now. How you doing, girl?"

"I'm good. Tank, that baby is *precious*. I can't wait to meet him and hold him."

They talked the entire drive, and Lizzie's mood had shifted from bleak back to merely somber by the time she got home just before six o'clock. Donny sensed it, and at once crossed the room to her for a hug.

"Rough day," he guessed, and she nodded silently against his chest.

"If you want, you can stay here and relax and I promise to bring you back some food," he offered.

"No," Lizzie decided, then lifted her head to look at him. "I really need 'normal' tonight to help wash away the horrible aspects of my day. Just let me get changed right quick and we'll go to dinner."

"Your call, Liz. We'll leave whenever you're ready."

"There *was* one awesome thing that happened today. I heard from Tank," she called out as she walked swiftly to the bedroom to change. "I'm an aunt. Renee had the baby this morning."

"That's great!" Donny exclaimed, following her down the hall to lean against the doorframe. "Everybody's healthy, I take it."

"Yep. Check out this picture," Lizzie said, and opened her text messages then handed Donny the phone.

"Man, that kid has a head full of hair, doesn't he?"

Lizzie grinned, her first one since before the trial started.

"I know, right? And he was over nine pounds. But Tank said everything went smoothly, no issues, and he and Renee are exhausted but thrilled. And they asked me to be Tucker's godmother."

"Sounds like we're making a trip to Houston soon."

"That we are. I was thinking next weekend. Give them a chance to get home from the hospital and get settled in."

Nathan Thomas had just pulled into his driveway when his phone rang.

"Good, you got my message about that profile," Nathan started to say, but Steve cut him off in an uncharacteristic show of impatience.

"Let's get to that in a minute. I just found out some information that you really need to know about."

Alarmed, Nathan leaned forward to rest his arms on the steering wheel and frowned.

"I know that tone. Whatever you're about to tell me isn't good."

"No, it isn't. Not at all. You know we kept the mole in place in Chicago, right?"

"Yes."

"I just got off the phone with the Director up there. She came to him late this afternoon and told him that she's been asked by her cartel handler for some information."

"As usual. And?"

"Nathan," Steve said gently, his voice tight with tension, "she's been asked to provide in-depth dossiers on you and the people on your team in Dallas."

Nathan lowered his forehead to the steering wheel, his mind racing as he processed the information.

"After all this time? Jones left the area months ago, so why is this happening *now*?"

"I know. It doesn't make sense to me either. I don't know what to tell you, Nathan."

"Can she even access that information?"

"No, she doesn't have the clearance to get into much of anything anymore – the Director made sure of that. But it worries me that the cartel even wants it – not to mention the steps they might take to get it. You watch your backs down there. Things could get ugly."

Chapter Two

Sᴏᴘʜɪᴇ ᴛʀɪᴇᴅ her best to remember to breathe normally the following morning as she found her assigned seat on row twelve, then buckled and tightened down the lap belt as far as she could without cutting off her circulation.

The flight's only an hour, she reminded herself. *One hour. You can do this.*

To distract herself, she reached down and pulled out a slender notebook, her iPod, a pen, and her earbuds from her backpack, then shoved the bag back under the seat in front of her.

She opened the notebook and reviewed the handful of notes she had taken during the phone interview.

Lighte Limited – based near Cundiff, Texas. Looking for a full-time permanent videographer. Position includes housing, transportation, and all meals, in addition to fifty thousand dollars per year as the starting salary.

She had tried her best not to gasp aloud like a complete rookie when the man she was speaking to told her all that, and she'd triple underlined the little tidbit of information about the pay in her notes.

Fifty thousand.

She still had trouble picturing it. That kind of money would be a huge step up. Her current situation was the odd bit of freelance work sandwiched between two waitressing jobs to make enough to cover the exorbitantly high rent for her efficiency apartment.

It's a chance to finally be able to focus solely on what I love for a living, and not *eat ramen every day,* she reminded herself. *Yes, for that chance, I can handle one hour on a plane.*

She inserted her earbuds, queued up her favorite playlist, and settled in for the flight toward her future.

———

Nathan gathered his team in the conference room at seven-forty-five and relayed the ominous news from Steve.

"That's not good," Ben muttered under his breath. "Not good at all."

"What's the plan, boss? Misdirection?" Lizzie asked.

"I'm not sure yet. We don't even know for certain that they will try anything, so, I don't think it makes sense for any of us to abort our day-to-day lives just yet."

He paused and looked at his team.

"But," he continued carefully, "this group was mentioned specifically. As a result, I *do* think it's an excellent idea for each of you to form an individual plan that can be activated at a moment's notice, should the worst-case scenario start to happen."

"A bug-out plan," Annie said evenly.

"Yes. And until further notice, no one goes into the field alone. We're pairing up in whatever we do for a while."

———

When the meeting adjourned, Ben motioned to Annie to wait for him. He murmured a few words to Nathan, then walked over to her.

"Can we talk for a minute?"

She shrugged.

"Sure."

They wandered down the hall until they found an empty office, and no sooner had Ben shut the door than he shocked the hell out of her by saying, "Move in with me."

"What?"

"At least until all this blows over. It will be safer."

Annie folded her arms across her chest and narrowed her eyes at him.

"Why are you looking at me like that? We'll be safer together, and you know it."

Unfazed, Annie jutted out her chin.

"Is that the only reason you want me to move in? Because some bad guy somewhere might come after us?"

"Well, no," Ben said, and Annie watched his ears turning uncharacteristically pink as he looked at the floor. "I, um…. I've been wanting to ask you for a while now."

"Is that why you've been so weird lately?" Annie blurted suddenly, and Ben's gaze jerked upward to meet hers.

"What? I have not been *weird*. I've just… got a lot on my mind lately, is all."

They stared at each other, Annie tapping one foot, and Ben frowning.

"Yes," Annie finally said, then marched around him to get to the door.

"Yes, what?"

"Yes, I will move in with you," she announced, and left quickly so he wouldn't see the megawatt smile beginning to form on her face.

Sophie gave a silent but heartfelt thanks when the plane's wheels touched down safely on the runway at Dallas/Fort Worth International Airport. Within ten minutes, the pilots had ferried them safely to their arrival gate, and the passengers disembarked rapidly, those around her bound for destinations Sophie could only guess.

She turned on her phone, then kept her promise to her big sister.

I'm here in one piece. Wish me luck!

Her phone chirped, and she grinned at Susan's response.

Good. Now go knock 'em dead. You got this!

Shrugging her backpack onto her shoulders, Sophie made her way to baggage claim to wait for her small black suitcase with the pink ribbon tied on its handle to appear on the conveyor.

Seven minutes later she was rewarded for her patience and hefted her bag off the carousel and down onto the floor, then extended the bag's handle to its fullest height for easier maneuvering.

Luggage in tow, she turned to make her way toward the car rental counters and was shocked to see a man with brown hair, who looked to be in his mid-forties, scanning the crowd – and holding a small sign with her name neatly printed on it.

Wow. How cool is that?

She cleared her throat, straightened her shoulders, and walked over to him.

"Good morning, I'm Sophie Drimmel," she said politely, and the man smiled.

"Good morning. It's nice to meet you in person. I'm Andreas," he answered, and stuck out his hand to firmly shake hers. "We spoke on the phone the other day. How was your flight?"

"Given that I'm not really a fan of flying, it was better than I expected," she remarked, and his smile grew.

"Well, welcome to Dallas. Right this way, please."

They walked side-by-side out of the terminal and into the parking garage, where Andreas loaded her suitcase into the back of a black SUV, then opened the front passenger door for her.

"Lighte Limited's headquarters is about sixty-five miles from here, so, it will take us about an hour," Andreas advised her. "Well, I say that. *Normally* it would. Rush hour traffic will add to that. But we should definitely be there by ten."

She nodded, smiled, and buckled her seat belt, ready to get her on-the-job audition underway as soon as possible.

It was Ben's turn to make an appearance in the gallery at the Jamesin trial on the team's behalf. Annie opted to join him, since per Nathan's announcement Ben could not go alone.

"Hopefully today will be easier to get through," she said wistfully as they exited the elevator and walked to Ben's car. "Yesterday was heartbreaking to witness."

"The families?"

"Yeah. Especially Mark Steward. He just looked so... *lost.*"

He reached over and squeezed her hand in understanding.

"That's the toughest part of what we do," Ben said solemnly. "Interact with those who are grieving and try our best to give them some sort of closure somehow. But a lot of times, it's just not enough."

"Do you ever think about doing something else?"

"Sometimes," he admitted. "But then again, I love this job. I feel like I can make a real difference. Keeping that in mind makes the bad stuff a little easier to deal with so I can focus on the good."

The conversation lapsed as they made the drive to the courthouse.

Andreas kept Sophie's mind occupied during what turned out to be a seventy-three-minute drive by asking her questions about herself. By nine-fifty-two they were making a left-hand turn from the main road onto a gravel side road.

As Andreas smoothly navigated the terrain, Sophie looked out the windows and noticed that the area did not seem to be developed much at all. Mesquite trees with a few oaks and pines scattered into the mix was all she could see past the barbed wire fence that lined either side of the road.

Man, I really expected that Lighte Limited would be in the city limits... I wonder how close the nearest town is...

Andreas speaking to her disrupted her musings.

"I'm so sorry, what were you saying?"

He grinned.

"I was saying, I bet you're wondering where on earth we're heading right now."

Sophie chuckled nervously.

"I was, actually. This seems very... rural. Undeveloped."

"The current surroundings, yes. Our company's location, no. You'll see."

A half-mile and a right turn later, Andreas rolled the SUV to a smooth stop outside an ornate, wrought-iron gate directly underneath a massive arch with more iron work that spelled out 'Lighte's Landing' in an elegant script.

He put the vehicle's transmission into 'park' then climbed out of the SUV and walked over to a little square panel mounted on a four-foot-high steel pole. He pressed some buttons, and the electronically controlled gate began to slide back to allow them to pass.

"Welcome to Lighte's Landing," Andreas said with a smile once he had climbed back in behind the wheel and driven through the now open gateway.

Sophie stared straight ahead through the windshield, willing her mouth to not drop wide open at the stark difference. The rough, untamed wildness outside the gate did not continue inside the property's parameters. Now, the trees lining either side of the paved driveway were orderly and well-maintained.

"How big is this place?" she asked, awe-struck.

"Two hundred ten acres total, including some lakefront."

"Wow," was all she could think of to say in response.

They drove another quarter of a mile, up a slight incline then down again, and Sophie's eyebrows raised as the main facility itself came into view – a surprisingly modest-looking, rectangular one-story structure of brick, wood, and glass in warm earth tones. The building's very design seemed to embrace, rather than overshadow, the natural beauty of its surroundings.

"That is really, really pretty," she blurted.

"Thanks. We wanted to honor the landscape as much as possible but still have great functionality."

Andreas pulled up to the front doors situated halfway down the front of the structure and parked.

"We can leave your bag in the car for now, if you'd like," he offered, but Sophie shook her head.

"It's got some of my equipment in it. I'll grab it."

"As you wish. Right this way."

Andreas retrieved her suitcase, then led the way into the building. He held the door open for her, and when she crossed the threshold, Sophie gasped as she gazed around at the lobby area.

Just off to the right, situated between two milk-chocolate-colored armchairs, was a huge wall-mounted natural stone fountain with rustic copper accents and beautifully colorful, smooth stones. The water trickling down the façade onto the stones made a soothing sound, and Sophie felt her shoulders relax in response.

In the center of the room two long, dark tan couches complemented the earth-toned color scheme and faced each other on the stacked stone flooring to allow anyone who gathered to easily engage in conversation.

Four grand windows, one on each side of the door she had just walked through and two more across the room, allowed for plenty of natural light, as did the two skylights overhead.

The decorative touches in the space were minimal, but effective – strategically placed live plants and flowers.

"This place is beautiful. So tranquil," she murmured as she took it all in.

"That was the goal. Pastor Lighte believes it is important for our surroundings to be a source of calm and comfort, even at work."

"*Pastor* Lighte?"

Andreas smiled.

"Yes. Lighte Limited is the legal setup for his ministry."

"Oh," Sophie said, brows knitting together, not sure what else to say for a moment.

"Are you all right? You look like you have a question."

"Yes," she responded quickly. "With him being a pastor and all, um... I mean... I guess you could say I've never been much on organized religion, so..."

"And that's okay," Andreas said gently. "Neither is he. You'll understand what I mean by that once you meet him."

He paused and glanced at his watch.

"Speaking of which, we need to get moving. You ready?"

Sophie took a deep breath, then nodded.

"I'm ready."

Andreas held out his hand, gesturing to the open hallway to their left. Sophie followed her guide down the hallway, growing more nervous with each passing step. He paused outside a beautiful mahogany door and knocked.

"Come in," Sophie heard a deep, rich baritone voice say, and Andreas motioned her forward.

Sophie stepped through the door that he opened for her, and her gaze was at once drawn to the man sitting behind the executive-style desk.

"Good morning," he said warmly, then stood and came around the desk to walk over to her, his hand outstretched in greeting. "It's so nice to meet you, Sophie. I'm Remiel Lighte."

She hesitantly took the handshake he offered, using the proximity to study him more closely. She guessed him to be in his late forties or early fifties, and a foot taller than her, with striking green eyes and wheat-blond hair.

"Nice to meet you, too, sir... Pastor... Mr. Lighte," Sophie stammered, and watched his green eyes sparkle with amusement.

"You can call me Pastor, or Brother Remiel, or even just Remiel – whatever is most comfortable for you, Sophie. No need for 'mister' – or 'sir' for that matter. Now, please have a seat, and let's talk about why I'd like you to come work for me."

Meanwhile, in the courtroom in Dallas, Ben and Annie were tucked side-by-side into a packed gallery. News of Dr. Jamesin's exploits, plus coverage of the emotional first day's activities, had caused a massive surge of out-of-state news agencies sending their reps to cover the trial, as well.

By ten a.m. Judge Burns, a typically genial man, had had enough. He formally paused the proceedings, had the bailiff escort the jury out, and then completely lost his temper – something unheard of in his twenty-nine years on the bench. His tirade ended with an invitation to several misbehaving members of the press to leave his courtroom and never, ever return – then he watched, glowering, as the banished offenders hastily gathered up their belongings and retreated from his sight.

That done, he issued a stern and crystal-clear warning to those media members left in attendance that he would brook no further nonsense.

"One more misstep from *any* of you, and I will kick every last one of you out and invoke a media blackout for the remainder of this trial," he growled. "Do I make myself clear?"

The entire media section of the gallery nodded its understanding simultaneously, and Annie had to stifle a grin at the sight of over fifty seasoned reporters with humbled – and chastened – expressions all bobbing their heads in unison.

"Good. Now, let's keep going. Bailiff, please escort the jurors back to their seats. Mister Prosecutor, please be ready to call your next witness the moment we get underway again."

Ten minutes later the trial resumed, and Ben and Annie were both shocked when the next witness called to testify was Mark Steward.

"Did you expect that?" Annie murmured.

"Yes, but not this early in the proceedings," Ben murmured back.

Once he had raised his right hand and was sworn in, Mark Steward took his seat in the witness box, and Annie swallowed hard when his heartbroken spirit was revealed in his expression for all to see.

The prosecutor gently led him through a series of questions, pausing on occasion to allow Mr. Steward to regain his composure. The gallery was dead silent, everyone in attendance riveted by the witness's obvious devastation.

By the time they wrapped up their first conversation, Sophie realized any preconceived notions she'd had about evangelists may not have been right.

Then again, I have never met one before. I have only ever heard about the ones that get in trouble for embezzlement or cheating on their wives. But Remiel seems like he is just a normal guy. Personable. His career is about his faith, that's all, she affirmed in her mind as they walked out of the main building and down the narrow sidewalk to the chapel on premises.

"Most of our current media platform centers around a weekly prerecorded podcast," he explained as they strolled. "But I'm definitely open to suggestions as to how we can expand on that – and our online presence in general. Live streaming, for example. Daily devotionals. Social media, even. Unusual ways to reach those who are hurting and help them."

He opened the door for her and ushered her inside.

"We've done most of the recordings in here so far," he said with a grin. "But I don't want to be one of those boring old preachers. Part of helping people is connecting with them in a way that speaks to them directly, and I know for a lot of people, it can be off-putting if it's too much like attending church."

Sophie could not help but grin back.

"Well, if nothing else, there's always a green screen approach, and then you just populate the background however you like. But if the rest of the property here is anything like what I have seen so far, I bet we could find some beautiful outdoor locations to record, as well. Andreas said you have two hundred acres here?"

"We do. The land was gifted to the ministry by one of the congregation's members. Brother Abel was a sweet, sweet man, God rest his soul. Loved meeting and interacting with people."

He showed her around the small sanctuary, then asked, "So, let's get started, shall we? I'm interested to see your work firsthand."

Once the prosecutor finished, the defense attorney rose and approached the witness stand to question Mr. Steward.

Annie clutched Ben's hand and waited anxiously, hoping that Jamesin's lawyer would tread lightly. To her immense relief, he did, handling his cross-examination of a grieving widower and parent with delicate empathy.

Finally, the defense counsel ended his questioning, and a solemn, sympathetic judge murmured, "You're free to leave the witness stand, sir."

Mark Steward made eye contact only long enough to nod his understanding, then stood and stepped out of the witness box, oblivious to most of the jurors fighting back tears after hearing his story.

During the natural pause between witnesses, Judge Burns and both lawyers were all perusing papers in front of them and not paying any attention as Steward walked slowly back toward his seat.

As a result, all three were startled when the panicked screams started.

Annie and Ben watched, horrified, as Mark Steward suddenly charged the defendant's table, toppled the defendant over backward in his chair, then stabbed Dr. Philip Edmund Jamesin to death in the middle of a courtroom in full view of over one-hundred-fifty people.

Two officers closest to Steward's position wrestled him into submission and seized the composite blade that he had managed to sneak past the metal detectors. Another police officer called urgently for an ambulance while more officers quickly emptied the courtroom of jurors and all spectators.

But Ben and Annie were allowed to remain once they displayed their badges, and Ben immediately pulled out his phone and called Nathan.

"Boss," he murmured, "you need to come to the courthouse. *Now.*"

"So, is this videographer position something new that's been created, or would I be filling a vacancy?" Sophie asked after they reviewed the short clip she had put together as her audition.

"You'd be filling a vacancy," Remiel said with a sorrowful smile. "Sister Marjorie passed on a few weeks ago."

"Oh. I am so sorry to hear that. What happened?"

"She had a heart attack in her sleep, from what we could tell. And she had no living relatives, so we had a little ceremony for her and buried her here. Many of our members are all alone out in the world, and as a result they live here on the property. It's convenient for them, but more importantly, here they have a family again, people they can count on."

"So.... everyone lives in the compound?"

"On the *property*, yes, most everyone."

Sophie's eyebrows raised and it was out before she could stop herself.

"Um... is this a cult?"

Remiel stopped dead in his tracks and stared at her intently before he began to belly laugh.

"Wow," he finally managed, wiping tears from his cheeks. "Most definitely *not* a cult - but that was hilarious."

"But you said everybody lives here," she began.

"Yes, but only if they *choose* to. Lighte's Landing is more like a commune than anything else. Everybody here is free to come and go as they please, and if the spirit moves them to leave for good, that is their choice. No one is here against their will. Besides, cults usually have some guy claiming to be a messiah or some sort of prophet. I am most assuredly not either one of those – and I don't want to be."

He paused and grinned, and she felt the corners of her mouth turning up in response.

"I'm just a guy who went through a lot, Sophie. But when I finally found hope again, I found peace, and the idea of helping others find it too has led me to where I am now. That is the whole reason I built Lighte's Landing. I am only a pastor who wants to help people, nothing more."

You sure are not what I expected, I know this much, she observed to herself.

"Speaking of - would you like to see the housing?" he asked. "Our little cabins are quite pretty. Matter of fact, you're welcome to stay the night in one, see what you think. In the meantime, let's head to the dining room. You must be hungry. You can have lunch with us and meet everybody."

"Sure, I'd like that."

Nathan Thomas arrived within fifteen minutes of Ben's call. He stood silently over the body sprawled out on the hardwood floor, looking down at the pale, still, very dead man whose face had haunted his dreams for months.

He will never hurt another living soul ever again, he thought to himself with grim satisfaction, no small amount of relief, and not one single ounce of sympathy.

He nodded curtly, once, then turned his attention to the two agents waiting for him.

"Where did they take Mark Steward?"

"County lockup, six blocks down."

"I'm going to go see him," Nathan announced. "You're welcome to come with me."

Chapter Three

NATHAN, Ben, and Annie signed in and checked their sidearms, then followed an officer down the hallway past the secured double-doors until they reached a visitation room. Several minutes passed before Mark Steward was brought in and seated across from them.

"Mr. Steward, I'm Nathan Thomas, a profiler with the FBI. I trust you remember Ben and Annie," he began, gesturing toward them.

"I do, barely," Mark said softly, holding Annie's gaze. "I think they came to see me at my house not long after Elaine and Timmy…"

His voice trailed off to silence as large tears began to fall once more.

Annie extended her hand across the table and Mark wordlessly accepted the tissue she offered him.

After a few minutes he sighed heavily, and muttered, "So I guess you're here to ask me why I killed him."

"I'm pretty sure I already know the answer," Nathan said gently. "But yes, I'd like to hear it from you."

"Because he was a monster," Mark replied, his eyes blazing, his entire body suddenly vibrating with anger. "Do *you* know what he did up in Minneapolis all those years ago? Because *I* do. The moment I found out his name I started digging into his background. And if those idiots in Minnesota had done their jobs and kept him in custody instead of letting him slip through their fingers, we would not be here right now. My family and all those other people might still be alive."

There was nothing that Nathan, Ben, or Annie could say, because the man had a completely valid point.

"I did my homework, and then I started building. You see, I am a mechanical engineer, Agent Thomas, and I am exceptionally good at what I do. I fabricated a weapon that could get through any security measures undetected, then just waited for my opportunity."

Nathan watched him from across the table, his face purposely blank while in his mind he was nodding enthusiastically.

Because I would have done the same thing if I am being honest. I started down that same road in a room very much like this one.

Thank God I had Lizzie and Ben there to pull me back.

Nathan leaned forward, rested his arms on the table, and spoke from his heart.

"Believe me when I tell you that I know *exactly* how you must have felt," Nathan told him quietly. "More than you will ever know. But we had him, Mark. And we were going to be able to send him to death row for his crimes."

He paused, making sure he had Steward's full attention.

"And now you have thrown *your* life away, too. There's no coming back from this," he said, echoing Lizzie's very words to him from not that long ago.

Mark Steward just looked at him for several moments.

"I know you mean well, Agent Thomas. And I appreciate your honesty. I really do. But here's the thing," he said wearily. "The moment my wife and child died, so did my reason for living. I have nothing left. But at least I will go to my grave knowing that the world is rid of him, so I have no regrets at all about what I did. I'd do it again a thousand times."

And with that, Mark Steward swiveled his head to look over his shoulder at the guard standing by the door.

"I'd like to leave now, please."

As the guard helped him rise to his feet, he nodded at Nathan before he turned his focus to Ben and Annie.

"I want you both to know how much it meant to me that you handled things the way you did when you came to talk to me that day. For that small handful of minutes, I did not feel quite so alone. Thank you for that. I won't ever forget it."

The three federal agents watched silently as Mark Steward was led from the room, shuffling along since he had been bound, hand and foot, with shackles.

The moment he was out of sight, a solemn Nathan looked over at Ben.

"I owe you and Lizzie both so, *so* much for stepping in that day," he acknowledged once again. "Because if you two hadn't, what we just saw could have been me."

"That poor man," Annie exclaimed as she grabbed another tissue and dabbed at her misting eyes. "I really wish he'd had someone there for him, too."

The group at Lighte's Landing consisted of forty-two people, including Remiel, and they ranged in age from eighteen to eighty-six. He introduced Sophie to them all en masse, then ushered her into line at the buffet-style table loaded with ingredients for sandwiches and tasty-looking side dishes.

"We grow a lot of our own food here," Remiel explained as they moved down the long table to fill their plates. "We got really lucky in that four of our members are experienced in agriculture, and they took point on making the property as self-sustaining as possible. Other members have backgrounds in ranching, air and solar power, construction, and other assorted things that have really enabled us to become our own little standalone community. We fulfill most of our own needs – so much so that we take some of what we grow into town once a week to sell at the farmer's market or exchange for the few things that we don't provide for ourselves."

She nodded, trying to take it all in as she scooped up a spoonful of pasta salad to add to her plate.

"Still others bring even *more* skill sets to the group," Remiel continued. "For example, Brother Andreas is very business savvy. For that reason, he helps with the financial and overhead side of Lighte's Limited, so that I can focus more on helping people. But he is also an *amazing* chef, classically trained, and knows how to make everything delicious. We even have a nurse practitioner here – Sister Joanna – that handles the day-to-day illnesses and injuries."

Plates in hand, they sat at a table and made small talk as they ate. Afterward, comfortably full, Sophie chatted with and got to know a few of them a bit better. She leaned back in her chair to listen to and watch the people around her that she had met only a half-hour before. Sophie could tell from watching them interact that a common desire to live in peace and serenity had formed them into a tight-knit community that transcended any differences between them.

Eventually, every one of them stopped by her table to say hello in person – with over forty people, a single table was out of the question, so the communal dining room consisted of six large round tables with eight chairs around each. And with each new person that came over with a welcoming smile and a heartfelt handshake, Sophie found herself warming to the group even more.

I never had this, she realized. *Never felt like I really belonged anywhere before. Until I found out about Susan, I was just – alone.*

She was enjoying the conversations so much that she was almost regretful when Remiel asked, "Would you like to see your cabin now?"

Remiel drove Sophie toward the cabins using a four-seater golf cart, stopping at the third little wooden structure on the left-hand side of the path.

"This one's yours for the night. If you decide to join us full-time, there are seven total that are currently unoccupied, and you will have your pick of them. Shall we go in?"

The tiny but cozy structures had each been built with lumber harvested from the property, and Sophie was entranced the moment she crossed the threshold of the one Remiel had unlocked for her.

The space was modest but still plenty big enough for one person – a open layout of kitchen and living room, complete with a dinette table, television, comfortable-looking armchair, and a three-shelf unit for books and movies. A short, narrow hall led to a full bathroom behind the door to the left and a surprisingly large bedroom to the right that held a full-sized bed and four-drawer dresser as well as a closet.

"Each of the cabins is laid out the same way. And we made sure that each one of them has a full kitchen," Remiel informed her as he opened cabinet doors to reveal plates, glasses, silverware, and cookware, then motioned to the microwave, oven, stovetop, and full-sized refrigerator. "I know sometimes not everyone's up to the crowd in the dining room. So, if you ever decide you need some space, you're all set."

"This is really lovely," Sophie told him earnestly as she looked around. "And peaceful. Been a while since I felt peaceful. I could get used to this."

"That is our specialty here, is living peacefully. So many of us had such rotten starts to life - or made some choices that stole our peace away. Like I said before, that's why Lighte's Landing exists. We would be delighted for you to be here full-time, Sophie. But if you need some time to think it over, I completely understand. Your current life is in Houston, yes?"

She nodded.

"And I totally get how uprooting from where you are and what you know to start over somewhere new can be nerve-wracking. It's a tremendous change."

"It *is* a little daunting," she confessed.

"So, think about it. It is entirely up to you. Stay the night, if you like, and head back in the morning. Just let me know what you decide."

———

"What did I miss?" Lizzie asked the moment that Nathan, Ben, and Annie stepped off the elevator and walked her direction. "I heard Nathan bolt out of here earlier, and I can tell by your expressions that something big happened."

"Remember when I pointed Mark Steward out to you yesterday?" Annie asked.

"Yes. Why?"

"He snuck a blade into court and stabbed Jamesin to death today."

"He did *what?*"

"Yeah," Ben confirmed. "The prosecutor called him to the stand, and he testified. Once the judge dismissed him, he made it look like he was returning to his seat. But at the last second, he changed direction and lunged for Jamesin and stabbed him to death in front of everybody."

Lizzie's gaze snapped over to Nathan.

"We went and talked to him in lockup, and yes, I am very, very aware that could have been me," he murmured.

"What did he say about it?"

"No remorse at all. None. He blames the people in Minnesota for letting Jamesin get loose in the first place."

"Can't say as I blame him on that part. Still..."

Nathan exhaled heavily.

"Yeah. Still. And I misspoke just now. That *would* have been me, if not for you and Ben."

Lizzie's expression softened and she nodded once in acknowledgement.

Annie cleared her throat.

"My question is, is there anything we can do?"

Nathan turned and looked at her.

"Such as?"

"What he did was premeditated, that much is obvious. But I just... I mean... the day we talked to him he was just so...so... Can't I make a statement on his behalf, or something?"

"He snuck a weapon into a federal courthouse and killed a man in cold blood in front of over a hundred witnesses, Annie," Ben reminded her not-so-gently. "I don't know that anything we could say will help him at all."

"But he only went after the man who killed his family, no one else. And he was a model citizen before his wife and child were brutally slaughtered," she retorted angrily. "One could argue diminished capacity, at the very least."

"Annie, if you want to make a formal statement on Mark Steward's behalf, then by all means go ahead," Nathan said simply. "I will make sure it gets to the District Attorney."

"Thank you," she responded, then cast a fulminating glare Ben's way before she stomped away down the hall.

"I really stepped in it that time, I guess," Ben muttered aloud as he watched her leave. "I wasn't trying to tell her *not* to do it. I mean, I feel bad for him too, you know? I just don't want to see her get her hopes up too high, that's all."

The look on Ben's face was one of utter dejection as he shoved his hands into his pockets, looked longingly in the direction Annie went, then turned and walked the opposite way.

By the time she gathered with the others for dinner, the peace Sophie felt wrapping around her soul like a warm blanket let her know she did not need any more time to think about it. The moment she entered the dining room, Sophie squared her shoulders and walked directly over to Remiel.

"I've decided. I formally accept the job offer, Remiel. I'd like to stay here tonight and fly back tomorrow. I can be back by next Friday with the rest of my belongings once I've squared things away down in Houston. My lease is up at the end of this month anyway."

He smiled and extended his hand.

"I'm pleased to hear it, Sophie. Welcome to the Lighte's Landing family."

***

The look on Nathan's face when he arrived home earlier than expected made both Bella's eyebrows arch upward sharply.

"Interesting day?"

The brief grimace he flashed at her question let her know that 'interesting' was the least of it.

"Something like that. Wait until you hear this one."

As he told her about the chaos in the courtroom, Bella was shocked - but not all that surprised.

"I wish I could tell you that I didn't expect something like that to happen, but *everyone's* emotions are heightened when kids are involved. You know that better than anyone."

Nathan gathered her up in his arms.

"Yes, I do. And I do sympathize with Mark Steward a great deal. But it was also a huge slap in the face for me. There but for the grace..."

"And your teammates," Bella chimed in softly.

"Yes, and my teammates," he agreed. "And I thanked them again for it."

"What will happen to him?"

Nathan sighed and rested his head on hers.

"After what happened today, the best he can hope for is life in prison. But I saw the look in his eyes when I went to talk to him, Bella. He had already given up - that happened to Mark Steward the moment he lost his family."

They stood, embracing, taking comfort in each other a moment longer before Nathan squeezed her gently and asked, "Wanna ride with me to go pick up our son?"

"I wonder how Sophie's interview is going," Susan mused out loud as she and Trevor settled in on his couch with their Chinese takeout. "She was super excited about it, so I'm hoping she'll call me and fill me in."

"Did she say when she thought she would be back?"

"No, she didn't, actually. And I have no idea what the details were, just that Soph said they were flying her up there for an onsite audition."

"I'm sure she will call you and tell you all about it at some point," Trevor assured her. "Now, what would you like to watch?"

Thirty minutes into their *Big Bang Theory* marathon, her phone buzzed, and Trevor paused the recording as she reached for it and navigated to her text messages.

I got the job!! I am going to fly back to Houston in the morning to pack up my stuff, and then I'll make the drive back up here. SO happy!

Susan laughed softly at the multiple smiley face icons that followed right after Sophie's message.

Way to go! Knew you could do it!! Susan texted back. *When do you start?*

Next week, Sophie responded, *because I need to tie up loose ends in Houston. But I should be able to be back up there by next Friday, at the latest. They said that was fine. And it pays fifty thousand a year, sis! Can you believe that??*

I can. You are exceptionally talented, Sophie. You just needed to catch a break. Sounds like it is finally happening for you, kiddo.

I know, right? I am so happy. Anyway, I will call you later and tell you all about it, okay? Need to charge my phone, it's almost dead.

Okay, Susan answered.

"Good for you, Soph," Susan murmured as she set her phone off to the side. "Good for you."

"Sophie must have shared some good news with you," Trevor quipped, and she smiled.

"Yep. She got the job."

"That's great! When does she start?"

Annie left the office a half-hour before he did without saying a word, opting to walk out with Lizzie instead.

When he got to his truck and texted her and Annie did not respond, Ben knew for sure that she was not in a talking mood – at least, not to *him*.

"Guess I'm on my own tonight," he grumbled, then dialed his friend Brody.

"Hey buddy, what's up?" Brody asked.

"Not much. Just got off work. Wanna go grab some hot wings?"

"Sure. Meet you there in about thirty minutes?'

"You got it."

Ben considered swinging by his apartment for a moment, then decided to continue straight to the restaurant instead. He and Brody arrived within two minutes of each other.

"Uh oh," Brody exclaimed the moment he saw Ben's face. "Someone's having girlfriend trouble."

Ben scowled.

"That obvious, huh?"

"Couldn't be more obvious if you rented out a billboard," Brody quipped as he clapped Ben on the shoulder. "Question is, what did you do now? You didn't call her 'teammate' again, did you?"

Ben sighed.

Gonna be a long night.

"Okay, okay. We don't have to talk about it," Brody conceded, his hands raised in surrender. "Come on, man. Let's get some beer and wings."

Three miles at a brisk run on her treadmill had done exactly nothing to cool Annie's temper, and she slowed the machine to a stop before climbing down and mopping her face with her hand towel.

I just do not understand him some days, she grumbled in her head as she took a long drink of water. *Lately it's like he makes it a point to make me angry - when he's not asking me if I want to live together, that is.*

How messed up is that?

She mimicked Ben's condescending-sounding comments and took a great deal of childish pleasure in voicing him in a simpering, petulant tone as she did so.

"He snuck a weapon into a federal courthouse and killed a man in cold blood ... blah blah *blah....*"

Annie showered, then dressed in sweats and a t-shirt before she went into her kitchen to figure out what to have for dinner. It was only when she glanced at her cell phone attached to its charger on the kitchen counter that she realized she had missed a text from him.

Hey, it said. *I'm sorry about earlier. What I was trying to say came out completely wrong. You have such a big heart, Annie, and you care so much about people. I just don't want to see you get hurt, that's all.*

She read it, set the phone down and started to open her refrigerator, then pivoted back to pick up her phone and read it again, then a third time, before she sighed and typed back a response.

Forty minutes later there was a knock on her door, and she opened it to find Ben standing there.

"I'm a jerk," he said at once, his eyes searching her face for any signs of hope.

"Yes, you are, sometimes."

"I speak without thinking and I can be too blunt, and I hurt you. Again. I'm sorry."

"Yes, you did," Annie countered, leaning against the doorframe.

"Does it help you forgive me if I tell you I love you?'

Her jaw dropped open.

"*What?*"

"I do," he said earnestly. "This isn't the way I wanted to say it to you for the first time, but there's no denying it anymore. I am in love with you, Annie. Have been for months. I've just been too scared to say it out loud until now."

He fell silent, watching her intently as she slowly reached forward to grab handfuls of his shirt, then pulled him toward her.

"I love you, too," Annie whispered before she pressed her lips to his, and in response Ben crushed her against his chest.

They moved together as a unit into her apartment and shut the door.

When Sophie returned to her cabin for the night, she opted to sit in the wooden slingback chair on the front porch for a while and enjoy the mild evening with its cloudless sky and beautiful stars.

In the distance fireflies danced and chased, their tiny lights dotting the dark landscape as far as she could see. They seemed to move in rhythm to the light breeze that gently rustled the leaves of neighboring trees.

The cabins were spaced just far enough apart to allow for some privacy, but still enable each resident to feel connected to the group. Sophie watched as one by one, each cabin's lights went out, each occupant headed for sleep, until at last only the fireflies, the stars, the wind, and Sophie remained.

She stretched, yawned, then sighed contentedly.

I am really going to like it here, she thought to herself. *For the first time in a long time, I feel centered – and optimistic.*

Yawning again, she stood and walked into her cabin.

Once she had put on her pajamas, washed her face, and brushed her teeth, she pulled back the handmade quilt and climbed into a bed with exquisitely soft sheets. She turned off the bedside lamp, rolled to lie on her left side so she could look out the window, and counted stars until she drifted off to sleep.

It was midnight before the meeting started.

Two words, spoken in an accusatory tone, floated across to him the moment he entered the room.

"You're late."

"I had to make sure I wasn't seen," he hissed as he poured himself a brandy. "Besides, it's not like you had anything better to do."

"So, what's the story with that Sophie chick?"

He shrugged.

"She's just a kid. Super tough time growing up, spent a lot of time in foster care. I don't think she's anything to worry about."

A raised eyebrow sent his direction had him snarling.

"Don't look at me like that. She is harmless – and broke. Nothing to gain there, so leave her alone. Now, let's get on with it. Who's our lucky lottery winner this time?'

"Brother Paul. Healthy checking and savings account balances, *huge* retirement pension, social security, the gamut. We're looking at thirty large, right off the bat, then residuals of five grand a month, easy."

Now it was his turn to lift an eyebrow.

"You don't say. Hasn't been that good a take since Abel. But Marjorie was not too long ago. Are you sure it's not too soon?"

A nod from his co-conspirator.

"Any underlying issues we can blame it on?"

Another nod.

"And what approach were you thinking?" he asked, then listened to the scheme his accomplice had devised.

He held up his snifter with a predatory smirk and an approving nod.

"Works for me. Cheers."

The next evening, while Paul's attention was focused on a closely contested football game on the big screen in the recreation room, a mysterious figure discreetly entered Paul's cabin and made a beeline straight for the kitchen cabinets.

Slowly, carefully, each tiny container on the bottom shelf of the cabinet next to the refrigerator had an extra special ingredient added to it. The gloved saboteur made sure that each little bottle was returned to its precise location before slipping out of the cabin again to return to the main building.

Chapter Four

By NINE A.M. the following Friday morning, an excited Sophie was loading up everything that would fit in her little four-door sedan. She had listed her furniture and the other bulky items that she couldn't take with her for sale through a popular website on Wednesday morning, and a young couple had just picked up the last piece left – her bed.

While she was sad to part with most of the possessions she had managed to collect, Sophie knew it was necessary. The whopping seven dollars in her bank account made that clear, as did her pride. Remiel had offered her an advance to cover any moving expenses, but she'd politely declined.

Not bad! Better than I expected, she realized now as she counted all the money that she had earned from selling off her stuff. *Two hundred and eighty dollars. Now I can afford the gas to drive up there and still have money left over.*

Sophie tucked the cash into the front pocket of her jeans, then hummed to herself as she made a series of trips from her apartment to her car. It was eleven before she wedged the last armful inside the cramped space and shut the doors and the trunk.

Although there was only enough space left for her to climb into the driver's seat – her belongings occupied every other available inch of interior and the trunk - she had managed to stack everything so that she would still be able to use her rear-view mirror.

But not by much, she thought with a satisfied grin. *Best round of Tetris ever.*

With the tiny apartment now emptied, she thoroughly cleaned as best she could, finishing just in time for the noon walk-through with the property manager.

Myra stepped inside the front door of the apartment and glanced around.

"I can *already* tell it's even cleaner than when you moved in," she said approvingly. "Where do you want your security deposit refund mailed?"

Sophie handed her a slip of paper.

"Send it here, please."

"You got it. I hate to see you go, kiddo," the little old woman rasped, "but I'm proud of you for taking this step."

"Thanks, Myra," she said softly, surprised when the woman reached over and gave her an affectionate – and uncharacteristic - hug.

"You take care of yourself, you hear me?"

"Yes, ma'am."

"Okay, now, off you go. Can't have the other tenants thinking I'm a softie," Myra cackled as she released Sophie and took a step back, and Sophie grinned and handed over the keys to the front door.

"Your secret's safe with me, Myra."

Sophie climbed behind the wheel and started her car. She paused only long enough to plug in her cell phone and fire up her navigation app.

"Your approximate travel time is five hours and seven minutes," the robotic voice announced, and Sophie smiled.

She waved at Myra for the last time, then pulled out of the parking space she had used for the last three years. Sophie headed toward her two former places of employment to collect her final measly paychecks.

Forty minutes later, after a trip through the bank's drive-up lane to deposit another two hundred sixty dollars and thirty-five cents in payroll earnings, she put on her turn signal and accelerated her little Honda so she could merge with the traffic on westbound I-10.

Tense and silent, she navigated her way through the downtown area with white knuckles – the myriad of major highways converging always made her palms sweaty.

"That's one good thing where I'm headed. Lots less people on the road," Sophie muttered, trying to find the bright side as her GPS guided her safely to US-290 West.

It was another fifty-four miles before the exit that she needed to finally start heading north on Highway 6 appeared. Once she was out of the city, she switched on the radio, then cranked up the volume when she heard the opening notes of Tom Petty's "Running Down a Dream" coming to her through the car's speakers.

Sophie grinned as she sang along at the top of her lungs, and thought, *so, this is what it feels like when your life finally gets started...*
Pretty darn cool.

She stopped in Hempstead to put more gas in the tank and grab something to snack on, then continued her trek northward, merging onto Interstate 35 when she reached Waco.

It was ten minutes to five as Sophie came into the Fort Worth city limits. Traffic on northbound I-35 had begun to fill in, and she was back to tense silence as she carefully watched the vehicles around her.

She shrieked in response to an extremely loud boom coming from somewhere up ahead of her and stomped on her brakes as the cars in front of her began to quickly slow down to a crawl.

She saw it at the very last moment when the car in front of her swerved - a huge chunk of tire tread, still smoking from the high friction of ripping itself apart, lying right in the middle of her lane.

Angling her car to the left or right was out of the question – other vehicles had her surrounded. With no choice but to stay in her lane and keep moving forward, she winced as she hit the debris dead center.

And immediately muttered a low curse as she heard another, much closer boom, then clanking as her car's 'check engine' light came to life.

Sophie sighed, put her blinker on, and began to try to get over to the far-right lane to take the next exit.

Please, oh please, just let me get off the highway...

Five o'clock, Cruz Delgado noted as he gently lowered the hood of the Toyota he had just finished working on, then walked over to the large sliding window that separated the garage from the office.

"The Camry's done," he announced to Miguel, the shop owner.

"Park it out front," came the directive, and Cruz nodded.

Define irony, Cruz thought to himself as he honked the horn to warn Javier and Ramon working below him in the oil change bay, then started the car and slowly drove it forward and out of the structure.

The only one of Dad's five sons that did not *want to be a mechanic like the old man. And what's my very first undercover assignment? Infiltrate the cartel - by working as a mechanic in one of their garages.*

Go figure. Thank God I paid attention when Dad was trying to teach me all this stuff...

But it was necessary. The DEA knew the Cortinas cartel was neck-deep in drug trafficking. And a solid tip about smuggling their wares out of Mexico and South Texas in car chassis had resulted in Cruz being hand-picked from a pool of qualified agents to try to get enough solid evidence to bolster their federal case.

He had been working in the cartel's south Fort Worth garage for eleven months, and in that time, he had firsthand knowledge of over a hundred vehicles coming through the shop that Miguel insisted on 'repairing' personally. Which was strange, since Miguel was quite possibly the laziest man Cruz had ever met.

And that was just *one* garage in the area. The DEA suspected that the Cortinas family had control of four other car repair shops along Interstate 35 in Tarrant County, as well.

Doing the math, Cruz was convinced that in the last two years alone, the five shops had been used as a front to smuggle well over thirty million dollars' worth of fine white powder out of South Texas and into the cartel's distribution pipelines that stretched all the way to the Canadian border.

But we're almost to the point of being able to raid their locations and shut it all down. Not much longer now, and this will have been worth it. And when all this is said and done, I swear I'm never working on another car as long as I live, he told himself as he circled the six-bay building, and grinned.

He pulled the Camry into one of the parking spots in front of the building, then climbed out and locked the door. When he walked back inside, Miguel beckoned to him.

"Yes, sir?"

"I need you here Sunday," the man said without preamble.

Cruz's brows knitted in confusion.

"But we're closed on Sundays."

Miguel's oily smile made Cruz extremely uneasy.

"Special client and a tight turn time," the shop owner explained as he laid his hand heavily on Cruz's shoulder. "Has to be ready first thing Monday morning. And I realized today that you might welcome the opportunity to make double-time pay."

"Sure," Cruz said casually, staying in character. "I appreciate it, boss."

"Be here at nine," Miguel intoned, then shuffled away.

Man.... If Sunday involves what I think it might, I will finally be able to prove out our theory, Cruz thought to himself, his mind racing even though externally he appeared unruffled and completely focused on the oil change he was in the middle of.

I need to make contact tonight and let the director know.

He had just stepped outside again when a horrible clanking sound caught his attention.

Cruz turned and watched as a 2005 Honda crammed with stuff limped into the parking lot.

"Hi," the petite blond driver called out when she got out of the car. "I need some help."

Cruz smiled and walked over to her.

"What seems to be the problem?"

"I'm not sure, to be honest," she answered, chewing her bottom lip. "What I *can* tell you is that up until a few minutes ago my car was running fine. I was on the freeway just south of here, and someone in front of me blew a tire. Debris went everywhere, and I ran over a sizable chunk of the tread. Then there was a loud boom, and this horrible clanking started, and then the check engine light came on. I took the next exit after that, to get off the highway as quickly as I could. Surprised I made it this far."

"Me too, from what you're describing. Happy to look at it for you and see if we can't get you back on the road. Can you pop the hood for me?"

She reached into the car and pulled the release mechanism, and he lifted the hood and braced it with the prop rod. The moment he did so, it became obvious what was wrong.

"See the pulleys, there and there?" he said, and pointed.

"Yes," she answered, moving closer.

"There's supposed to be a belt going around them. It's called a serpentine belt. What happened was, that chunk of tire you hit knocked the belt off. I don't see it anywhere in here, so, it's probably lying out on the highway."

Her nose wrinkled.

"Oh. That's not good."

"No, it's not. Fortunately, we have one in stock, and it shouldn't take me long to put it on for you."

"How much?" she asked, wincing.

"It's thirty-five for the belt and a half-hour of labor, so seventy-five bucks plus tax."

"Oh," she said again, this time happily. "Okay, that's not too bad at all. Can you please fix it?"

"Sure. Let me grab the belt and my tools. I'll be right back."

Cruz retrieved what he needed and returned to her car.

"So," he began, making small talk to make her comfortable, "it looks like you're on quite a trip with all that stuff in your car."

She grinned.

"I am, actually. I'm moving for a new job. Super excited about it."

"That's great!"

"Yeah," she sighed. "I'm Sophie, by the way. It's nice to meet you."

"Likewise. I'm Cruz."

They chatted some more as he worked to install the new belt.

"Where's the new job, exactly?"

"A little over an hour northwest of here? At least, that's what the GPS was showing."

"And what is it that you do?"

"Until recently, waitressing until I could catch a break," she quipped with a laugh. "But my passion is videography, and this job I'm relocating for is a full-time permanent one doing what I love."

"That is fantastic to hear, Sophie. Most people are not lucky enough to have their dream job," he said sincerely.

"Man, don't I know it," she answered, and laughed again. "I look forward to *not* dealing with a bunch of starving drunks at two a.m. anymore."

Cruz chuckled.

"Yeah, I can see how that would get really old, really quickly."

Twenty minutes later, he said, "Okay, Sophie. Start the car for me, and let's have a listen."

The smooth purr he heard after Sophie turned the key made him smile.

"I can also check the fluids and tire pressures while you're here if you like. No charge," he announced once she'd turned the motor off and returned to stand by him at the front of her car.

"Thanks, I'd appreciate that."

Cruz was glad he checked those things for her because both the front driver's side and back passenger side tires were low. He added air to each of them to solve the problem, and Sophie's smile warmed his heart when he turned to her and said, "You're all set."

He escorted her into the office where she paid for the belt and his time, then walked her back to her car.

"Thanks again, Cruz," she said, holding out her hand.

He took it and shook it gently.

"Anytime, Sophie. Good luck."

She waved as she pulled away, and he watched her little Honda disappear around the corner.

By the time Lizzie arrived home at six o'clock, Donny had an overnight bag packed and ready to go.

"Figured you'd want to get underway as soon as possible in the morning," he confessed with a grin when she noticed it sitting on the narrow table by the front door. "The only thing we'll need to add to the bag are our toothbrushes."

"See? That's just one of the many reasons I love you," she told him. "You understand all too well that I *cannot wait* to get down to Tank's house and hold that baby."

"Yes, I do," he replied. "But first things first. You hungry? I was just about to pull the enchiladas out of the oven."

The moment he got home from work, Cruz locked his front door and headed straight for his bedroom to pull out the burner phone stashed in his dresser.

He turned it on only long enough to send a burst of carefully worded text, then powered it down again and put it back underneath the clothes in the drawer to conceal it.

He had just left his bedroom and was en route to his kitchen when he heard a knock at his front door.

"Hey, man," Ramon said with a grin when a surprised Cruz answered the door. "We're heading out for burgers and beers. Wanna come with us?"

We have never *hung out together after work before... wonder if this is connected somehow...*

"Um, sure, sounds good. Let me grab my keys."

It was almost seven o'clock by the time Sophie reached the beautifully crafted gate leading to Lighte's Landing. She drove up close to the panel mounted on its steel pole, rolled down her window, and pressed the button labeled 'intercom'.

"Hello there," a friendly voice said.

"Hi there, it's Sophie. Remiel's expecting me?"

"Glad you made it safely. Come on in and stop at the main building so we can get you a set of keys."

She heard a muted buzzing sound, then watched as the gate slid effortlessly out of her way. She navigated through and headed straight for the main building as instructed.

Andreas was waiting to greet her.

"Hello again, Sophie," he said. "Welcome back. Did you have a preference of the available cabins?"

"Hi, Andreas. Remiel said they all had the same configuration, so, any of them will work."

"How about you take the one you stayed in before?"

She nodded.

"That will work just fine."

He handed her a pair of small silver keys.

"Would you rather eat first, or unpack first?"

"Food, definitely."

He chuckled.

"Good choice. The popular vote was for Italian food this evening. I made fettuccine alfredo, chicken parmesan, and a huge pan of lasagna. I think you'll like it."

"You're speaking my language, Andreas – Italian food is my absolute favorite, hands down. Lead the way."

In the DEA's Dallas division office, a computer tech decoded Cruz's encrypted message, then routed it to the director, who scanned it and grinned.

Looks like our patience is about to pay off. Cruz finally got asked to the dance, he thought with satisfaction.

Annie and Ben held hands and followed the host through the restaurant toward the corner booth they had requested.

Once they'd been handed the menus and ordered drinks, Annie asked, ""When is Brody coming over tomorrow?"

"He said he'd be at my place by nine," Ben answered.

"Sweet of him to offer to help us move my stuff."

"He didn't."

"Let me guess," Annie interjected. "You bribed him with free pizza and beer?"

Ben smiled.

"You are one astute woman, you know that?"

"I've been known to figure stuff out," she teased, then turned her attention to the menu. "Except what to order for dinner, evidently. Everything sounds equally good."

"Why don't we start with an appetizer and go from there?"

Annie smiled.

"You are one astute man, you know that?"

———

Claire and Paul, two of the members she'd talked with the longest during her earlier meals with the group, both beamed when Sophie entered the dining room.

"Hey kiddo! Welcome back!" Paul boomed in his rich baritone as he walked over to hug her. "I take it you decided to join us full-time?"

"That I did," she answered with a smile. "And after we eat, I'll get settled in."

"Want some help?" Claire asked as she too greeted Sophie with a warm smile and a sincere hug. "It's no trouble at all."

"That'd be great, thanks."

"I'm happy to help, as well," Paul chimed in. "It will give us even more time to visit, too."

She stood looking at the two of them – Paul in his late sixties, with silver hair and piercing sky-blue eyes, and Claire, a slender brown-haired beauty in her late fifties – and Sophie thought her heart just might burst from all the unconditional love and acceptance she could feel emanating from them.

They already feel more like parents to me than anyone I stayed with in foster care...

She filled her plate then sat with them, catching them up on her activities for the past week as the three of them ate.

"I never cared much for Houston traffic either," Paul commiserated. "I drove a semi-truck for years, and it was *always* more challenging with a big rig than a passenger car."

"Really? Did you travel all around, or was it all locally?"

"All over the United States," he said proudly. "I've been in every state at least once except for Alaska and Hawaii, and those are on my bucket list."

Sophie grinned as she listened.

"Speaking of big rigs, I didn't tell you about my big excitement on the way here," Sophie confided, and told them about hitting the debris and having to have the serpentine belt replaced, finishing with, "The piece I hit was huge. Had to have been from a big truck."

"You got lucky, it might have been worse," Paul replied. "I've seen big pieces like that bounce and hit someone's windshield before."

There was a slight pause as Paul drained the last of his iced tea.

"Be right back," he said, and lumbered up out of his chair to go refill his drink. When he returned to the table, he pulled a small plastic bottle out of his shirt pocket and squirted a bit of its clear contents into his glass, then stirred it briskly with his spoon.

"Liquid sweetener," he explained when he saw Sophie's curious expression. "I put it in just about everything, and I find I don't have to use near as much as crystallized sugar."

"Is it kind of like that stuff you can add to water to give it flavor?"

"Exactly. And I use those a lot, too."

After dinner, Sophie returned to her car and drove down to her cabin with Paul and Claire leading the way on one of the property's golf carts.

Claire grinned as she watched Sophie exit the car.

"That's quite the packing job," she observed.

"I know, right? I'm just glad I didn't have anything else. I would have had to strap it to the top of my car somehow."

The three got to work, and within a half-hour Sophie's car returned to its more spacious state. They had just carried in the last box when Sophie noticed Paul suck in a quick breath then frown, close his eyes, and run both his hands through his silver hair.

"Are you all right?"

"Headache coming on. I get migraines sometimes," he managed with a wince.

"I can stay and help her set up," Claire offered. "Why don't you go get some rest?"

Paul glanced at Sophie, who softly agreed, "Yes. Go rest. Migraines are the worst."

She crossed the room to hug him.

"And thanks for helping me unload the car. I really appreciate it."

"Anytime, kiddo. See you two in the morning."

"Is he going to be okay?" Sophie asked as they watched him leave.

"Yes," Claire said as she patted a concerned Sophie on the shoulder. "Paul told me last week that Sister Joanna put him on a new blood pressure medicine that she felt would work better. I'm not a doctor by any stretch, but I suspect that his blood pressure being all over the place might be what causes his migraines. He just needs to keep taking the new medicine, and he'll be fine."

"That's good to hear," a relieved Sophie confirmed.

"Now, where would you like me to start?" Claire asked as she waved a hand at everything they'd brought in from the car.

"I think I want to get my clothes and bathroom stuff put away, then go to bed. I can unpack the rest tomorrow."

"Sounds like a plan."

Twenty minutes later, Sophie's clothes hung neatly in the closet and all four drawers of the bedroom's dresser were filled and organized. In the bathroom across the way, her towels were hanging from the sleek four-hook rack she'd mounted on the wall, and her toiletries now occupied their proper places.

"Thanks again, Claire."

"It was my pleasure. Happy to help. Good night," Claire responded with a wink before she left.

Sophie was headed for a hot bath and then her soft bed when it hit her.

Crap! I forgot to text Susan that I got here safely!

She dutifully did just that, along with a promise to call in the morning, then plugged her phone in and left it on the kitchen counter for the night before she resumed her path to first soak and then sleep.

Chapter Five

Lizzie bolted upright, wide awake of her own accord, at five a.m. on Saturday morning and turned her head to see Donny sleepily smiling at her.

"I guess you're ready to go, then," he murmured with a smirk.

"Dibs on the shower," was her saucy response as she flung back the covers and raced to the bathroom.

Donny chuckled as he got up and followed her.

Thirty-five minutes later they were dressed and heading out the door with travel mugs filled with coffee.

"You sure you don't want breakfast here?" he asked her.

"We can hit a drive-thru or a donut shop on the way," she responded gaily.

"Your wish is my command, milady."

After some discussion they decided to stop at the donut shop down the street, and not long afterward Donny navigated their SUV up onto the deserted freeway as Lizzie opened the box of sugary goodness and handed him one of the apple fritters he'd ordered.

"Thanks, baby."

"No problem," she said around a mouthful of chocolate-covered fried dough.

"Good morning, Sophie!" Remiel said with a smile when they crossed paths in the lobby of the main building. "I am so sorry I wasn't here to greet you when you returned yesterday. I traveled a bit this week and just got back last night myself. How was your drive up?"

"Mostly uneventful," she confirmed. "I thought I'd come talk to you and find out if there's anything you need me to do today. I don't believe we discussed when my first official day would be."

"Well, I hadn't planned on coordinating with you until Monday, and I do have some calls I need to return here shortly. But if you are ready to start today, then I think we should plan on touring more of the property this afternoon to try and put together a list of locations we can use in the videos. I really liked that idea. Say, around three?"

"Yes, sir. I'll meet you back here."

He smiled warmly at her.

"What did I say before about the 'sir' thing?"

"Sorry, Remiel," Sophie said, her cheeks turning pink. "It's a habit."

"See you this afternoon, Sophie," Remiel said gently, then walked away.

Sophie returned to her cabin and set about liberating the rest of her things from their boxes and bags. She started with her books. An avid reader, the books she carefully collected were not only her most prized possessions, but in many ways the only companions she had to turn to for much of her life.

She scooted the first box over to rest beside the bookshelf, sat cross-legged on the floor, and began to lovingly unpack and arrange them on the shelves. With each book she touched, she smiled at the memories – where she was when she found it, the thrill of that first devouring of a story, the subtle nuances discovered with every re-read after that.

When the first box was empty, she repeated the process with the next one, until all five boxes that had held her treasures were reduced to flat panels and stacked in a corner.

The drive south was uneventful, and by ten a.m. Donny and Lizzie were pulling into the driveway of Tank and Renee's home in the suburbs just south and west of Houston.

Tank met them in the yard, shook Donny's hand, then picked Lizzie up and spun her around in a hard hug.

"Man, I missed you, skinny white girl," he announced with his booming voice and his trademark megawatt smile as he called her by his usual nickname for her. "How have you been, Zim?"

"I missed you too, Tank. Now put me down so I can go hold that godson of mine," she fired back as she kissed his cheek, then began to squirm until he gently set her on her feet again.

He laughed, throwing his arms around hers and Donny's shoulders.

"Wait 'til you see him. He's perfect, and I'm *not* just saying that because I'm his daddy."

He ushered them in through the front door and into the living room.

"You guys want something to drink? Renee will be out shortly. She's changing him right now."

"Sure."

They settled in on the couch with iced teas.

"How's the job?" Lizzie asked, and Tank sighed.

"Gang activity is picking up in the city lately, Zim," he admitted, his tone grim. "Every shift is tense."

"You on days?"

"Nights, right now," he answered. "I still don't get to choose my shifts yet, being one of the new kids down here, you know. But I'm thinking I'll work up to days before the year is out."

"How does it feel, being a parent?" Donny asked, and Tank's smile returned.

"I've never been so satisfied – or sleep deprived – in my life," Tank confessed with a laugh. "We're trying to get into a rhythm, but Tucker's got his days and nights mixed up."

A blur of motion in her peripheral view caught Lizzie's attention, and she turned her head to see Renee walking into the room with a tiny bundle in her arms.

"Hi, Renee," she said as she rose and crossed the room to give her a carefully placed one-armed hug so as not to disturb the infant.

"It's so good to see you, Lizzie. I want to introduce you to your godson," Renee told her, and gently transferred the baby into Lizzie's arms.

Lizzie glanced around and selected the nearest armchair to sit in, then looked down at a tiny, perfect human with soft jet-black hair, caramel skin, and long eyelashes framing the most beautiful brown eyes she had ever seen.

"Oh," she gasped, tears forming as her heart melted with love. "He's *gorgeous*."

The baby scrunched his eyebrows together in a fierce scowl as he stared up at her intently for a long moment.

"Hello, Tucker, I'm your Aunt Lizzie," she crooned softly, and in response Tucker's serious expression morphed into an adorable smile that made Lizzie's tears overflow.

Once she had composed herself a bit, Lizzie slowly stood and walked over to sit beside Donny on the couch so that he could see the baby, too. She snuggled close and he draped his arm around her shoulders and leaned in to look at Tucker.

"What a little angel," Donny murmured as he brushed one

diminutive fist with his index finger, then smiled as Tucker grabbed it and held on tightly. "Got a good strong grip, too."

"Oh, yes he does," Renee chuckled. "I was burping him a couple of days ago and he got a little fistful of my hair and yanked it – *hard*. That little boy *already* has some of his daddy's muscle."

Tank just beamed, a deep pride radiating from him that filled the entire room.

"So how long are you guys here?" he asked, and Lizzie shrugged.

"Until you run us off, or until tomorrow afternoon, whichever comes first."

Renee laughed out loud before she favored Lizzie with a warm smile.

"Girl. You know better than that. You're family. So, you two are staying in our spare bedroom overnight."

She looked over at her husband.

"You said you were gonna grill, right?"

"Yes ma'am, got the steaks all seasoned up and ready."

Lizzie glanced down at Tucker and noticed that the infant's eyes had closed.

"I think he's asleep," she said softly.

"Come with me, I'll show you his room and we can put him in his crib," Renee said as she stood up.

"Be right back," Lizzie told Donny, then leaned over and kissed him before she slowly rose to her feet again and carried Tucker down the hall and out of sight.

When their wives were out of earshot, Tank looked at Donny and solemnly said, "Lizzie's a natural with kids."

"Yep, she sure is," Donny agreed.

"Ya'll thought about having any?"

"We talked about it a while back, then tabled that discussion for another time," Donny confided. "And to be honest, it hasn't come back up yet."

"Huh," Tank said, and waited.

"It's just... back when it first came up, she was worried about being able to be both a mom and a federal agent, you know?"

"I understand that completely, man," Tank answered.

Meanwhile, Lizzie crept into a room that was cleverly decorated with baby animals. The wallpaper, the toys, even the mobile hanging over the crib carried the same motif, with accent colors of light and dark blue.

"Wow, this is really cute!" Lizzie exclaimed as softly as she could, and made Renee laugh again.

"Another thing my son got from his father is the ability to sleep through anything if he feels like it," Renee told her, using her normal speaking voice. "Trust me, we could yell right now, and that child won't wake up unless he's good and ready. That's part of the reason it's been a bit difficult to get his sleep schedule straightened out."

"Yikes," Lizzie said, and Renee nodded.

"Indeed."

Lizzie walked over to the crib and paused.

"Should I lay him down on his tummy or his back?"

"On his back."

Lizzie gently kissed Tucker's forehead before she leaned over and placed the sleeping child in his crib, then stood upright again and sighed happily.

"He's beautiful, Renee."

And as she watched her brand-new godson sleep and dream, an intense, unfamiliar longing sprang to life and took root in her soul with enough force to steal her breath away.

I really do *want a child of my own...*

"Hey, we have a question for you, Donny," Tank began once Lizzie and Renee returned to the living room.

"Shoot."

"Well, we want to set up some sort of college fund for Tucker. Would you be able to help us with that while you are here? And look at our current setup on insurance policies and stuff too? We need to make some changes."

"I'd be happy to help with that."

"Great," the new father said with relief. "Because we weren't sure how to get all that started."

"Matter of fact, my laptop is in the car," Donny revealed as he rose to his feet. "I'll go out and get it and our suitcase right now."

The two couples settled in around the dining room table so that Donny could help the proud new parents with vital changes to their financial planning.

By the time she finished putting the rest of her things away it was twelve-thirty, and her stomach was rumbling. Sophie stepped out of her cabin, locked the door behind her, and began to walk to the main building for lunch.

"Want a lift? We have a seat left," she heard from behind her, and turned to find Paul, Claire, and Joanna approaching on a golf cart.

"Sure," Sophie said, and Paul slowed enough to allow her to hop in.

"Nice to see you again, Joanna," she said to the woman who looked to be in her late thirties sitting to her right.

"You too, Sophie. Did you get your cabin set up?"

"I did. Feels like home already."

"That's good to hear."

"Paul, how are you feeling today? Did your migraine go away?"

"Nipped it in the bud, fortunately. I got back to my cabin and took my headache medicine in time," he replied.

It startled Sophie when Joanna frowned and leaned forward suddenly.

"Still having trouble with those?"

"On occasion," he gritted through his teeth, his dislike of all things medical clear in his voice.

"Oh, come on now, Brother Paul, don't growl at me like that," Joanna chided in a light tone. "You know I can help you if you'll let me. Your last blood pressure check was beautiful, right where it was supposed to be."

"Yes, I suppose it was," he begrudgingly admitted. "Sorry, Sister Joanna. My aversion isn't directed at you at all."

"It's all right. I don't take it personally. Besides, hardly anyone I know actually *enjoys* spending time as a patient in a clinic."

She glanced over at Sophie and winked.

"This thing's kinda heavy," Ben grunted from his end of the treadmill that he and Brody were trying to maneuver through Annie's front door.

"Yeah," Brody grunted back, "and you're on the *light* end of it. I think we're missing something."

"Use the wheels, guys," Annie called out, shaking her head.

"What?"

"Set it down for a minute, and I'll show you," she said as she approached.

They did, and their jaws dropped open as she first pressed a little lever that unlocked the belt section and allowed her to lift it up and lock it into an upright position next to the control panel. Then she tilted the machine toward her slightly and rolled it easily back and forth.

"See? Wheels."

Brody mumbled, "Never owned one, I always use the great big ones at the gym. Had no idea these things could bend like that."

Ben looked sheepish.

"Not gonna live this down, are we?"

"Nope," Annie said with a mischievous grin.

***

They had just finished eating and Paul was halfway through his third glass of iced tea when he mentioned he did not feel well.

"Your head again?" Sophie asked, and he slowly nodded.

"Okay, let's get you back to your cabin. You can take another migraine tablet and lie down," Sophie suggested, and was relieved when Paul agreed.

With Claire on one side and Sophie on the other, they aided the six-foot tall, two-hundred-sixty-pound bear of a man walk back to the golf cart as best they could. Claire took point on the driving while Sophie sat beside the man on the rear seat.

"I'm sorry you don't feel well, Paul," she said softly, and he patted her hand.

"I just need my pill and a nap, and I'll be right as rain," he assured her.

Slowly, carefully, they helped him into his cabin. Paul, steadying himself by placing one hand on the wall, headed for the bedroom as Claire got him a glass of water and one of his over-the-counter migraine pills.

"What kind do you want?" she called out, acknowledging that Paul never drank water without flavoring added to it.

"Peach," came the answer, and Sophie retrieved the little bottle from the cabinet and handed it to Claire.

Once his glass of water was to his liking, Sophie carried it and his pill to him, with Claire right behind her.

He popped the pill in his mouth, took a big drink of water, and swallowed.

"That should work pretty quickly. I hope," he said as he eased off his shoes and stretched out on the bed.

"I hope so, too," Sophie answered as she squeezed his hand. "We'll come check on you at dinner time, and if you're not feeling up to joining us, we will bring dinner to you. How does that sound?"

"Thanks, Sophie. Thanks, Claire. I'll see you two later."

Chapter Six

BEN, Annie, and Brody all agreed that it was well past breaktime.

They had loaded the moving truck, taking care to place the items headed for storage in an area closest to the roll-up door since the storage unit was on the way to Ben's place. The guys drove the moving truck to the storage unit while Annie scrubbed her empty apartment until it shined, then turned in her keys and headed over to Ben's apartment.

The trio met up again at Ben's at half-past one, and all three were starving.

"I vote we order the pizza and eat before we get the rest of that stuff out of the truck," Brody mentioned, and the others agreed.

"Luckily, I called the order in on the way over here," Annie told them with a big smile. "Should be here any minute."

A grand total of three minutes elapsed before the doorbell rang. Annie met the delivery driver at the threshold and tipped him generously before she carried the two large pizza boxes into the kitchen.

After reviewing their current plans and policies, Donny explained the best way moving forward to achieve Tank and Renee's goals.

Lizzie was reluctant to join them at first – she felt uncomfortable being privy to their private financial discussions – until Tank reminded her that as the godmother, it was important for her to be aware of anything involving Tucker.

"Besides, you've been one of my best friends for how long now? Fifteen years, give or take?"

"Something like that," Lizzie replied.

"You and I went through the police academy together, and we've worked side by side and gone through doors together, and you've *always* had my back. Always. We trust you as much as any blood relative, Zim, and we would like you to be involved here."

So, she sat with them, quietly observant and becoming fascinated as her husband listened to, and then worked to address, their hopes and concerns for the future.

By the time little Tucker woke from his nap, both his mom and dad were smiling.

"I'm so glad we're taking care of this," Renee admitted. "It's been weighing on me that we didn't have everything updated and in place. This eases my mind, Donny, more than you know. Thank you."

"Me too, sweetheart," Tank readily agreed. "Now that we've got all this lined out, we can concentrate on other things – like if he'll take after his old man and play football and baseball when he gets bigger."

"A child of mine won't play *any* of them if he doesn't make good grades," Renee pointed out before she left the room to get Tucker and feed him.

Tank chuckled, his eyes full of adoration, as he watched his wife walk away.

"That woman is *fierce*."

Over in Pantego, Nathan muttered under his breath in his home office. A courier had knocked on his front door at seven a.m. and handed over a thick packet.

Inside were four case files and a handwritten note that said, *I really need to know if you think these incidents are in any way connected. Look them over. We will discuss when I call you at nine a.m. Monday – Steve.*

As a result, Nathan had spent all morning in front of his dual monitors, comparing the papers to other items contained in the FBI's secured database and trying to figure out if the puzzle pieces he had been handed had any discernable pattern linking them together.

A gentle knock on the doorframe had him looking up from his work.

"It's almost two, honey, and we said something about taking Charlie to the p-a-r-k, remember?" Bella reminded him, spelling it out to avoid Charlie, who was currently contentedly watching cartoons, whooping in excitement.

"You're right. I can continue this tonight," he admitted with a rueful smile as he saved his work and shut down his computer. "I get tunnel vision sometimes."

"You certainly do, and I know it's part of how you're wired, but you're definitely in your own little world today, baby," she replied, pointing to the untouched sandwich still sitting on the plate that she had placed on his desk around twelve-thirty.

Nathan looked where she was pointing, frowning when he saw the food perched on the corner of his L-shaped desk.

"When did you bring me that?"

"Over an hour ago, mister 'ninja-like FBI man'," she teased. "Fortunately, it should taste just the same, unlike if I had brought you anything that is meant to be eaten hot."

"You mean I didn't even notice you come in? Wow. Sorry about that, honey," he said earnestly.

"What are you working on that's got you so in the zone?"

"Hey," he retorted in jest, "I'm *always* in the zone."

"Yes, but usually not to the point of oblivion."

"Touché. Steve overnighted me some files and asked me to research them and find a common denominator, if there is one," Nathan said on a heavy exhale. "He wants to round-table about it all first thing Monday morning."

Bella closed the distance between them and took both of his hands in hers.

"Well, you look beat. Take a break with us, honey. Go with us and spend an hour or two in the fresh air and sunshine, and then, come back to it. You know as well as I do that sometimes you have to walk away from something for a bit to reset your focus so that you can find what you are looking for."

He smiled then stood up and kissed her.

"Wiser words were never spoken, honey," he said with a twinkle in his eye before he leaned around her and hollered, "Hey, Charlie! Wanna go play on the swings?"

A delighted squeal of "*Swings!*" barreled back to them from down the hallway.

Another feeding and diaper change later, and Tucker was a smiling, happy baby once more. Lizzie scooped him up again for some more aunt/godmother time and chatted with Renee as Tank went to start the grill and Donny traveled with him to talk sports.

"How's the doctoral program coming along?" Lizzie asked as she carefully untangled her hair from Tucker's grasp.

"Brutal some days. But I am determined to conquer," Renee said as she flashed a confident smile. "It's a goal I've had for years, and now it's within my reach. I can't stop now; I am much too close to getting it done."

Something in Lizzie's expression must have betrayed her thoughts because Renee leaned forward to touch Lizzie's arm.

"What's on your mind, honey?"

Lizzie sighed.

"I'm conflicted. For years, I had a 'career first' mindset. And what I do is dangerous. I'm sure Tank told you about my house exploding a while back."

"He did, and I was so thankful to hear that you and Donny were all right," Renee confirmed.

The seasoned agent sighed again.

"Yeah. I mean, I am good with the risk involved – and so is Donny. I have known since I began my career in law enforcement that the danger level was extremely high, and so I chose to focus solely on my job, because anything less than one hundred percent focused can get somebody hurt."

Renee nodded as she pointed to herself.

"Cop's wife, remember? And he and I have had this same discussion more than once. But I love him for who he is, and part of who he is as a person is being a police officer."

"*Exactly*. And Donny knows that about me, too, and he is super supportive, so I have continued down the path I chose. But then I met Nathan's little boy, Charlie. And he is adorable. I love him to pieces. And now this little one has my heart, too," Lizzie paused to glance down at a smiling Tucker.

"And it just has me thinking – what if I didn't make the right choice? I am thirty-seven years old, Renee. What if it is too late for me to be a mother? And even if it *is* still possible - how would I be able to do that and still work in the career I chose, that I *love*, when there's such risk involved of not coming home to my family one day?"

"I can't answer those questions for you, Lizzie, as much as I wish I could," Renee said gently, her eyes full of understanding and concern. "I mean, my husband weighed those *exact* same concerns when we found out I was pregnant. Should he stay in law enforcement or transition out to something safer but with less passion for the work. I told him I would support his choice no matter what, and I did. I still do. But even so, it is still a *vastly* simpler choice for men than women when you are talking about whether to have children. We are the ones physically invested from the jump. So only *you* can decide what you want and how best to proceed here."

Their conversation stalled out as the men came into the kitchen.

"We've got the grill ready, baby," Tank told Renee. "Where are the potato packets? I'll get them going first."

"They're ready for you. Seasoned and wrapped in foil. Second shelf of the fridge."

"Thanks," he said as he moved across the room to grab them, then headed outside again.

But Donny lingered, gazing at his wife.

"Lizzie," he murmured. "Are you okay?"

"I'm good. Catching up with Renee and loving on this sweet little baby," she said, injecting happiness into her face and voice so that he would not worry.

He raised an eyebrow.

"Okay, then. I'm going back outside. We've been trying to decide who the best utility infielder is this season."

"Oh, no, you're one of *those*," Renee teased. "Go on outside, then. My husband is probably thrilled to have somebody else around besides him that cares about that stuff."

Donny grinned, then left, and Lizzie slowly exhaled.

"He can tell that something is bothering you," Renee observed. "And he loves you. I can't really give you advice on what we've talked about. Like I said, you need to make those choices for yourself. But what I *will* tell you is, don't shut him out of this, Lizzie. Talk to him. Tell him what is going on and everything you are feeling. Tank shut me out at first when he was wrestling with his decision, and it caused some problems between us."

"I think this area is really pretty," Sophie said as she and Remiel stood at the water's edge. "We could shoot this just as it is, with the tree line over your shoulder, and the water behind you. And if we can catch it at the right time of day that would be even better."

"Which would be?"

"An hour or so after sunrise, or about a half-hour before sunset. There's still plenty of natural light to work with, but without the glare on the water that we're seeing right now," Sophie answered, gesturing at the lake to illustrate her point.

"I agree. Shall we come back down here after dinner?"

"Absolutely. Speaking of which, I need to stop in and check on Paul on our way back."

Remiel frowned.

"Why? What's wrong with Brother Paul?"

"He's had really bad headaches the last couple of days, and Claire and I told him we'd check on him and bring him some dinner if he doesn't feel up to joining us in the dining room."

"I'll come with you."

When they reached Paul's cabin, Remiel led the way inside.

"Hey there," he said softly as he approached the bed. "Sophie tells me you've been having more headaches again."

Paul managed to sit up.

"Yeah," he admitted. "It's been years since I've had more than one a month. Seems like they're ramping up again."

Remiel sat on the side of the bed and gently patted the older man's shoulder.

"I know you're tough as nails, Brother Paul, but there's no reason to suffer needlessly. I think you should make a visit to Sister Joanna and let her help you get rid of your headaches. Please."

"Okay," Paul grudgingly conceded after a long moment. "I will tomorrow."

"You up to coming to dinner?"

"My medicine kicked in, but I still don't feel that great," came the murmured answer.

"Do you want another pill?" Sophie offered. "I read the label. You can take up to eight of them in a twenty-four-hour period."

"Yes, please," he replied. "And more water. Cherry flavored, this time."

Sophie refilled his glass as directed and brought him another over-the-counter pill.

"I'll bring you some dinner in a little while."

Chapter Seven

THREE WEEKS PASSED, and Sophie's concern for her new friend continued to grow. Rather than Paul's headaches subsiding as she, Claire, and Paul had hoped, they had gotten worse – and lately, the typically genial man had become increasingly foul-tempered, to boot.

The trio were having breakfast on Friday morning when he uncharacteristically snapped at Claire to the point that she left the table in tears.

Sophie was shocked.

"I know you haven't been well," she said gently, "but still, she didn't deserve to be spoken to that way, Paul."

The usually gentle giant sighed.

"I know. I just... I don't know what's wrong with me lately, kiddo," he confessed as he reached into his shirt pocket and pulled out a little bottle to add his customary dose of liquid sweetener to his third glass of iced tea.

Sophie glanced over and frowned in alarm.

"Paul, you're trembling."

"What?"

"Your hands. They're shaking."

He looked at her, the concern she was feeling mirrored on his face.

"My eyes," he murmured, blinking rapidly.

"What?"

"Your face is blurry, Sophie."

"Don't move. Stay right here, I'll be right back," she urged, then raced out of the dining room to go find Sister Joanna.

On her way out she saw Claire sitting in the lobby area, wiping her eyes with a tissue.

"Hey, are you okay?"

"I will be. I know he didn't mean it. He just doesn't feel good."

"Can you go back in and sit with him? I need to find Joanna."

Claire's eyes widened.

"What happened?"

"He's got tremors and he just told me his vision is blurring."

Claire immediately rose from the couch.

"Yes, I'll stay with him."

"I'll be back as quick as I can," Sophie assured her before she ran out the door.

It was a little after eight a.m. when one of his bodyguards rapped on his bedroom door, causing Estoban Cortinas, eldest son and heir of cartel king Silvadore Cortinas, to growl in response.

"*What?*" he snarled, enraged that anyone dared to disturb his slumber.

"Patrón," came the respectful reply, "you have a phone call. Your father."

"Tell him I will call him back in ten minutes."

"But Patrón, I-."

"*Tell him!*" Estoban yelled, then winced as the pain it caused reverberated through his head.

"Sí, Patrón," his bodyguard replied before hastily retreating.

Esteban blearily looked over at the clock.

"Dios," he grumbled under his breath. "Does my father ever sleep?"

Only one way to proceed here if I want a clear head quickly, he thought with a smirk as he sat up in bed and reached into the little drawer of his nightstand.

With a practiced hand he quickly worked the powder he'd sprinkled onto the mirror into two tightly formed lines, then snorted them, one line into each nostril.

Ahh... there we go....

Estoban grinned as the superior-quality coke raged through his bloodstream like a freight train and jump-started his adrenaline.

"Now then. Let's see what dear old Papa wants of me now," he murmured, sniffling, as he reached for the phone on his nightstand.

"Good morning, Papa," he at least had the presence of mind to say when Silvadore picked up the call. "You needed me?"

"Yes," his father said without greeting, then launched at once into the reason for his call.

Estoban listened, anger growing, the hand that wasn't holding the phone fisting itself tightly against his silk sheets.

"I want you to handle it personally. Today. If our information is correct, take care of it – *discreetly,*" his father finished, stressing the word 'discreetly' and making Estoban roll his eyes.

"Yes, Papa."

He set the handpiece back on its cradle and pondered it for a moment, then picked it up again and dialed.

"I will be at your establishment at seven p.m. tonight. Be ready for my arrival," he announced in a commanding tone when the other person answered.

"Sure, Patrón, we'd be delighted to –."

Estoban interrupted, his voice steel.

"This is not a social call by any means. You have a rat in your midst, and you will assist me in catching it."

A surprised, stammered, "Yes, of course, Patrón," made him smile as he abruptly cut the groveling man off mid-sentence and hung up the phone.

Estoban Cortinas laughed, then shrugged, and threw the covers back to get out of bed.

"Better look my best," he murmured aloud as he sauntered toward his private bath. "Exactly what *does* one wear to set a rat trap?"

By the time Sophie found Joanna and returned to the dining room, Paul was beginning to realize something was very, very wrong with him. No matter how much he blinked, his eyes simply refused to focus enough for things around him to be sharp and legible.

"I think it's time we take him to the hospital," he heard someone say, and Paul started to protest but suddenly found himself almost too exhausted to even speak. He could only nod.

"I'll bring the car around," he thought he heard someone else say, but they sounded echoed and distant, like Paul was standing at the bottom of a well. He couldn't even tell for certain if the voice was male or female.

The pain in his head that had become a constant companion over the last three weeks bloomed full force again as he struggled to his feet, and Paul felt hands clutching at him before he succumbed to merciful darkness.

"Any plans tonight?" Javier asked Cruz on their lunch break.

"Nope. Not feeling that great. Just gonna stay in, order in a pizza, and watch the game. You?"

Javier held his gaze.

I need a break from you guys, so, please say no, Cruz pleaded internally. They'd gone from not including him at all in after-work activities to monopolizing his evenings lately – beginning with that first Sunday he'd been allowed to 'work' on one of the mule cars.

"Nothing planned, at the moment," he said cryptically, then walked away, leaving Cruz confused.

What was that about?

All three of them – Javier, Ramon, and Miguel – had been acting strangely toward him all morning.

He absentmindedly reached up to touch the Saint Christopher medallion hanging around his neck from a thick gold rope chain. While he always carried one with him, this medallion was one of a kind. It had been fitted with an almost impossibly tiny camera by the DEA's IT gurus, and he'd swapped it out for his usual medallion and started wearing it the first Sunday he worked at the shop.

As a result, he'd been able to secretly record irrefutable evidence of every drug-concealing vehicle that had passed through the shop for the last three weekends.

Oh, God... Cruz realized as he crumpled up his sandwich wrapper. *Have they figured out I'm a cop? But how could they possibly know? My cover identity is airtight. Enough truth to be believable and still offer some protection... unless they've been tipped off somehow?*

To his credit, he never let any of the swirling emotions he was feeling show on his face – especially since he knew all too well that the security camera mounted in the corner of the dingy breakroom wasn't there just for show.

He stood, threw away the sandwich wrapper, and headed back out to his work area to clock in and finish up the transmission service on the Ford F150 he'd been assigned.

I need to make a call tonight, he decided as he worked. *Hank's been deep undercover before. I can run this by him and get his take on things. I trust his opinion.*

And after that, he thought ruefully, *maybe it's time I ask to be extracted.*

"Earth to Lizzie," Annie said for the third time before Lizzie realized someone was speaking to her.

"Huh?"

"I said, what's the status on your part of the Baker case profile?"

"Sorry, Annie. Got a lot on my mind lately."

She pressed some buttons on her keyboard, then hit 'enter'.

"Just emailed it to you."

"Thanks," her younger teammate responded. "Are you okay?"

"Yep, never better."

"Uh huh," Annie retorted. "Sure. Hey, let's grab some sushi, my treat."

"Um, okay."

They opted for a sushi place not far from the office and settled into the booth that was tucked into a corner by itself.

The moment their order slips were turned in Annie looked at Lizzie and said, "Spill it."

Lizzie's brow wrinkled.

"What? There's nothing to spill."

"Look," Annie replied, pointing the chopsticks she'd just unwrapped, "I'm a lot of things but dumb isn't one of them. Wanna try again?"

Lizzie laughed and held up her hands.

"Fine, I surrender. Just between us, right?"

Annie looked offended.

"It hurts that you think you even have to say that to me."

"Sorry. It's just... it's big."

"Like how big?"

"Like, an 'I think I want to tell my husband I want to try for a baby' level of big."

"Oh. *Oh*," Annie exclaimed, eyes wide. "That's quite a decision, especially doing what we do, Liz."

"I know it. Which is why I'm wrestling with it so much."

"Are you worried about what Donny will say?"

"Not so much. I know he'll support whatever I decide. For me, the issue is more about what it would mean if I *do* get pregnant. I'm having trouble picturing how that would work out with my being a federal agent."

"I don't think it would be as impactful as you fear it might," Annie told her honestly. "Stay in the office and at your desk versus going in the field for a while, that's all."

"The question is, can I be okay with that?" Lizzie rejoined. "And right now, my answer to that is that I'm honestly not sure. I've always been happiest being on the frontlines, at Seattle PD, and now here. Hanging back doing paperwork has never really been my thing, you know?"

Annie shrugged.

"There are other female agents that have kids. Maybe talk to them, get their take? But when it all comes down, only you and Donny can decide to take that path or not."

"Thanks. Your turn," Lizzie remarked as the server returned with their drinks and spring rolls. "How's cohabitation so far?'

Annie flushed scarlet but couldn't prevent a mile-wide grin from forming.

It was late afternoon when Paul slowly, painfully returned to awareness as a faint voice said, "I know you don't feel well, but we need to get some papers signed so we can treat you."

He blinked rapidly then opened his eyes wide, trying his best to read at least some of the words on the pages being held in front of him.

"So tired," he mumbled.

"I know you are. Just sign these for me and we can help you feel better."

He managed to grasp the pen that was offered and scrawled his signature everywhere the blurry finger was pointing.

"There you go. All done. We can get started now. I need you to drink this for me. It will ease your pain," the voice instructed, and Paul felt two sets of hands guiding him to a sitting up position as the edge of a cup brushed his lips.

He swallowed and swallowed until the voice purred, "Good. Very good, Paul. Now just lie back and relax."

The hands maneuvered him downward gently until he was flat on his back again.

The ten-ounce cup of water and liquid poison at once began to wreak its lethal havoc on Paul's body, and he found himself gasping for air while his blood pressure skyrocketed. As he focused his full attention on desperately trying to catch his breath, he didn't even notice the sharp pinprick of a needle full of succinylcholine sliding into his vein.

Brother Paul was dead six minutes after he scrawled his last signature.

"Hi, honey," Donny said when Lizzie got home a little after six. "How was your day?"

"We need to talk," she replied, and he raised his eyebrows.

"O...*kay*," he answered warily. "Does this have to do with why you've been so.... preoccupied lately?"

"Yes, it does."

He crossed the room to her for a hug.

"You know whatever's going on, you can tell me, right?"

She hugged him back, hard, and whispered, "I know."

Lizzie stepped back from him only long enough to take his hand and lead him to the couch. They sat down, side-by-side, then pivoted to face each other, and she reached over to grab his other hand, too.

After she exhaled deeply, Lizzie dove right in.

"Do you remember when we were driving down from Seattle in that crappy moving truck and you asked me how I felt about kids?"

Both Donny's eyebrows shot up.

"Yes," he murmured, a cautious tone creeping into his voice. "I *also* remember freaking you out – well, both of us out, to be honest - because I brought the subject up way, way too soon."

"And it *was* too soon. Back then, I mean," Lizzie confirmed. "And we said we would table that discussion and come back to it later."

"I remember. And I remember you said kids were a level six and we had only barely reached a level two."

"Well," she said, "now that we're at level five, being married and all, I think it's time to bring that topic back into play and discuss it."

Senior DEA agent and serial skirt-chaser Hank Myers leaned back on his couch, flipping channels and lamenting his lack of female companionship on a Friday night. When his cell phone rang, he checked the caller ID, then muted his TV and answered with a grin.

"Hey there, buddy! Long time no talk. How's it going down there?" he asked his best friend.

"Almost there, I think," Cruz Delgado murmured quietly. "I think within the next two weeks or so, we'll be able to make our move. But I don't think I will be able to talk anymore until then. Tonight's a fluke. It's the first time I haven't had one of them stuck to my side like glue in almost a month."

"Do they suspect..." Hank's voice trailed off in concern.

"I don't know for sure, but they *were* acting really strange all day today. My gut says there's trouble brewing."

"How so?"

"Nothing I can really put my finger on, man. Just a whole vibe, and...".

"What's wrong?" Hank asked when Cruz paused his sentence.

"Pizza's here," Cruz answered. "That was fast. Normally it takes forty minutes, at least. Hang tight, I'll be right back."

"Sure."

Cruz set the phone down on the coffee table beside the TV remote and went to his front door.

"The big boss wants to see you," he heard his unwanted visitor say when he swung the door open, fully expecting to see a teenager holding a pizza box.

"Okay, sure, I can be there first thing in -" a confused Cruz started to answer but was cut off mid-sentence.

"No," Miguel said firmly as he stepped across the threshold, closed the door, and began to walk toward Cruz. "*Now, ese.*"

Sensing trouble, Cruz backed away slowly from Miguel, his pulse and mind racing so fast that when he felt a malevolent presence behind him, he almost yelped. A split-second later Javier, who had both a height and weight advantage on him, had wrapped him in a crushing bear hug that pinned his arms to his side as Ramon roughly shoved a burlap hood over his head.

"Stop, Ramon! You're forgetting something, pendejo," Miguel admonished as he stepped forward and lifted the hood long enough to apply a wide swath of duct tape to Cruz's mouth. Then he lowered the hood and grunted.

Cruz's hands were forced behind his back, the cold, impersonal steel of handcuffs closing around each wrist in response to Miguel's unspoken command.

"There. Much better. Proceed," Miguel directed.

Cruz felt himself being lifted, then carried, and began to struggle mightily. He felt the grip around his ankles loosen and used the small reprieve to his advantage, pulling one leg free then kicking as hard as he could. A sickening crunch followed by a scream of angry, pained surprise made the corners of his mouth twist upward into as big a smile as he could manage behind the duct tape.

At least I got one good lick in, it sounds like. Maybe I will get lucky and get a few more.

But a sharp pain exploding at his left temple brought a sudden and painful rush of stars into his limited vision before his world swam into grey. The last conscious thought Cruz had was of the pain radiating through his head before he felt himself flying forward then downward into blackness.

Chapter Eight

On the other end of the open line, Hank heard rustling as Cruz set the phone down, then footsteps.

He went to answer the door, Hank realized.

Hank could hear Cruz and another man talking, but their distance from the phone was too great; he could not make out what was said.

His heart raced as he heard multiple footsteps, somehow menacing, faint at first, then more loudly. Next came a muffled shout, followed by what sounded like a struggle of some sort.

He overrode his natural instincts to call out to his friend, instead willing himself into silence as he strained to hear every scrap of background noise coming to him across the tiny speaker. Hank held his breath, hoping that Cruz would pick up the phone and tell him he was all right.

Instead, he heard multiple footsteps again, coming closer from the sounds of it, a pause, a scream of pain, then more footsteps fading away again before there was another rustle.

The hair stood on the back of Hank's neck as the sound of

someone breathing filled the line. He closed his eyes and swallowed hard when a gruff, mysterious voice spoke ominously into his ear.

"He's going to have to call you back."

The last thing Hank heard was a crash, like the phone had been dropped, before the call disconnected completely.

Hank sprang into action and was putting his shoes back on with his phone pinned between his ear and his shoulder.

"Patch me through to Dallas," he barked as he stood up and marched into the bedroom to retrieve his service weapon and badge and pack an overnight bag before he tromped to the kitchen to grab his keys off the counter.

"Senior Agent Myers here," he said to the man who'd picked up the line, "and you've got a big problem with one of your undercover operatives. You need to check on Cruz Delgado. Turn his camera on."

He paused, listened, then snarled, "I don't give a *damn* what your title is! Don't you dare take that tone with me. I was on the phone with him just now when he was abducted. He's been my best friend for twenty years and I *will* find him, with or without your help. *Sir*."

He hung up the call, muttered a string of profanity, then dialed another number.

"Roscoe, I need to get to Fort Worth, Texas. How fast can you get me there?"

Once they'd gotten their prey loaded into the customized panel van parked in the alleyway behind Cruz's house, Ramon pulled out a handkerchief and clapped it to his face.

"I *told* you we should've tied his feet together," he lamented, trying his best to stem the flow of blood that streamed down from his broken nose. "He has on steel-toed boots."

"Stop complaining, ese. He actually made your nose look much better," a usually silent Javier teased with a grin, which earned him a laugh from Miguel and a deep-throated growl from Ramon.

Still chuckling, Miguel produced zip ties and quickly stripped their victim of his dangerous footwear before he bound an unconscious Cruz's ankles together.

"Done. Let's get moving. The boss will be at the shop in twenty minutes. He will be really pissed if we are late."

***

"Have you heard any updates on how Paul is doing?" Sophie asked Claire when they met up again in the dining room at dinnertime.

"No, not yet. Have you?"

"No," Sophie confirmed. "And I'm worried about him."

"Me too," the older woman said, wringing her hands.

"Maybe we can go to the hospital and check on him after dinner. See if we can't cheer him up," Sophie suggested, and Claire nodded enthusiastically.

Their mood improved at the thought of going to see him, and they chatted all through the meal with the others at their table. They'd just finished eating when Remiel entered the room, his face ashen.

"If I could have everyone's attention, please," he called out, his voice solemn.

Once the group members were all looking at him, he cleared his throat.

"I'm so sorry to have to tell you all that we've lost Brother Paul this evening," he announced, his voice breaking.

Sophie gasped with shock and grief before she burst into tears.

Remiel paused, both to acknowledge his group's stunned reactions and to collect himself, before he continued speaking, his voice trembling with emotion.

"He was a fine man, and a good and faithful friend, and he will be greatly missed. As he had no family, I'd like for us to have a memorial service for him here, and I will let you all know once that has been arranged."

With that, he turned and slowly walked out of the room. Sophie was on her feet and following him before she even realized what she was doing.

"Remiel, wait," she called out as they entered the lobby.

He turned slowly to face her, and she noticed his eyes were misted over with tears, too.

"What... what happened to him?" Sophie stammered, her sorrow flowing freely down her cheeks. "How can he just be *gone* like that?"

"I don't know, Sophie," he said gently. "I don't know."

"It's not fair," she wailed, her heart breaking.

He stepped forward and enveloped her in a warm hug.

"No," he whispered, patting her back as she sobbed. "No, it's not."

Cruz Delgado's brain gradually climbed up and out of the unconscious stupor that the attack had thrust upon him. The first sensation that registered was a still-throbbing pain at his left temple from whatever they'd used to hit him in the head.

Willing to bet that even a seven-day bender wouldn't cause this kind of headache...

The next thing he became aware of was a smooth, cold surface underneath his right cheek. He slowly opened his eyes to realize that the hood they'd put over his head was gone.

Maybe not a good thing... man that light is bright...

Wincing at the intensity of the beam that rained down from somewhere overhead and reflected sharply off the dull gray surface under him, he instinctively tried to bring his hands up to shield his eyes. Cruz was puzzled at first when they wouldn't move, until he remembered that his abductors had bound them behind his back. He tried a frown and realized that the wide swath of extra-sticky tape across the lower half of his face was still in place, as well.

Okay, he thought, taking inventory of his situation. *Monster headache, hood's off, tape and handcuffs are still on, and I am lying on my side on a concrete floor.*

He closed his eyes again and willed himself to concentrate on his surroundings, straining to hear something, anything, that would give him a clue as to where Miguel and his goons had taken him.

Cruz wasn't destined to question very long. Mere moments passed before a slow, deliberate slap...slap...slap of what he suspected were leather- soled shoes against the hard surface serving as his resting place reverberated through the stillness.

He tensed, waiting, as the owner of the footsteps came closer, walking behind him and then around his head to stop in front of Cruz's face.

"Funny," a heavily accented voice said drolly. "He doesn't look like a cop."

His mystery host tapped Cruz lightly on the left cheek a few times, then said, "I know you're awake, ese. Might as well look at me."

Cruz opened his eyes, less to follow orders and more to confirm his own suspicions about the man's footwear – which was the only thing he could see clearly. The rest of the man was obscured in shadow.

I knew it... they're Testoni, Cruz, himself a bit of a clothes hound, realized with satisfaction. *Well, whatever else he is, at least he has good taste in men's dress shoes...*

The nerve-shredding scrape of metal across the floor interrupted his tangent and alerted him that someone was dragging something closer to his position. Cruz kept his focus on the pricey shoes, watching as the man wearing them crossed one leg over the other so that his right foot dangled in the air dangerously close to Cruz's face.

They brought him a chair, Cruz realized. *Which means whatever is about to happen won't be quick.*

His system flooded with fear at the thought.

"Take the tape off," came the brusque command, and rough hands ripped it away, taking a good part of Cruz's skin cells with it.

Instinctively, he poked his tongue out and ran it across his lips, wincing at the raw flesh that he could tell was already beginning to swell.

Play dumb, he reminded himself.

"Nice shoes. Why am I here?" he croaked in a raspy voice.

The mystery man's right shoe swayed back and forth, back and forth, before suddenly changing direction and making such hard contact with Cruz's nose that a starburst bloomed in his vision.

Okay, maybe not a fan of Testoni anymore, Cruz admitted when he felt and tasted blood pouring from his broken nose and his stomach clenched with nausea.

"I ask the questions, not you," the man growled.

As the clock crept toward midnight, and while most of the residents of Lighte's Landing slept, the two responsible for Paul Bingman's untimely demise held snifters of ten-year-old brandy aloft in celebration.

"To another successful – and profitable - conclusion," one of the co-conspirators announced with satisfied glee.

"Hear, hear," answered the other, before they lightly clinked their glasses together. "But I do think we ought to wait a while before we pick the next lottery winner. And Paul's death hit the group hard, so, maybe you should pick one that's not so... *beloved* next time."

"I could choose Sophie," came the snarky reply.

"I've already told you she's off limits."

"Why? You want her in your bed?"

A crack and a gasp of surprised pain as hand struck cheekbone.

"Know your place," his angry voice threatened, "or there *will* be consequences."

A noise in the hall stopped all conversation.

"What was that?"

A finger to his lips clearly conveyed the message to his companion to remain quiet, and the one in charge crept silently over, then flung open the door.

For several tense moments, there was no movement or sound, and the door was closed again.

"I think we might want to find another place to meet, just to be safe," he solemnly pronounced.

Lizzie tossed and turned but could not get her brain to throttle back enough to allow her to rest. She turned her head to the right and grimaced at the alarm clock's display.

Twelve-oh-nine a.m.

She sighed quietly, then drew back the covers and was about to ease out of bed so she didn't wake him when Donny murmured, "Where are you going?"

"I can't sleep."

"Me either. Wanna talk about it?"

"I don't know that there's anything more to talk about, honey," she told him. "I mean, you said you're good with whatever I decide."

"And I am."

"So, all the pressure is on *me* to make a choice that impacts *both* of us," she pointed out. "See why I can't sleep?"

"I didn't mean it like that, Liz. I was just – I'm trying to make sure you know that I am very aware that it's *your* body, and possibly *your* career, which could change the most. That's all," he said, gently caressing her face. "Would I love for us to have a child together? Absolutely. Do I want you to feel forced to abandon the career you've worked so long and hard to build? No. I don't."

"But here's the thing," he continued, sitting up now. "I don't think it's as drastic a decision as that. At least, not for the long term. If we decide to try for a child, the most vulnerable time concerning your job would be through the pregnancy, right?"

"Right. Especially the further along I get."

"Okay, so, while you're pregnant, you might have to adjust your approach and not be in the field for part of it. But that's not a forever thing, Liz. Once the baby gets here, if you wanna go back to being in the middle of the action, then I think you should."

"Really?"

"Yes. Of course. Why wouldn't I? You excel at kicking ass and taking names – it's one of the many reasons I fell in love with you. Harder to do that stuff from a desk, honey."

"But wouldn't you be worried?"

"News flash, Liz. I *already* worry every time you leave for a shift," Donny admitted as he sank back into bed and pulled her close. "But I knew from day one that you're a cop through and through. Federal, city, doesn't matter. It's part of who you are, and I'm proud as hell of you. You make it sound like this is an either/or thing. It's not. Being a kick-ass agent is *not* mutually exclusive to being a parent. Just look at Nathan."

She snuggled closer to him, their conversation at a lull.

"Donny?" she whispered.

"Yes?" he whispered back, one hand tracing warm, soothing circles on her back.

"I really want a baby."

"Then we'll start trying."

She yawned, and he chuckled and brushed his lips against her hair.

"Later, that is. You're exhausted, honey. Let's get some sleep, for now."

"Definite rain check," she murmured as she laid her head on his chest and dropped off to sleep.

Sophie and Claire were sitting at Sophie's tiny table in her cabin, each with a cup of hot tea to help soothe their souls.

Neither one had been able to sleep, and Sophie was grateful when she'd opened her door a little past midnight to find Claire standing there. She'd reached forward and grabbed Claire in a fierce hug before leading her inside and shutting the door.

Now they sat across from one another, and the misery on Claire's face precisely mirrored Sophie's feelings.

"I just... I can't believe he's gone," Claire said sadly as she absent-mindedly stirred the tea in her cup. "He was so full of life, so healthy."

Sudden awareness widened Sophie's eyes.

"Claire," she said carefully, "were you and Paul... you know... more than friends?"

Claire flushed a deep pink.

"We.... we realized we had some feelings for each other going on, and we were exploring that," the older woman managed to say before starting to cry again. "And now..."

Sophie reached over and squeezed her hand.

"I'm so sorry, Claire."

"He wanted things between us to move at a faster pace than I did," Claire revealed with a wan smile. "But he was a gentleman. He knew I'd been badly hurt before, and he said he was willing to take things slowly if it made me more comfortable. Now I wish I'd just dived right in."

A sudden knock on the door startled them both. Sophie raised an eyebrow at Claire, who shrugged in confusion.

Her heart racing, Sophie slowly walked over and opened the door and stepped out into the night air.

"No one's here," she called out to Claire, then pivoted to go back inside her cabin.

It was then that she saw the note that had been tacked to the cabin's exterior wall just beside her front door. Sophie carefully pulled the piece of paper down and quickly moved back inside to close and lock her door.

"Who was it?" Claire asked.

"I didn't see anyone," Sophie replied. "But whoever it was, they left me this."

She sat down again and carefully unfolded the paper to find an ominous message awaiting her. She skimmed it once, paled, then looked up at Claire with terror in her eyes.

"What is it?" Claire demanded, and a shaken Sophie thrust the note into her hand.

"I overheard part of a conversation tonight that I'm pretty sure I wasn't supposed to," Claire read aloud. *"I didn't hear all of it, but from what I did hear, I don't think what happened to Brother Paul was natural, at all. I think they might have killed him."*

Claire's free hand stretched out toward Sophie, and she clutched it tightly and watched as Claire closed her eyes, clenched her jaw, and swallowed hard before she recited the rest.

"There's more. The other part I heard... I think you might be in danger too, Sophie. I am getting the hell out of this place, and if you're smart, you will leave, too."

The two sat, stunned and silent, for a long moment.

"Whoever this person is... if they're right, you should run, Sophie," Claire urged her. "Get as far away as you can, as fast as you can."

"*No,*" Sophie protested, her soul-deep need to avenge her friend beginning to stride past her fear and take control. "If Paul was murdered, I'm not leaving until I find proof."

Meanwhile, the primary player in what had been overheard waited until his co-conspirator was gone, then slid back a wooden panel to reveal a bank of computer monitors.

A simple press of a button rewound the electronic recording, and the predator smiled as the security system's extra features that no one at Lighte's Landing knew about but him clearly revealed the eavesdropper hovering in the hallway. He watched the figure press one ear against the door, then dash away suddenly out of the camera's range.

"Sweet Brittany," he sighed, and licked his lips in anticipation of her punishment that he planned to mete out personally to the inquisitive eighteen-year-old. "So young. So full of promise. So... *ripe*. It's a shame you had to be so nosy."

He tapped a few more keys and smiled again as he watched the live video feed from Brittany's cabin.

"Well then, guess I'd better get a move on. Wouldn't want you to disappear on me," he murmured before he slid the panel closed again and left the room to intercept the would-be runaway.

Chapter Nine

CRUZ WAS BEGINNING to sorely miss being laid out on the chilly and uncomfortable floor.

After what felt like days of brutal kicks to the head, stomach, and back, the man interrogating him had opted to switch tactics, and with a simple wave of his hand, his goons sprang into action.

Javier and Ramon were all smiles as they roughly hauled a battered and bloodied Cruz up to a standing position. Ramon ensured his cooperation via a gun muzzle touching the back of Cruz's head. Meanwhile, Javier forced his feet as far apart as possible and clamped thick iron shackles around each ankle, then repositioned his hands over his head and attached the handcuff chain to a large hook that conveniently dropped down from the ceiling.

The whir of an electric motor cut through the temporary silence, and Cruz felt himself being lifted and stretched. He gritted his teeth, unwilling to give them the satisfaction of crying out, but as the whirring continued an unspeakable agony crept into his body. Any sensation in his hands and arms dissipated, replaced by what seemed like a thousand needles pricking his skin as the hoist pulled him upward.

The needles were almost immediately replaced by a bone-searing white-hot pain as Cruz's ligaments and joints bore the brunt of two opposing forces – the shackles securing him firmly to the floor while the hoist continued lifting him toward the heavens.

His pain had reached a fever pitch by the time the whirring noise finally stopped. His vision blurring with agony, Cruz managed to open his swollen eyelids wide enough long enough to finally get a brief look at the face of the man in charge.

What he saw killed any hope, however small, that Cruz had left of getting out of his current situation alive. He'd memorized the DEA files, and he'd seen that face and read the background enough times to know that Estoban Cortinas, second-in-command of the entire cartel, was about to personally ensure that he met his maker.

Cruz held Estoban's gaze until the man moved out of his narrowing field of vision, then closed his throbbing eyes again, sank his chin to his chest, and accepted his fate, whispering a fervent prayer for it to be over quickly.

The first and second massive strikes of heavy lead pipe that broke both kneecaps made him scream behind the fresh swath of tape that someone had clapped over his mouth.

The third and fourth strikes that broke four ribs, ruptured his spleen, and punctured his left lung sent Cruz Delgado hurtling back into the darkness.

He never felt the lethal blows to the back of his head.

***

After packing up everything she owned, Brittany sat on the edge of her bed and wrestled with her next steps since she didn't have her own means of transportation.

I'll have to try to talk someone into taking me to town in the morning, she realized. *Even if it wasn't a twenty-minute ride by car, there's no way in hell I'm gonna try to walk out of here in the middle of the night. It's creepy around here in the dark.*

Resigned to her wait, she sighed, pulled off her shoes, and stretched out on the bed. She turned out the bedside lamp and rolled toward the window, her mind racing.

She was so preoccupied with thinking through what her steps might be once she was away from Lighte's Landing that she never heard the intruder enter her cabin and creep up behind her.

The next thing Brittany knew she'd been flung forward onto her stomach with her arms pinned underneath her, and a heavy weight was pressing the length of her petite frame into her mattress. One huge hand fisted in her hair and yanked backward roughly as another clamped a horribly smelly cloth down tightly over her mouth and nose.

"We're gonna have some fun now, just you and me," a deep male voice filled with unadulterated evil whispered lustily in her ear before she felt hot breath and then a wet tongue moving down the back of her neck. In her dazed state Brittany didn't know what to make of it at first.

But when her unknown assailant began to grind his body provocatively against hers, she realized his intentions for her and began to tremble violently, her eyes wide with terror.

The big breath of air she tried to take in to scream for help only served to aid the chloroform-soaked rag in finally working its magic, and the fumes she inhaled so deeply sent Brittany spiraling downward into oblivion.

Estoban carefully wiped his prints from the pipe before he leaned it against the wall, then gestured for a second towel. He used it to wipe first his brow, then the rest of his face, then his bare upper torso where some castoff blood spatter had landed.

"Get rid of him," he muttered to the three men staring, pale and wide-eyed, at the cartel boss they'd just watched beat a man to death.

As he stalked toward the tiny bathroom in the corner to try to clean up, the rest did as he commanded.

Javier at once moved to unshackle the corpse's ankles while Miguel took point on the hoist controls, leaving Ramon the gruesome task of cradling the body in front of him as the slack was increased enough to lay it down on the floor.

"But where should we..." Ramon grunted and was cut off by the big boss, who had returned to the chair and picked up his shirt.

"There," Estoban directed calmly and pointed, as if he was advising where best to hang a painting rather than dispose of another human being. "No one will find him."

Javier grabbed the legs, and an increasingly nauseated Ramon placed his arms under each shoulder while Miguel lumbered across the space and lifted a two-foot diameter hatch.

Together the two flunkies wrestled the body over to the opening of the eleven-foot deep, three-thousand gallon used motor oil reservoir under the shop and dropped it inside, then watched as it disappeared beneath the liquid's inky black surface.

"You... you sure no one will find him?" Ramon blurted out, forgetting his place as he looked down with dismay at his favorite – and now, blood-soaked and ruined - shirt.

Estoban closing the distance to slap him hard across his face silenced any further questions.

"When the truck comes to empty the tank, what diameter is the hose?" he asked softly as he buttoned up his dress shirt again, his voice in direct contrast to the fire flashing in his eyes.

"Three inches, four, at most," a cowed Ramon answered as he rubbed his stinging cheek.

"Trust me, our little rat won't fit through that," Estoban snapped tersely. "Unless you'd like to see for yourself?"

Ramon took two steps backward, shaking his head furiously.

"Good. Do us all a favor and stop thinking."

"Y-y-yes, sir."

Estoban turned his attention to Miguel.

"You've proven valuable – for the most part," he intoned, sending a caustic glance Ramon's way before he continued. "I have another task for the three of you, one that means a great deal to me personally."

The shop owner bowed low before he replied, "Patrón, whatever you ask, it's yours."

Estoban strolled back over to the chair to retrieve the custom-made suit jacket that he'd taken off and set aside.

"Very well. Let us adjourn to your office, perhaps open some tequila."

The three men followed Estoban into Miguel's office, where Estoban promptly reiterated his ranking in the group by claiming the single chair for his own and beginning to speak as Miguel poured out four shots of tequila.

"Now then," he said, fingers steepled, "some months ago my little brother Izan was murdered. Shot down in cold blood by an FBI agent in Chicago. You're going to find the man responsible and bring him to me in Reynosa - alive."

Miguel's brow creased in confusion.

"Forgive me, Patrón, but you wish us to go to Chicago?"

Estoban slowly shook his head.

"That agent fled south and was last seen right here in Fort Worth. Other agents in this area helped him hide. I want you to persuade the ones that helped him run away like a spineless coward that it is in their best interests to hand him over peacefully."

He took the next few minutes to brief them on the details of their assignment, then rose and stepped around the desk and handed a business card to Miguel.

"You can reach me at this number, day or night," Estoban said as he buttoned up his suit jacket and straightened his cuffs. "You have two weeks. After that, I will find another to fulfill this task and the three of you will join the rat. Understood?"

Three heads nodded vigorously.

Estoban reached out to pick up the small glass of liquor Miguel had poured for him.

"Do not fail me, gentlemen. I will take it as a personal offense," he announced with a malicious smile, then downed the shot and handed the empty glass to Miguel. "Good night."

With that, Estoban leisurely strolled out of the office to return to the stretch limo waiting for him.

Once they were certain he was gone, Ramon glanced at Miguel.

"Dios, ese," he whispered, "what have you gotten us into?"

"It will be fine," Miguel assured him.

"You mean you *hope* it will," Javier chimed in from his position in the corner with a dull, flat monotone. "He beat Cruz to death with a pipe based on a rumor, a *suspicion*, nothing more. We have just seen with our own eyes what he is capable of. If we do not find this Agent Jones, we are all dead men. That much is certain."

"Then I guess we had better not fail," Miguel said grimly.

In the Dallas regional office, the tech on overnight shift that had remotely activated Cruz's medallion camera refreshed the connection, then frowned as he reached over and dialed his supervisor's extension.

"Sir, I think we have a problem."

It was almost five-thirty a.m. before he made it back to his own cabin for a much-needed shower. As he peeled off his dirt-crusted clothes, he wrinkled his nose.

Not salvageable, I don't think. And it's not like I can just take them to the laundry room. What will I say if someone sees me? Better to throw them away...

"But it was *so* worth it," he murmured with a sated smile as he relived – and relished – the night's activities. "And her bags are in the lake. No one will ever know she didn't actually leave."

Decision made, he carried the jeans and t-shirt over to the trash can, then hustled to the shower to soothe the overworked muscles he'd strained from hastily digging a shallow grave by moonlight.

Afterward, he hurried through the breaking dawn back toward the main building with the express purpose of editing a certain cabin's recording. He closed and locked his door and moved swiftly over to the wall of monitors.

Once he'd made a copy of the specific footage that he wanted to be able to watch again privately at his leisure, he deleted the primary recording and replaced it with a duplication of the previous day's benign video.

That done, he slid the panel closed again, made sure his door locked firmly behind him after he stepped out into the hall, and headed to the dining room.

Chapter Ten

Agent Hank Myers' private flight landed at Meacham Airport at six-forty in the morning. Dangerous weather systems between their origin and their destination meant that Roscoe, an experienced pilot and one of Hank's poker buddies, had to improvise on the fly to skirt the huge thunderstorms once they'd finally been cleared for takeoff.

"Thanks, Roscoe," Hank said, extending his hand to his friend in gratitude.

"Anytime, buddy. Hope you find him. Watch your back, man."

Hank gathered his overnight bag and hustled down the narrow steps to the waiting car he'd called ahead to arrange.

He climbed into the back seat and rattled off the address to the driver, finishing with, "As soon as possible, please."

"Just so you know, traffic is already heavy," the driver replied, holding Hank's gaze in the rear-view mirror. "Rush hour around here starts early. But I'll do the best I can."

"I appreciate it," Hank replied, then turned his gaze eastward to watch the sun climbing higher into the sky.

Hang in there just a little longer, Cruz. I will find you. No matter what it takes.

Sophie woke with a start around eight a.m. and rubbed her eyes.

"Huh. Guess I managed to get some sleep after all," she muttered under her breath as she kicked back the covers and stood, stretched mightily and yawned before she headed for a shower.

While her body moved on autopilot to complete her morning routine, her mind gnawed on the suspicions planted in her head by the mysterious letter.

Shame whoever gave me that didn't name names. If Paul was killed as the letter claimed, then it could be anyone at Lighte's Landing. That's a huge suspect pool. How am I going to figure out who's responsible? I have no idea where to begin.

She tilted her head back to rinse out her shampoo.

If Susan were here, she'd know exactly where to start... she's excellent at digging into things and finding the truth. That's what makes her great at her job...

Her hands stopped working conditioner into her hair as she considered it.

But how can I get her advice about this without freaking her out? I can't tell her the whole story. She'll show up here pounding on the gate if she thinks I'm in danger.

Sophie frowned, even as the recollection of how protective Susan could be of her warmed her heart.

I need to think this through some more before I start anything. Right now, the only one here that I know for sure I can trust is Claire, since she was with me when I got that letter. But she's suffered enough, and I don't want to put her in harm's way. Better if she stays out of it.

Sophie rinsed out her hair a final time then turned off the tap, stepped out onto her bathmat and reached for a towel.

Lizzie had just walked to the bank of elevators in the lobby when she heard someone call her name. Confused, she turned and watched as a tall, muscular man carrying a duffle bag walked toward her. When she realized who it was, her jaw dropped open in surprise.

Hank Myers? You've got to be kidding me. What the hell is he doing here?

The six-foot-three, muscled, blond-haired and blue-eyed DEA agent had been very reluctant to accept the word 'no' the last time she'd seen him. Donny had taken it well under the circumstances, because her telling Myers off had led directly to Donny and Lizzie professing their love for the first time. But now that she and Donny were married, she knew her husband would not hesitate for an instant to cause Myers bodily harm if he messed with her again.

I suppose it's too late to pretend I didn't hear him. Shame.

"Agent Myers, nice to see you again," she murmured politely, then braced herself for one of the inevitable pickup lines that she was certain the man lived to invent.

But as he approached, she immediately noticed the clench to his jaw and the tension in his frame.

"Detective Zimmerman. You look well. What are you doing in Dallas?"

"It's Special Agent Zimmerman now, actually," she informed him, "and I transferred down here. My question is, why are *you* here?"

He stared at her intently for several moments.

"Can we go somewhere more private and talk for a minute?"

Great, here it comes, Lizzie thought to herself, barely stopping her eyes from rolling. *Some people never change.*

But something of her emotions must have escaped her will and flitted across her features, because his response was terse – and surprising.

"This is a strictly professional conversation, Lizzie. You made it very, very clear to me that is where things would stay between you and me."

She relaxed her guard.

"Follow me."

They took the elevators to the eighth floor, where Lizzie escorted him to a small conference room and shut the door behind them.

"What's going on?"

Hank dropped his duffel bag on the table and ran both hands through his hair.

"My best friend was on undercover assignment down here and he's gone missing. I'm here to find him."

Intrigued, Lizzie's eyebrows raised.

"How do you know he's missing?"

"We were in the middle of a conversation last night when he set the phone down to answer the door. I heard a struggle, a shout, a scream, then silence. After that someone else got on the phone – I didn't recognize the voice - and said Cruz would have to call me back. Then the line went dead."

"Oh."

"And he's not working just any case, Lizzie," Hank said earnestly. "They hand-selected him to infiltrate the Cortinas cartel's network in Fort Worth."

"There's a lot of chatter about them lately," Lizzie shared. "They've gone so far as to target our team down here."

"*What?*"

Lizzie read him in on the history involving Agent Jones and Izan Cortinas, finishing with, "So we've been briefed to be even more aware of our surroundings than usual. No one goes into the field alone until further notice."

"Just pairing up won't be enough. Do you have any idea what Estoban Cortinas is capable of, Lizzie? Because I do. He's pure evil walking around in human form. And one of our sources got word to us that confirmed what we've suspected for some time now. He doesn't just help his father's empire make and peddle cocaine. He's become addicted to it. That makes him ten times as lethal. Rumor has it that the old man is finding it harder and harder to keep Estoban under control."

"Why are you telling me all this?"

"Because I know I can trust you."

"How can you be so sure, Myers? We only worked together on one case for a couple of weeks – if that long."

He took a step toward her.

"Yes, but even in that short time, I realized how professional you are and how seriously you take being on the job. I also realized that I could trust you with my life if need be."

Lizzie pinned him with an appraising stare.

"Does your branch director even know you're here?" she asked softly.

"No," came the surly answer.

Lizzie sighed.

"So, you're just gonna buck all rules and regs and charge right in, is that it? I know you are worried about your friend, but that's a half-baked plan, Myers. It's not only dangerous, but it could cost you your career."

He swiftly closed the distance between them and gripped her shoulders tightly.

"Don't you understand? I don't give a *damn* about my career," he snarled as he shook her, his ice-blue eyes alight with raw anger. "Cruz Delgado is the best friend I have ever had, and I *will* save him, Lizzie, with or without anyone's stamp of approval."

"How about you take your hands off my agent and step back?" a voice thundered ominously from the now open doorway. Lizzie and Hank both turned their heads to see a furious Nathan braced for a fight, one hand on the service weapon at his hip.

Hank released her, then lifted his hands in the universally under-stood sign of surrender and backed away quickly to put some space between himself and Lizzie.

"That's better," Nathan drawled as he stepped into the room, flanked by Ben and Annie. "Now, you want to tell me who the hell you are and why you're here?"

Hank glanced over at Lizzie, and she could see the question in his eyes.

"You can trust them," she confirmed.

"Well, then. You all might as well have a seat," Hank said as he took one himself. "And I will start from the beginning."

"How did you sleep? Did you manage to get any rest?" Sophie quietly asked Claire as they sat down to breakfast.

"Not much," Claire confessed. "It still seems surreal to me, to be honest. I keep thinking he's going to walk through that door and yell 'gotcha'."

"I know. Me too," Sophie commiserated, squeezing her friend's hand.

"I need to keep busy, try not to dwell on it," Claire said. "I volunteered to make the run to the farmer's market today. You want to go?"

"I'm supposed to meet Remiel later today, so, as long as we're back by six, I'm in."

Sophie glanced around the room, silently counting occupants in her head.

"Not everyone's here this morning," she remarked.

"No," Claire confirmed. "There's a group of about seven of them that eat early then get out to the garden to harvest and load the truck for the trip into town."

Maybe that's my place to start, Sophie realized. *Build a list of who typically does what and when around here, then work backward and see if I can't find a variance in the patterns that might explain what happened to Paul.*

The realization made her feel more centered.

Maybe it's time I volunteer for some things, too. That should give me more access so I can take a deeper look around.

And I know just where to start.

"I'll be right back," she told Claire. "I need to talk to Remiel for a moment."

Sophie finally found the leader of the group in the tiny office in the chapel and knocked softly on the doorframe to get his attention.

"Hello, Sophie. Nice to see you. Come on in. I was just writing out some thoughts to share at Paul's service tomorrow morning."

"Oh. That soon."

Remiel nodded.

"Yes. At nine a.m."

She briskly walked forward and took a seat in the right-hand chair facing his desk.

"Everything all right?"

"Well, I had a couple of questions," she began.

"Sure. What's going on?"

Sophie took a deep breath.

Make this convincing.

"I'd like to volunteer to take care of packing up Paul's things," she announced. "He was a good friend to me, Remiel. He was one of the first people to really make me feel welcomed here. And I'd like to repay that kindness by making sure his belongings are cared for properly. Not that I don't trust others, but..."

"I get it," Remiel said gently. "You need it to help with closure."

She nodded.

"Yes, that's it exactly."

He smiled warmly at her before he replied, "I completely understand, and I think you should do that. What was your other question?"

"It's about volunteering, in general. I'd like to pull my weight around here more. Is there a list somewhere?"

Remiel grinned.

"As a matter of fact, there is. Andreas maintains it, so he can help you with that. I know for a fact he's going to need more help in the kitchen while Brittany's gone. How do you feel about cooking?"

Sophie's eyes widened with surprise.

"Brittany left? When?"

He shrugged.

"Sometime last night. But as I said before, members come and go as they please."

"Interesting," Sophie mumbled. "She seemed happy here."

"Yes," he agreed. "But I do know that her grandmother's health has deteriorated lately. Brittany and I talked about it just a few days ago, and she mentioned going to see her."

"Well, I hope all that turns out okay."

"I'm sure it will all work out as it's meant to. While you're here, Sophie, I wanted to ask – did you have a specific location in mind for this evening's video shoot?"

He was halfway through sharing the history of Cruz's involvement with gathering intel on the Cortinas group when his phone rang.

Hank looked at the phone, then grimaced.

"It's my director. Up in Seattle. I'd better take this," he said apologetically, then answered the call.

"Good morn -" he began, then listened, closing his eyes, and holding the device away from his ear as his boss shouted at him.

Across the table from him, Lizzie and Nathan glanced at one another.

"Guess they got wind of his trip down here," Nathan murmured from the side of his mouth, and Lizzie nodded.

After several minutes, Hank snapped, "Understood," hung up on his boss, then hurled his phone against the wall.

"What just happened?" Annie asked softly.

"They're trying to tie my hands, that's what happened," Hank growled as he stood and paced the floor. "It's a chest-thumping match. They're angry that I called down here last night demanding that the locals check on Cruz. I've been threatened with suspension if I don't return to Seattle as soon as possible."

"What are you going to do?" Lizzie queried.

"What do you think? I'm gonna go up to the tenth floor of this building, turn in my badge and service weapon, fill out a personal leave form, and find Cruz on my own. I've got six weeks of vacation stored up. They can't stop me from using it – or from looking for him. My badge is a small price to pay for making sure he's all right."

"Besides," he continued, shaking with rage, "the conversation I just had made it crystal clear to me that they really don't care what happens to him, so long as their precious case isn't damaged."

He leveled his gaze at Lizzie and his tone softened.

"I understand now."

"Understand what?"

"How you felt about Jessica, and why you got so angry when I said what I did back then," he told her. "I'm so sorry."

Lizzie dipped her head downward once as a sign of acknowledgement.

"You might as well sit down and tell us the rest before you go," Nathan prompted. "Because I have a feeling that whatever's happened to your friend and the threats against our team are all interconnected. The more information we have, the better."

"I agree," Hank rejoined, "because I have a lot of details to share about these people."

"Such as?" Ben piped up.

"Such as, we toppled the previous regime responsible for cocaine distribution in the western half of the country a little over a year ago. But it turned out that our victory was short-lived. The Cortinas clan resurrected those routes and old man Cortinas put Estoban in charge of it all. Their exploits since he started running things have already made the first group that we busted look like Boy Scouts by comparison. He's got a hair trigger temper, and he is paranoid even when he's *not* high as a kite, so the fact that he's a coke addict makes him even more unstable. It's what I was telling Lizzie earlier – if you guys have landed on Estoban's radar, just making sure you travel in pairs will not be sufficient to keep your team safe, Agent Thomas. You are going to need all the intel you can get."

"Once we're done here, I think I will come upstairs with you – after we take a brief detour to speak with *my* director, that is," Nathan said suddenly, causing Hank to stop his pacing mid-stride. "Then we can come back down here, and we'll talk some more."

"Why?"

Nathan grinned, a gleam in his eyes.

"Because I have an idea."

The profiler looked over at his teammates.

"Plan to meet back in here sometime after lunch. By then, I should at least have a working outline to share with you all."

By the time Sophie ended her conversation with Remiel her mind was racing, processing everything she'd just learned.

Brittany just up and left? That doesn't feel like a coincidence to me. And based on what she's shared with me before, her and her grandmother have never gotten along that well...

Maybe I can find a sample of her handwriting somewhere and compare it to the letter. But where?

"The menu board," she suddenly remembered, and raced back to the dining room, phone in hand.

She entered the room cautiously and looked around. She could hear activity in the adjoining kitchen, but for the moment she had the dining room all to herself.

Sophie quickly walked over to the dry-erase board that she had seen Brittany using the previous afternoon to list out the week's lunch and dinner menus. She swiftly took four pictures of it, two up close and two further back, then tucked her phone into her pocket and left the room to find Claire.

It didn't take her long. Claire was helping load up freshly washed produce into the truck.

"You still coming with me?"

"Yes," Sophie assured her.

"Are we good?" Claire called out when she turned back to the group that had just placed the last bushel basket in the bed of the truck.

"Yep, ready to go," one of them answered, and closed the tailgate.

Claire moved around the front of the truck to climb in behind the wheel while Sophie settled into the passenger seat.

Once they were past the front gate, Sophie said, "I wanted to let you know that I asked to be the one to pack up Paul's things, and if you'd like to be involved, you're welcome to join me."

Claire's eyes got misty.

"I just... I don't think I can, Sophie," she murmured, and reached over to pat Sophie's hand before she wiped her eyes. "But I appreciate the offer, and I'm glad you're the one that will be doing that for him. He thought of you as the child he never had, you know."

***

Meanwhile, Nathan and Hank spent some time in the Dallas division FBI director's office, where Nathan lined out his plan.

"If it helps keep our people safe, I'm all for it, Agent Thomas. I take it you'd like me to accompany you?"

"If you can, sir, I believe it would be helpful."

The director smiled.

"This ought to be interesting. He's got a bit of a reputation around here as being very... well, territorial is a good word for it. So, you both need to understand that we may have to kick this request further up the chain before we get cooperation."

"I've heard the same, which is why I'd like your direct involve-ment," Nathan confirmed, his face impassive.

"And if nothing else, maybe we could bring Agent Myers here in as a consultant. After all, if he's on his own time... that would still achieve what you're looking for, would it not?"

"Yes, sir, it would."

"Well, then," the director said as he stood, rolled down his sleeves, and buttoned them before he moved to the coat rack in the corner to put on his suit jacket. "Let's go make some noise up on the tenth floor, shall we?"

Chapter Eleven

"Tiny town," Sophie noticed as they made their way down the narrow two-lane road that wound its way past a church. "There can't possibly be a hospital here."

"You're right," Claire confirmed. "Technically, it's not even considered a town, more of an unincorporated community. There's not even a post office here anymore. The closest city is Jacksboro, about fifteen miles from here. That's where everyone goes for most things like groceries, gas, and medical treatment. Fortunately for us, the farmer's market is a huge draw. People come from all around. It's the one thing that helps this area thrive."

Claire pulled into a large open grassy lot with canopies and long wooden tables set up every few feet. Sophie noticed quite a few other vendors in place already, setting out their wares. Claire waved at them as she drove slowly past, then parked behind a two-table setup at the end of the row closest to the street.

"Here we are. We're a bit behind schedule, so we need to hustle and get set up," Claire instructed as she glanced at her watch. "Things will get really busy within the next hour or so. But once we've got everything unloaded feel free to look around a little if you like. There are some pretty cool things that show up for sale here."

"Like what?"

"Pretty much anything from homemade jellies and fresh honey to windchimes and hand-blown glass figurines – and everything in between. We've even had an author or two show up with some of their books to sell."

"Really? That's interesting. I've never been to a farmer's market before. I guess I just assumed it would be, you know, all about food."

Claire winked. "Yep, some pretty good variety here, usually. That's what enables us to barter sometimes."

"That went about like I thought it would," Nathan's director said wryly an hour later once they'd returned to the eighth floor. "Let me make some calls. We'll get this done. That much I can promise you. I happen to know for a fact that the head of the DEA is a huge proponent of inter-agency cooperation."

"He might want to impress that point on the guy we just talked to – *and* my director in Seattle," Hank muttered. "Because neither one of them like to share worth a damn."

"I've got this," the director assured him and Nathan both. "Go grab some lunch, and let's meet up again around two. Agent Thomas, make sure your entire team joins us, please."

"Will do, sir," Nathan replied, then turned to Hank.

"How do you feel about chicken fried steak?"

"I'm a fan."

"Good. There's a great place just down the road. Let's go."

On their way to the elevator Nathan asked, "Got a place to stay?"

Hank shrugged.

"I hadn't even thought about it yet. Figured I'd just wing it when the time came."

"You're welcome to stay at my house, if you like."

"You have a wife? Kids?"

"Yep," Nathan said proudly. "Bella's the light of my life, and our little boy's name is Charlie."

"Then the answer is no. I appreciate the offer, Agent Thomas, but if things go down like I have a feeling they might, it will be much safer for your family if I don't."

"Fair enough," Nathan said, then waited until the elevator doors were closed before he asked, "So, how do you know Lizzie?"

"Why do you want to know?"

"Just curious. It was obvious earlier that you two have some sort of history."

Hank hunched his shoulders when he answered.

"She was working a murder case that tied into my undercover ops up in Seattle. Matter of fact the very first time I saw her, she approached me to ask me some questions in front of some of the cartel members. I had to stay in character, so, I tried to get rough with her."

"And how did that work out for you?"

Hank chuckled at the recollection.

"I will be honest, she handed me my ass, and I never even saw it coming. And trust me, everyone who was there to see it gave me a ton of shit about it later, too. But that first interaction with Lizzie intrigued me, I guess, because I've had a thing for her ever since."

Nathan laughed.

"She's tough as nails, all right."

"Yeah," Hank agreed. "She's tiny but fierce. Then later I was able to tell her who I really was, and then, um, well, I may have hit on her a couple times."

Nathan raised his eyebrows.

"Wow. You *do* like to live dangerously. So, given all that, you staying with her and Donny while you're in town is out of the question."

"Is that the same guy she was with back then? He came down here too?"

"They're married now, so yeah, it would have been weird if he didn't," Nathan replied drolly. "Didn't you notice her wedding rings?"

"Oh. No, I didn't, to be honest. Didn't realize they'd gotten married," Hank said sheepishly and ran a hand through his hair. "All my focus lately is on finding Cruz."

A long silence ensued, which Hank finally broke by saying, "So, yeah. Probably good that I didn't ask her out again then, huh."

"You think?"

Lizzie waited until Nathan and Hank were gone, then called her house.

"Hey, honey," she said when Donny answered.

"Hi, Liz. Everything all right?"

"Yeah," Lizzie said on an exhale. "But something interesting has happened today that I will need to fill you in on when I get home, all right?"

"O...kay," Donny murmured, confused. "So why call me now but not tell me about it? That's a little strange, honey."

"You have a point," Lizzie conceded. "Okay. Here's the thing. Hank Myers showed up here."

"Who?"

"Hank Myers. The DEA guy I told you about?"

"Oh. *Oh*," Donny exclaimed. "The one that came to your house when we were packing up your stuff that day and hit on you?"

"That's the guy."

"Don't tell me he was dumb enough to..."

"Nope. Strictly professional the whole time he's been here. But I wanted to let you know about it up front. No secrets. Especially since it looks like he's going to be around for a while."

"I'm not worried about *you*, at all. My question to you is, do you trust *him* to keep things professional?"

She answered without hesitation.

"With what's going on? Yes, I do."

"Then everything should be fine. We can still talk about it tonight if you like. Now, since we're on the phone, what would you like for dinner? I'm thinking Italian."

Nathan, his team members, and Agent Myers assembled as scheduled with the branch director at two p.m. in the main conference room.

The director looked around the table and announced, "I'm very pleased to report that the DEA has graciously agreed to an official joint task force, to be run completely out of this office. Moreover, Agent Myers, you'll be the DEA's lead and run the team jointly with Agent Thomas. Now, we'll wait for a few more minutes while the others they've requested to be added to the task force join us. They should be on their way down already."

A few minutes later there was a discreet knock on the door and three men stepped past the unit secretary that had escorted them and entered the room.

"Good afternoon, all," said the first one. "My name's Agent Baker. These are Agents Wilford and Evans. Nice to meet you all."

"Nice to see you again, Patrick," Hank Myers chimed in as he stood and moved around the table for a handshake. "Been a while."

"How about we get started?" the director suggested and glanced over at Nathan once everyone was seated.

Nathan rose and went to the oversized dry-erase board.

"Okay, here's what we were thinking," he said, and began to write out a skeleton of the rough plan he'd formed with Hank over lunch.

It was almost five before Claire and Sophie made it back to Lighte's Landing, and Sophie made use of the spare hour she had by retreating to her cabin.

She pulled the letter out from its hiding place – tucked discreetly into one of her books – and unfolded it, smoothing the page out and laying it on the kitchen counter. Then she pulled up the pictures on her phone and laid it down next to the letter.

"Well," she grumbled, "it *sort* of looks the same..."

And then she noticed something.

She zoomed in on one of the close-up pictures she'd taken, then picked up her phone and held it, side-by-side, against several lines of handwriting across the page.

All the air rushed from her lungs in a whooshing exhale, and she began to tremble as Sophie felt the first puzzle piece click into place.

"Brittany wrote me this letter," she murmured aloud in shock. "I *knew* it."

That's great. Now what?

She quickly tapped some keys on her phone and took another picture – but this one was a nice, clear shot of Brittany's handwritten note to her. Next, she opened her email account and sent all five of the pictures to herself before removing all of them from her phone.

"Can't be too careful," she said on a sigh as she carefully refolded the paper. She started to put it back where she'd been hiding it, then thought better of it and tucked the note into her front jeans pocket for safekeeping.

The last thing she did with her phone before she shoved it into her back pocket was set up a passcode so that it couldn't be accessed by just anyone.

Feeling only marginally safer, she grabbed her video equipment, then locked up her cabin and returned to the main building for a quick dinner before she met with Remiel.

Unbeknownst to her, in the upper west corner of her living room the new smoke detector with the tiny wide-angle camera that had been installed the day after Sophie's interview dutifully continued recording everything that came across its path.

Once the task force kickoff meeting adjourned, Hank returned to the tenth floor to requisition a company car. After that, the next order of business for his first night in town was finding a place to stay. He lucked out and found a small, upscale hotel not too far removed from Dallas's downtown nightlife. Hank prepaid for four weeks to get a better rate and hauled his duffel bag to his room on the twelfth floor.

He unpacked and stowed away his gear, which took all of five minutes, then changed clothes and wandered back downstairs. His melancholy mood improved slightly when he realized the hotel's gym was extremely well-equipped, keycard access controlled, and available twenty-four hours a day.

He put in his earbuds, then ramped up the treadmill for a bruising four-mile run that he hoped like hell would clear his head, if only for a little while.

He'd put a mile and a half on the treadmill's progress display when his phone rang.

"Hey, buddy," Patrick Baker said when Hank answered. "Got plans tonight? I thought maybe we could hang out, catch up."

"Sure," Hank said as he pressed a button to slow the machine to a stop. "Let me get showered and changed. Where do you want to meet up?"

"I can swing by and get you. Where are you staying?"

Once Hank gave him the address, Patrick said, "Nice digs. And there's a great rib joint within walking distance. What do you say to barbeque and beer?"

"Sounds good. How long?"

"I will meet you in the lobby in forty minutes."

"I'd ask how your day was, but..." Donny said with a teasing smile when Lizzie got home.

"A little surreal, for sure," she answered with a wry grin. "Never thought in a million years I'd run into Agent Myers again."

"I can imagine," he agreed. "So, what happened today?"

"Well," Lizzie said as she sat on the couch to remove her boots, "I'd just walked into the building from the garage and was waiting for the elevator when he saw me and came over to talk. And I'll be honest – at first, I was *not* happy to see him, at all. I figured he was gonna be pushy again, like he was before."

"Obviously something changed your mind."

She nodded as she dropped her boots and socks to the floor and wiggled her bare toes.

"Yeah. The short version is, an agent friend of his has gone missing, and he came down to look for him. He talked with all of us, including Nathan, and now we're all part of a joint task force. FBI and DEA working together."

"For how long?"

"As long as it takes to bring the bad guys down."

"So, where's he staying?"

"No idea. Why?"

"Well," Donny said thoughtfully, "we *do* have a spare room here."

"No," Lizzie said at once. "That, I am *not* comfortable with, no matter how well-behaved he happened to be today. Besides, the last time another agent stayed with us this place got blown up, remember?"

"Like it was yesterday, actually."

"Granted, it wasn't really the kid's fault, and at least Jones never hit on me. Are you really saying you'd be okay with someone that kept pestering me to sleep with him staying here?"

"Honestly?"

Lizzie crossed her arms over her chest.

"Absolutely."

"No, I wouldn't. I was trying to be polite," Donny admitted with a devious grin. "But I'm much, *much* happier that he's not going to stay with us. Unless, of course, you'd like to be able to rub in his face how happy we are."

She threw a small accent pillow at him.

"That's awful."

"It's how I feel. But I do have to say, if Agent Myers hadn't done his full court press that day, you might have never admitted you love me, so...."

"That is so not true! I would have!" Lizzie interrupted. "Eventually, I mean."

Donny scooped her up into his arms.

"Very funny. But I guess I actually do need to tell the man 'Thank you' at some point for helping to move things along between us."

"Where are you taking me?" she asked, then yelped as he jostled her.

"To reaffirm my claim on you," he said cheekily.

Lizzie snorted back a laugh since she knew he was only teasing.

"Your *claim*? What are you going to do, pee a circle around me?"

"I think I can come up with something more romantic than that," he intoned before he began to nibble her ear.

Her shrieks of laughter echoed through the house as he carried her to their bedroom.

The two DEA agents settled in around the high-top table in the bar area and flirted with the server that took their order and brought them two frosted mugs of beer.

"So how long has it been, exactly?" Patrick asked. "Five years? Six?"

"Something like that. Before I transferred up to the Northwest division, for sure," Hank confirmed once he'd thought about it. "How many of the old gang are still around?"

"A few," Patrick admitted. "But not very many. Blake retired, and Kevin got married and quit. His wife didn't want him working such a dangerous job anymore. And you heard about Nelson, right?"

"No. I was in deep on a three-year assignment until just recently. Why? What about him?" Hank responded, leaning forward in concern at Patrick's tone.

"He's been missing for almost two years now."

Hank felt a chill trace up his spine as he stared at his old friend in complete disbelief.

"What?"

"Yeah," Patrick said, shaking his head sadly. "He was chasing down a lead in south Texas. I think the drug runner he was investigating had something to do with it, but nobody's ever been able to prove conclusively what happened. Especially without a body."

"Oh, man. No, I hadn't heard about that," Hank replied, and solemnly lifted his beer in the air.

"To Nelson," he said softly, and as they tapped their mugs together before each took a drink, a silent but fervent prayer crept across Hank's consciousness.

Please, dear God, let me find Cruz alive.

Once Sophie and Remiel finished the video shoot, he went with her to her cabin to retrieve some packing supplies, then walked her to Paul's cabin and unlocked it for her.

"Let me know if you need more boxes. I bet we can rustle up more from somewhere," he told her, and she nodded, then stepped over the threshold with the collapsed boxes and the roll of packing tape she'd brought from her cabin.

"Are you sure you don't want any help?" he asked softly.

She shook her head.

"No. I'd like to be the one to do this for him."

"Understood. I'll leave you to it then," Remiel answered, and patted her gently on the shoulder. "Good night, Sophie."

"Good night."

As he walked away, she used her elbow to close the door and flip the switch right next to it before she made her way to the dinette table to set down what she'd brought along with her.

She paused a moment, taking in her surroundings.

Where in the world do I start? Sophie thought to herself and felt a little overwhelmed at first, then shrugged her shoulders.

I suppose it doesn't really matter since it all needs to be sorted through. I'll start in the back and work my way to the front door, I guess. That's as good a plan as any.

She taped up the bottom of the first box, restoring it to its natural shape, then flipped it over and carried it into the bedroom to start clearing out the contents of Paul's dresser.

Before she began in earnest, she slipped her wireless earbuds in place and queued up her playlist. The beginning strains of "Wish You Were Here" by Incubus filled her senses and conveyed the loss she felt so deeply as she gathered up Paul's things, piece by piece, and lovingly placed them into the box.

It wasn't long before the first box was filled, and she taped it closed, then carried it into the living room and set it down in a corner. Sophie readied the next box and returned to her labor of love.

By the end of the third box, Paul's room and bathroom were bare, emptied of all personal possessions save the clothes hanging in his closet, and she turned her focus to the living room.

She'd gotten about a third of the living room packed up when she ran out of boxes, so Sophie glanced around at what remained in place in the living room and in the kitchen to try to calculate how many more she would need.

But opening the cabinet next to the fridge and seeing Paul's immense stash of liquid sweeteners and water flavoring brought fresh tears to her eyes, and Sophie took a few minutes to simply grieve for her friend.

Once she'd composed herself, she returned her attention to the items still not packed up.

I need another three boxes, at least? But it's already after ten o'clock, and I am already worn out, she realized with a start as she glanced at her watch, then yawned. *This has been a lot harder on me than I thought it would be. I will finish this tomorrow afternoon sometime. But tonight, I'd better get some rest. I must be strong for Claire at the service tomorrow morning. She's going to need me.*

Sophie turned off the lights, locked the door, and walked to her cabin, using the brilliant light of a full canopy of stars overhead to find her way.

As she walked, she recalled a particular conversation she'd shared with Paul as they'd walked in the cool night air and looked at the stars. He'd pointed out constellations one after the other, then went on to share facts and myths about each that left her completely fascinated.

Sophie felt the wet warmth of more tears trickling as she sought out those same stars now for comfort, and whispered, "I won't ever forget you, Paul, and I *will* find out what happened to you. I promise."

She slowly walked into her cabin, locked the door behind her, turned out the lights, and paused only to remove her shoes before she crawled into bed and cried herself to sleep.

Chapter Twelve

After a subdued breakfast the following morning, the residents of Lighte's Landing gathered en masse in the chapel to say goodbye to one of their own.

Sophie walked next to Claire and offered up her hand as a silent show of support. Together, they approached the front of the room, where a simple bronze urn and a picture of Paul sat side-by-side on a small table.

Claire discreetly kissed her fingertips, then softly touched them to the picture before she allowed Sophie to guide her to a seat in the third row.

Once everyone had paid their respects and taken their seats, Remiel walked forward to stand behind the little table.

But as Paul's memorial service began, Sophie's mind became more and more distracted by the certainty that someone in attendance was only *pretending* to grieve in this moment – and was directly responsible for Paul's sudden and unexpected death. She found herself casting subtle glances all around, trying to figure out who the culprit might be without making it obvious that she wasn't listening to Remiel's words as much as she should be.

At one point she'd become so focused on her search that Claire gently squeezed her hand to get her attention. When Sophie looked over at her, Claire furrowed her eyebrows and mouthed *'not now'*, and Sophie's cheeks tinged with embarrassment at being caught. She nodded once solemnly, then reformed her focus on the group's leader at the front.

"One of Paul's favorite songs was 'Abide with Me'," Remiel intoned. "So, I believe it's fitting that we now sing it in his honor. Would you join me, please?"

Later, once the chapel service ended and everyone began the walk toward the cemetery on the property, Claire dawdled, holding back until she and Sophie were at the back of the group and out of earshot of the others.

"What were you *doing* in there?" Claire whispered.

"I was trying to see if I could figure out who did it," Sophie whispered back. "But everyone looked genuinely sad."

"Well of course they would," Claire murmured. "They'd be too smart to *not* blend in at a funeral service."

The older woman stopped suddenly, turned to Sophie, and grabbed both her hands.

"Let it go, Sophie. Let it go. *Please.* I know you want answers, honey. I do too. But I don't want to see anything happen to you."

"I can't do that, Claire," Sophie responded quietly, her eyes resolute. "Paul's gone, and you and I both know that he shouldn't be. Someone needs to answer for that."

"But Sophie," Claire started to say, then stopped talking when she noticed Remiel had walked up to join them.

"I know the two of you were closest to Paul," he said, his eyes full of sympathy. "And when I saw you weren't with the group anymore, I thought I would come check on you both. Most of the others are at the gravesite already. Do you need a few moments? We can wait as long as you need."

"No need, Brother Remiel, but thanks. We were just about to join you all," Claire assured him, and the three strolled down the path to where the others had gathered.

A few more words and a simple prayer precluded Paul's urn being lovingly placed in the small hole that had been dug. Then each group member stepped forward to toss a handful of dirt down into the hole. One by one they finished their personal goodbyes and walked away until only Remiel, Sophie, and Claire remained.

"Take as long as you need," he gently told them, then stepped back to give them a measure of privacy.

Claire broke down, clutching at Sophie, who in turn wrapped her arms around her friend and mourned as well. They stayed for a time, grieving, leaning on one another for support, until Claire finally wiped her eyes and looked over at Remiel.

"I'm ready," she whispered, and nodded at him.

He walked forward with the small shovel, and slowly, carefully replaced the rest of the upturned soil into the hole. When he was finished, he looked up at them both.

"His headstone hasn't been ordered yet. I thought the two of you might like to have some input as to the design."

The women smiled at him through their tears.

"We'd really like that," Sophie replied. "Thanks, Remiel."

"Yes, thank you for being so thoughtful," Claire agreed. "Would it be all right if we do that sometime tonight or tomorrow? I think I'd like to lie down and rest a bit."

"Of course. Whenever you'd like," he answered. "Just let me know."

The trio walked from the cemetery back toward the main buildings, slowing their steps as the side path leading toward the cabins came into view.

"I can come check on you this afternoon," Sophie offered, but Claire waived her off.

"Meet for dinner at six?" she suggested instead.

"You got it. Go get some sleep."

Claire turned onto the side path and walked away, leaving Remiel and Sophie to continue side-by-side toward the main building.

"You look like you could use some rest, too," he noted.

"Can't. My mind's going all over the place," Sophie admitted. "So, I thought since I have all this nervous energy, I'd grab some more boxes and finish packing Paul's things."

"As you like," Remiel said. "I've located some empty copier paper boxes. Will those work?"

"That will be fine. I'm guessing five should be more than enough."

"Then we'll get them, and I'll walk with you to open Paul's cabin for you."

They stepped inside the main structure long enough to grab the boxes, then made the short trek to Paul's cabin.

"You still want to do this by yourself?"

Sophie nodded.

"Understood. See you later, then."

She closed the door once Remiel was gone and went to work loading up the rest of Paul's living room items. Three boxes later, the living room held only its furniture, and Sophie turned her attention to the tiny kitchen.

She began on the far end of the row of cabinets but realized quickly that most of the contents – plates, bowls, cups, and glasses - needed to stay in place for future use by a new tenant. She picked up the box and moved to the other end of the counter, then opened the last cabinet door by the fridge - and froze, staring, with her mouth hanging wide open.

Certain she was seeing things, Sophie blinked rapidly to clear her vision. But no matter how quickly her eyelids moved, what was in her field of vision remained constant.

The entire bottom shelf of the cabinet, which just last night had been filled almost to overflowing with Paul's sweeteners and water additives, was completely empty.

But... but... they were just flavorings and liquid sugar, Sophie's brain rationalized. *Out of all the stuff in his cabin, why in the world would anyone take...*

And then it registered - and her jaw snapped shut again from a fresh wave of surprise.

Oh, my God. Maybe that's how they killed him! Someone tampered with them somehow.

But who? And when?

Frantic, she opened the cabinet door hiding the open space under the sink and pulled out the tiny trash can that was still full.

"Please, oh please," she murmured over and over as she rummaged through its contents, then hissed in triumph when she felt her fingers curve around a familiar object. She withdrew her hand and stared at her prize – an almost empty clear plastic bottle of Paul's sweetener.

"Dammit... probably shouldn't have touched it with my bare hands," she muttered to herself, belatedly recalling all the true crime shows she'd binged on.

Three steps to the left helped her find an open box of quart-size plastic freezer bags. Sophie grabbed one, tucked the bottle down inside it, sealed the bag, and set it on the counter. Then she picked up another bag, but this time she turned it inside out to slide over her hand.

"At least *one* of them won't have my prints on it, anyway," she grumbled as she resumed her search and found two more bottles, another liquid sugar, and the peach-flavored additive container, at the very bottom of the can. She closed her hand around them and pulled them to the surface, then flipped the bag right-side out around them to enclose the bottles before she sealed it, too.

Using a third bag as another makeshift glove, Sophie carefully picked through the rest of the trash can to make sure no other pieces of evidence remained.

Now what do I do? It's not like I can just run these bottles over to the police and say, 'good morning, there's been a murder, test these'. I have no proof. They will laugh me out of the station.

"Susan would know what to do next," she pondered aloud. "But how do I ask her what I need to know without freaking her out?"

Hank Myers and Nathan Thomas remained in their seats side-by-side in a conference room on the tenth floor once the three-hour long video ended.

"Run it again, please," Hank said tersely after a long and weighted silence.

"You sure?"

"I said run it again."

The tech shrugged, turned back to his keyboard, and started to press 'play' a second time when Nathan spoke.

"How about we take a break before we watch it again?" he suggested as he placed a sympathetic hand on Hank's shoulder. "Come on, come with me. Let's eat and come back to it. We'll notice more details with fresh eyes, Hank."

Hank nodded reluctantly.

For him, even watching it once had been particularly difficult – the video streaming on the massive wall display was the one that the tech had recorded from Cruz's medallion camera's live feed. And when they'd watched it the first time, Hank's sudden, deep shock was too far forward for him to glean any useful data besides the obvious – based on the footage he'd just seen, Cruz was most likely dead already.

But now he roughly shoved the shock and bone-deep grief to the back of his mind to let a white-hot rage take their place front and center. Now, he wanted – no, *needed* – to watch the footage as a federal agent, not as a devastated friend.

"But not longer than an hour," Hank conceded. "And we get the whole team in here for the second round. More of us seeing it means more chances to pick up some clues."

"Agreed."

Nathan turned to the tech.

"Can you please edit the video to exclude the first forty-seven minutes of pitch-black screen, please?"

"Sure thing."

"Any way to boost the audio?"

"I tried, several times, but for whatever reason the microphone didn't function correctly."

Hank and Nathan exchanged a look.

"Very well," Hank told the tech. "When you're done with the edit, put it on a flash drive for us."

"Will do."

The two agents walked side-by-side to the elevator.

"I know one thing for sure, Nathan. I'm glad there's no audio," Hank said grimly. "I don't think I could bear to hear it if there was."

"Hey, kiddo! How's the job going?" Susan said when she answered Sophie's call.

"I love it," Sophie replied, injecting a cheeriness she did not feel into her voice. "You got a minute to talk? I need some advice."

"Sure! What's up?"

Play this up, Sophie. You need this information.

"Well, this area up here's got a lot of really cool history," she began, and winced at lying to her sister. "So much so that I've been thinking about putting a video documentary together. The camera work I have down to a T, but what I do *not* have a lot of experience with is research. Any pointers?"

"Girl you are speaking my language," her big sister retorted with a laugh. "The two best places to start will be the local library and the county clerk's office. You should be able to get copies of old newspaper articles, birth and death certificates, things like that."

Sophie gripped her phone a little tighter.

"I can get someone's death certificate?"

"Sure can. It's public information. That's where the county clerk's office comes in. They file all that stuff for the official records. And then the library would have the old articles, obituaries, and so on."

"Okay, that's really helpful, thanks."

They chatted for a few more minutes until Susan said, "Hey I'd love to talk longer but I need to get ready. I have a videoconference coming up in about twenty minutes. It's a job interview with a magazine up in Dallas. Wish me luck."

"I thought you liked where you were working?"

"I used to," came the sharp retort. "I guess I didn't fill you in on all that, huh. Suffice to say I'm done with some lecherous old creep using my job as leverage to try and worm his way into my bed."

"*Wow*. Yeah, you need to tell me all about that at some point, for sure. Good luck on your interview, Susan. Love you."

"Love you too, Soph. I'll keep you posted."

Sophie stared at the phone in her hand after the call ended.

Local library and county clerk's office, she repeated in her head, then checked the time.

It's past noon already. Better get moving.

Sophie untucked her long shirt, then settled the bagged bottles just inside the waistband of her pants, leaving the shirt out to help camouflage them as best she could before she left Paul's cabin.

When she reached her own cabin and walked inside, she moved straight to her bedroom to trade in her funeral attire – her best slacks and blouse - for more casual clothes. Sophie pulled the bottles from their hiding place and laid them down on her bed before moving to the closet for a clean top to wear.

I can't leave them in here – or the letter, for that matter. It's not safe, she mulled as she quickly changed into her new shirt and then put on the jeans she'd worn yesterday. *I mean, Paul's bottles didn't just walk off by themselves. It's obvious that someone's been rummaging through other people's houses.*

But I can put them in my car, she realized. *And lock them in the glove compartment. That way only I can get to them.*

Sophie absentmindedly reached into her front pocket to make sure the letter she'd tucked in there was still where it was supposed to be and nodded in satisfaction when her fingers grazed it. Then she retrieved a small paper bag from her kitchen, unfolded it, and set the wrapped bottles down inside it. That done, the paper bag went into the new, larger purse Susan had bought her for Christmas, along with her wallet.

Once she'd put on her tennis shoes, she slung the purse strap across her shoulder, locked her front door, and slipped her sunglasses on before she went to her car.

Sophie turned the key to start the engine then laid her purse on the passenger seat. She was about to move the bottles she'd found to the glovebox but hesitated.

No. Not yet. Not here, her inner voice urged. *Someone might see you. Wait until you're off the property.*

Her hands trembling, she buckled her seat belt, then stepped on the brake and shifted the transmission into drive.

When she reached the property's exit, Sophie rolled down her window and pressed the button to activate the gate. Once it rolled back along its track, she eased her car through, then paused for a moment.

"Nope, not yet," she murmured, her instincts on high alert. "Could be a camera somewhere."

She picked up her phone and activated GPS, then thought for a moment.

Probably ought to hit the clerk's office first, I guess. Pretty sure they close at five.

She typed in '*county clerk's office in Jacksboro, Texas*' and waited.

In moments, the directions had loaded - and had also confirmed her suspicions about their hours of operation.

Sophie pressed the 'start' button, and as instructed she took a right-hand turn. Twenty minutes later she was in downtown Jacksboro and parking in front of a squat tan brick building.

She looked around first to make sure no one was watching her, and quickly removed the bag holding the bottles from her purse and locked them in the glove compartment. Then she slung her purse strap across her body and exited the vehicle.

The woman behind the counter had a warm smile and friendly face, and Sophie found herself smiling back when the county employee said, "Good afternoon, how may I help you?"

"Hi," Sophie said. "I need a copy of a death certificate, please."

The woman tapped some keys on her computer.

"Name of the deceased?"

"Paul Bingman."

"Just a moment," the lady said, and typed in Paul's name.

"That record isn't pulling up by name. Date of death?"

"Three days ago."

The woman behind the counter gazed at Sophie, her eyes full of sympathy.

"I'm so sorry, miss, but one that recent won't even be in our database yet. It can take up to thirty days to be officially recorded."

"Oh. Wow. I didn't know," Sophie blurted. "Sorry to bother you."

"It's okay, a lot of people aren't aware," the woman said kindly. "The Bureau of Vital Statistics has to send a verification notice to the medical examiner to complete their portion, then it goes back to the state, and only *then* does it get sent to the county clerk's offices."

"Good to know," Sophie answered. "I guess I will see you in about a month, then. Could you give me directions to the library?"

"Sure. It's about six blocks down on the left. And here," the woman said as she handed Sophie a pamphlet labeled '*Vital Statistics – Frequently Asked Questions*'.

"That should help you," she continued as she pointed to the trifold paper. "It lists acceptable forms of ID needed for family members and authorized representatives to get a copy of a death certificate."

Sophie's brows knitted in confusion.

"But I thought death records were public information?"

The lady shook her head.

"Not all of them. Access to death certificates in Texas are restricted for the first twenty-five years from the date of death. Only a qualified applicant can get a copy of one that falls within that time-frame. Read that pamphlet, it explains a lot, dear."

"I will. And thanks for your help."

Sophie waited until she was outside to stop smiling and mutter, "*Dammit.* How am I gonna find out the 'official' cause of death if I can't see the certificate?"

She stomped back to her car, every cell of her being humming with frustration. And as she started the engine for the drive to the library, she began to question her entire approach to solving Paul's mysterious death.

Six blocks later Sophie was still stumped.

"Should I even bother with the library today?" she wondered aloud. "I mean, Paul's death was so recent. Would it even *be* in the obituary section yet?"

Her eyes went wide with a sudden realization.

Probably not – but all the others should *be, right? So, I need to start with the oldest headstones in the cemetery and work forward to Paul's death. That should let me know how long it takes for the newspaper to announce them.*

Emboldened, she parked her car and walked up to the front doors of the library long enough to note their hours of operation, then climbed back into her car.

"I'll just make a list and come back," she assured her reflection in her rear-view mirror.

Chapter Thirteen

THE TASK FORCE gathered in the main conference room of the eighth floor just after one p.m. at the request of the FBI Director.

Nathan sidled up to him as the rest of the team members took their seats and murmured, "Was there a reason for moving this to our floor?"

"It's a bit of a strategic move on my part," Nathan's director admitted. "I said the task force would be run from *this* office, and I meant it."

Nathan raised an eyebrow before he went to stand at the head of the table. Immediately the room went still, everyone watching him expectantly.

"Agent Myers and I have already seen what you're about to watch. We wanted you to view it, as well. More pairs of eyes on this means we have more chances to identify useful information," Nathan announced solemnly, then paused for a moment.

"However, I do need to mention before we get started that this video is a recorded feed from an undercover agent's camera and has some disturbing content. Unfortunately, we need to examine it in detail if we're going to get to the truth, particularly since for some reason there's no corresponding audio to help us make sense of it."

He paused again and swept his gaze over each team member to make sure no one had formed any questions, then gestured to Hank to take point.

"The original footage was three hours. It's been edited to exclude a large chunk toward the beginning that had no discernible movement. This new version of the video is approximately two hours in length," Hank told them. "We'll pause playing it as needed to discuss possible clues and intel we can glean from it. I should hope it goes without saying that nothing about what you're about to watch leaves this room."

Another visual sweep around the room confirmed that every agent on the team understood.

"Very well," Nathan said.

He stood and moved to the bank of light switches on the wall to turn off the room's center and front lights, then gestured to Ben, who staffed the controls of the sleek laptop that was connected to the overhead projector equipment.

"Roll tape, please, Ben."

On her drive back to Lighte's Landing, Sophie's thought process bounced around in her brain like a ping-pong ball as she tried her best to line out a solid plan for gathering the information she wanted.

It would be weird to just randomly wander up to the cemetery, I think. Especially if I am trying to take pictures. That is going to look odd. Maybe I should use a little notepad and pen instead. But if I go at night it is going to be harder to see. Speaking of – at night will draw more suspicion, but there is much less chance of being seen than during the day...

She sighed loudly.

This is crazy-making, and I haven't even gotten started yet.

Claire... should I take Claire up there with me? Might be less questions that way, since losing Paul is so new. We'd have a valid reason for spending time there. But then again, I don't want her involved, for her own safety.

"Ugh," Sophie grunted to herself in frustration. "Maybe I should just sleep on it."

Before she knew it, she was already back at the property's fence line and pulling up to the gate. She rolled down her window and pressed the intercom button. But before she could even speak a slightly tinny sounding *"Welcome back, Sophie"* emanated from the speaker as the gate opened for her.

She rolled her car forward through the gate, then raised her driver's side window and mumbled, "That was creepy. Guess my guess about a camera was right."

***

In the privacy of his office, the homicidal mastermind who was becoming more and more obsessed with her watched Sophie's little Honda as it drove through the gate and down the long driveway toward the main building.

"Where did you go, little one? And what are you up to?" he murmured as her car passed out of sight of the camera's range.

Hmm. Maybe I ought to review some footage from her cabin...

***

The first place Sophie went was to Claire's cabin to check on her.

"Did you get any rest?" she asked when Claire answered the door.

"Not really," Claire admitted with a wan smile. "Tired body but a restless mind, you know?"

"I know."

"How about you?"

Sophie hesitated.

If I tell her about the items missing from Paul's cabin she is going to worry...

"I was too wound up to even try to lie down, so, I went over and got the rest of Paul's things packed up," she revealed.

Technically, that's not a lie... I did pack up everything of his that wasn't stolen, she thought wistfully, then turned her attention back to what Claire was saying.

"I think we ought to go take a look," the older woman finished, and looked at Sophie expectantly.

"I'm so sorry, Claire. I spaced there for just a moment, I guess. What did you say?"

Claire reached over and patted her shoulder.

"That's all right, dear. What I said was, I have no clue what the design for Paul's marker should be, so I think I'd like to go to the cemetery and look at some of the other headstones in the next couple of days. If you're up for it, that is."

"Of course, Claire. I think that's a good place to start," Sophie replied, and thought *and since we'll be looking at design ideas, I can get away with taking pictures. Problem solved.*

"But for right now, I probably should try to eat something," Claire told her. "I know we said six o'clock, but..."

"That's fine," Sophie assured her. "I missed lunch too. Did you want to walk up to the dining room? If you'd rather stay here, I'm happy to bring something back to you."

"Why don't we split the difference? I'll come with you, but we'll grab our food 'to go'," Claire suggested. "I really don't feel like being around a lot of people right now."

Twenty-two minutes into the shortened medallion camera video, Hank signaled to Ben to press 'pause' then got up, walked over to the end of the room, and pointed to a spot on the oversized screen.

"Can we zoom in here, please?"

Ben tapped some keys and magnified the image.

"What *is* that?" Lizzie murmured.

"Looks like some sort of machine?" Ben offered.

"That is a tire changer, to be exact. It's used to take off or put on tires on rims," DEA Agent Wilford declared, then shrugged when everyone looked at him.

"What? I spent four summers working at a tire shop back home when I was a teenager."

"Okay," Hank said. "So, from that it's pretty obvious that when they grabbed him they took him to a garage someplace. My assumption is that it's the same one where he's been working undercover."

He glanced over at Baker.

"Got the file?"

"I do. Hang tight," Baker said, and scanned the pages. "Yep, right here. It's a place in south Fort Worth, just off Loop 820 and Interstate 35."

Hank smiled a predator's smile and looked at Nathan.

"We have any fleet cars that could use some work?"

"I think we can get our hands on a junker, yeah."

"Noted. Let's keep rolling, please, Ben."

The video resumed.

"Hold it there, freeze it and enhance," Nathan barked suddenly.

"Those shoes look like they're custom made," Ben commented.

"Yep, I noticed that too. Copy that image to a separate file. We'll see if we can't get more information on them," Nathan directed. "Now, let's keep moving."

The roomful of agents didn't need any audio to help them interpret what they saw next – a foot swinging back as far as possible before rushing past the camera - and then the video shook violently. As it did, the vibe in the conference room plummeted into shocked silence.

"Pause," Lizzie said grimly. "Just for the record, where was this agent's camera placed?"

"He was wearing it. The tech confirmed it was embedded into a Saint Christopher medal on a chain," Agent Evans answered softly.

"So, he had it around his neck," Lizzie murmured, her jaw set but her eyes haunted as she glanced over at Hank.

"Yeah," he managed, fists clenched. "Keep going, Ben."

Play resumed, and both Hank and Annie flinched involuntarily with every subsequent jostle that occurred in the video.

For another twenty minutes the group watched the unique shoes land blow after blow. Then there was a long pause, and suddenly the video swam drastically out of focus before correcting itself.

"Freeze," Hank hissed, and Ben abruptly paused the feed.

They all stared at the screen, taking in the face that had unknowingly loomed closer to the camera.

"That is Estoban Cortinas in the flesh," Hank announced, his voice steely with anger. "I'd know that face anywhere."

"We'll run it against the database, just to confirm," Nathan chimed in. "We want this as airtight as possible."

Hank nodded as Ben captured a still shot of the screen, then let the footage continue.

Over the next several minutes, the camera angle changed and became higher. The group watching could tell from the video that Cruz had risen – or been lifted - to his feet. More images were appearing now in the background that confirmed an eye-level view of the agent's surroundings, but not much else at first.

Then Nathan was out of his chair and striding quickly over to the screen.

"Pause, Ben. Enhance upper left corner."

Ben did as he was directed, and Nathan pointed.

"Security camera. Wonder if it's operational."

"And if they're lazy about keeping the footage longer than they should," Hank replied. "We can certainly find out. If their system isn't just for show, we should be able to hack it and work backward to glean more information. Hopefully we'll find more video that's useful. Maybe even another view of the scene we're watching now. That would tighten up our case, don't you think?"

Nathan's single nod in acknowledgement was a solemn one as he returned to his seat.

With a gesture from Nathan, Ben pressed 'play' once more, and Annie gasped aloud as Estoban Cortinas strolled back into view, but this time it was a full body-length image. He was naked from the waist up and brandishing a long piece of pipe like a baseball bat. The look on his face was feral, evil incarnate.

"He's wearing the shoes we saw earlier," the Director pointed out gently. "So, at least we know he was the one doing the kicking."

"Pause, please," Annie gulped. "I'm sorry. I just... I need a moment here before we continue this."

Lizzie, seated to Annie's left, reached out and squeezed Annie's hand as the younger woman steeled her nerves for what they were about to watch.

After a couple of minutes Annie looked over at Ben.

"I'm ready," she said simply, her voice carefully neutral.

The video continued with a blur of what looked like metal rushing toward the camera lens, then angling downward out of sight, then violent shaking. The sequence repeated three times. After that the mechanics of the assault moved out of the camera's view, but the violent shaking continued.

Next was a long pause, and gradually the video's viewpoint drifted upward, as if the man wearing the camera had laid down on the floor on his back.

More jostling happened, and then a gentle swaying and a shot of the ceiling overhead before another rushing blur of movement as the camera's viewpoint violently shifted from ceiling to wall to a murky, inky nothingness.

By the time the video ended, every face in the conference room had paled, and no one spoke.

Nathan slowly stood again and turned the lights back on, then took a deep breath.

"Two things. We need to look around the shop Agent Delgado was assigned to, and we need to get a tap into that security system," he announced and looked over at the Director.

"Agreed. I'll get a warrant for the electronics. Who do you want on the tech side?"

"Mitch is on vacation," Nathan responded. "But we can pull Rick in. His skill level is first class with stuff like this and we already know he's got the clearance."

The Director rose from his seat.

"I agree. I'll see if I can't get that warrant pushed through by tomorrow morning at the latest. And I'll walk it through my back channels so that it stays off the radar. No telling what other connections the cartel has. Now, who did you want to send to check out the place?"

Lizzie raised her hand.

"I'll do it. They'll never suspect that I'm a cop."

"I'll go too, but on a separate visit," Annie volunteered. "I can wear another wig and play up the ditzy blonde routine, get a little flirty. They won't know a thing."

"Are you sure?" Nathan asked as he looked at them both.

Annie cleared her throat.

"Cortinas took a lead pipe to one of ours," she said firmly, "and he needs to pay for it."

Everyone around the table nodded in agreement.

"Let's get a plan lined out, then," Nathan directed, and lifted the drop-down video screen up so that he could access the whiteboard.

Once the meeting adjourned a half-hour later, Lizzie walked over to Hank.

"I'm sorry about your friend, Myers," she said softly.

The tic in his jaw and his clenched fists directly contradicted his neutral tone when he answered, "Yeah, thanks. But we still need to find him so that I can get him back to his family, at least."

"Yes. And we will," she reassured him, and patted his shoulder.

When Claire yawned a second time, Sophie realized it was time to give her friend a bit of space and quiet.

"How about I take some pictures of the headstones?" she suggested. "That way we can look at them any time we need to, and we can take them with us when we go into town to place the order. It might be helpful to be able to *show* what we're talking about rather than trying to describe it."

"That's a great idea," Claire responded, then stifled a third yawn.

"You rest for now, okay? I will see you in the morning."

Sophie saw herself out and made a beeline for the cemetery, phone in hand. She quickly opened the waist-high chain-link gate and moved to the back of the oversized lot to begin her quest.

To support her cover story of capturing images for ideas for Paul's stone, she took four pictures of each of the nine headstones in the Lighte's Landing graveyard – two far views and two close-up views – then checked the time.

Three p.m., and the library closes at nine.

Sophie Drimmel resolutely marched out of the cemetery and back toward where her car was parked in front of her cabin.

As she entered her lodging, a high-pitched beeping assaulted her ears. Sophie frowned and made a slow circle, trying to find out where the sound was coming from. Finally, it registered with her that it was the smoke detector in the living room making the noise.

"Man, that's annoying," she murmured. "Hopefully it's just the battery."

She scooted a chair over against the wall and stood on it, then reached up and worked the cover off the device.

"I need two double A's," she noted, and stepped down to move over to her kitchen area. She rummaged through the drawers until she found what she needed, then stepped back up on the chair and changed the batteries out.

Immediately the noise ceased, and she grinned.

"That's more like it," Sophie said, and was about to replace the cover when she noticed something strange. The exterior side of the cover had what looked like a small black dot that seemed to catch and reflect the room's lighting.

Intrigued, she looked more closely at the interior of the cover, and what she saw caused her pulse to skyrocket.

It's a camera. There's a camera in my living room...

Her hands shook so badly with fright that she barely managed to get the cover back into place. She purposefully schooled her expression into one of routine calm before she stepped down off the chair again.

Wonder if the bedroom has a camera, too...

"Well, usually when one battery goes out the others go out too. Better check the one in the bedroom," she said out loud to lull whoever might be watching and listening into a false sense of security.

Sophie grabbed the chair and moved it into her bedroom to get a closer look at the smoke detector in there, too. It didn't take her long to confirm that she was being monitored in her sleeping quarters, as well.

That realization caused anger to surge forward and mingle with the fear.

Her jaw set, she walked over to her dresser to retrieve two items before she left her cabin again for the drive to Jacksboro.

Game on, whoever you are.

She had no way of knowing that her lethal secret admirer had reviewed her every movement at Lighte's Landing to date, and because of it had added a tracking device to the undercarriage of her old Honda while she was visiting with Claire.

Chapter Fourteen

Twenty minutes later Sophie pulled into the library's parking lot. She dropped her phone and the flash drive and spiral notebook she'd retrieved from her cabin down into her oversized bag and went inside.

After she signed the visitor register at the reception desk, she was handed a slip of paper with the library's wireless network login information and directed to a bank of computer terminals along the far wall.

Sophie purposely selected the setup at one end and sat down. She pulled her phone, her notebook and a pen from her bag then set the purse on the floor next to her chair.

She picked up her phone, scrolled through the pictures and copied each headstone's information down in her notebook, then logged in and navigated to the county newspaper's website.

"Okay, let's see what we can find," she muttered under her breath, and typed in the first name on her list – Abel MacKensie, the man Remiel said had gifted land to Lighte Limited, and who had died five years earlier.

The search results were instantaneous.

Error - Record not found.

Confused, she checked the spelling on the picture to make sure she hadn't written it down wrong, then tried again.

Error - Record not found.

"Hmm. Archives, maybe?" she mused aloud.

Two more clicks to navigate to the 'archives' link of the paper's website brought up a new screen, and she selected 'Obituaries' and tried Abel's name again.

Error - Record not found.

Sophie then tried including the date of death in an expanded search for Abel's public death notice.

Error - Record not found.

She paused, her mind reeling as a knot of dread began to form in her stomach. Her hands began to tremble as she then tried to pull up records for each of the other eight names. In every single instance, she was rewarded with the same error message.

Sophie switched tactics and navigated to the library's internal system to pull up and look at electronic copies of old newspaper clippings. She selected a date range of up to two weeks after each death date, then painstakingly opened each file and perused each PDF thoroughly from beginning to end.

Another hour passed before she was able to confirm that the paper's website wasn't the only place where the death records simply did not exist.

Nine people. Nine. And none of them had obituaries published?

She leaned back in her chair and mentally sifted through her discoveries to date.

So, there's a whole cemetery of people buried out there, but no one outside Lighte's Landing seems to even know they've died. Not to mention Paul dies mysteriously and is cremated quickly, and Brittany sends me an ominous note then disappears... and to top it off, I've got not one but two hidden cameras in my cabin that watch every move I make... What the hell is going on?

Other thoughts crept suddenly into her head, ones that stole her breath away.

Oh, my God... did they hear Claire and me talking about Brittany's note? Does Paul's cabin have cameras, too? Did they see me find and bag up the bottles?

Sophie reached down into her purse and brought forth the little flash drive. Once it was firmly seated in the USB slot, she repeated every search she'd done in both the library system and on the paper's website and saved each result onto the drive.

Next, she opened her email app on her phone and sent herself the headstone pictures. Then she opened her email account on the computer and ported every single picture she'd sent to herself – the headstones, the menu board, and Brittany's note - onto the little portable drive stick as well.

It's not safe for me to keep any of this stuff with me anymore, she decided as she worked quickly to wipe all traces from both her email account and her phone's picture gallery. *And there's only one person that I know I can trust with all this.*

She carefully logged out of everything she'd navigated to before clearing the computer's search history. Then she gathered up her things and headed toward the door, pausing only long enough at the reception desk to ask where the nearest shipping services place was.

"There's a little mom-and-pop store not far from here. They can ship a package out for you, and they don't close until seven tonight," she was told.

"Thanks," Sophie managed with a normalness she wasn't feeling and walked out to her car.

She climbed in, locked her doors, and closed her eyes to take a moment to just breathe and think. Then she pulled out her notebook, flipped to a new page, and began to write out everything Susan needed to know.

Once she'd gotten everything she'd learned so far - and her thoughts about it all - out of her head and onto the pages, she set her pen down to re-read the letter she'd just finished. Sophie nodded once in satisfaction, then carefully tore the three-page letter from the notebook as well as the prior page of names and dates.

She folded them up and tucked them into her purse. Then she retrieved Brittany's note and the bottles from her glove compartment and added them to her purse, as well.

"Okay," she said on a deep exhale. "Let's send Susan a package."

She started her little car and left the lot. Sophie never noticed that a black SUV across the lot from her timed its exit about ninety seconds after hers.

Sophie found the shipping store right where the library clerk had said it would be. She grabbed her purse and hustled inside.

"Good afternoon! How can I help you?" a genial man with salt-and-pepper hair boomed from behind the walk-up counter.

"I need to mail some things out, but I don't have a box."

"Sure thing. What size?"

She frowned.

"I'm not sure, to be honest."

The man pointed off to her right.

"They're right over there. I've got a sample of each set up so you can see what the sizes look like when they're assembled. Take your time, and just let me know when you're ready."

"Thanks," Sophie replied, and dutifully moved over to the shelves the man had pointed out.

Let's see... the biggest part of all this are the bottles. Six-by-six inch, maybe? Six-by-nine?

She grabbed the six-by-six-by-four-inch sample box, placed the bottles, flash drive, and pages inside to test it out, and was pleased to see that it would serve her needs well. She removed her items and set the sample box back on the shelf, then retrieved a flat one in that same size to assemble.

"I've got tape, if you need it," came a drawl from the counter.

"Yes, please, thanks," she answered and went back over to take the roll he'd offered.

Sophie quickly taped the box into its usable format, then placed everything that needed to find its way to her big sister down inside the packaging before she sealed the box and carried it over to the counter.

"Here's your tape back," she said, and returned the roll to him. "I need to get this to my sister pretty quickly. How much is overnight shipping?"

"Let's see... what's the zip code it's going to?"

She told him, and he typed that into his computer, then weighed the box she wanted to ship.

"Priority overnight comes to thirty-one dollars and seventy-two cents," he announced. "And it should get there by three p.m. tomorrow."

"Works for me. Do you have a label? I need to write her address."

"No need," he revealed. "I can type it right into the computer here and print it out, easy as pie."

Five minutes later she was returning to her car with her receipt that included a tracking number. The first thing she did was lock it up in the glove compartment.

Should I call Susan and let her know to be expecting a package? Sophie wondered as she turned the ignition key of her Honda.

She pondered that for a moment.

Part of me says no. She'll bombard me with questions, and then I will have to explain everything. But part of me says yes, because the package will rattle her the moment she opens it...

She'd driven almost two blocks when she noticed that the SUV behind her was mimicking her movements, and the hair on the back of her neck stood up. When she switched lanes, the SUV did too, but it never tried to overtake or pass her.

Concerned, Sophie made a sudden left, only to find the SUV following behind her. She tried a few more evasive maneuvers like the one she'd read about in books, but the SUV never wavered from its course.

Finally, she pulled over abruptly and parked in front of a little ice cream shop on the south side of the town square. To Sophie's surprise and relief, the SUV continued its drive down the street, then turned at the corner and disappeared from her line of sight.

"Oh, thank God," she murmured, her head resting on the steering wheel.

But that tells me one thing for sure. I need to call Susan and give her a heads up.

She turned off the engine and picked up her purse, then made her way inside the old-fashioned establishment. As she looked around she could make out an actual full-sized telephone booth shining like a beacon for the weary in the far left-hand corner of the shop.

"I hope that thing works," she muttered under her breath. "Because I don't know that I can even trust my cell phone to remain untampered with at this point."

Sophie walked over to the counter and addressed the cashier.

"Hi there. I'd like a small chocolate shake, please," she began, to give herself time to come up with some subtle way to find out whether the phone booth was functional, or purely for decoration.

"You know, I don't think I've ever seen one of those," she said when the lady handed her the milkshake a few minutes later.

"Seen what?"

"That," Sophie said, thumbing over her shoulder at the telephone booth. "I thought they didn't exist anymore. Everyone's got cell phones now."

The lady behind the counter smiled.

"I know, right? The owner has a thing for antiques, so he rescued that one - and it actually works! But you don't need change like you did for most of them. That one he found has a slot where you can swipe your card, kind of like an airplane phone."

"Oh, that's cool! I may have to try it. I remember my grandma talking about pay phones growing up," Sophie lied through her teeth.

She paid for her frosty drink, then made her way to the beautifully restored wood and glass phone booth. When she stepped inside and slid the bifold door closed behind her, she felt claustrophobic, even though the walls were made of clear glass.

"Ugh. I don't see how people did this," she mumbled to herself as she pulled out her wallet to get to her credit card.

Sophie used her card, then dialed Susan's number and waited, nervously checking her surroundings every few seconds while the phone rang and rang.

"Come on, Susan, pick up," she muttered under her breath. "Pick up, dammit, I need you."

When the call went to voicemail, she leaned forward in despair to rest her head gingerly on the glass wall. She closed her eyes and the words tumbled out in a low, desperate rush.

"I think I've stumbled onto something here," she said the moment the long beep stopped sounding. "I just overnighted you a box. If my gut is right, what's happening is horrible and it's big, Susan, really big. I can't talk much longer right now, but I'll call you back later and by then I should have even *more* evidence to blow this thing wide open."

A sudden certainty that she was being watched sent a tingle from the back of her neck all the way down her spine and made her shiver.

"One last thing," she murmured, consumed with a bone-deep urgency. "I think someone is following me. If you don't hear back from me in two days, I want you to reach out to *Claire*, understand? Come up to Jack County and go to the farmer's market that happens every Friday and find Claire and talk to her. I love you, sis."

Defeated and scared, Sophie reluctantly hung up the lifeline in her hand, then closed her eyes again and took a deep breath to steady her frayed nerves before she opened the creaky bifold door and stepped out of the quaint little phone booth.

The silky, deceptively calm voice that murmured in her ear almost made her yelp with fright as a huge right hand reached from behind her and closed tightly like an iron shackle around her left wrist.

"Sister Sophie, *there* you are. I was wondering where you'd wandered off to."

Her first instinct was to scream, to fight him off, but it was squelched at once by the feel of cold, thin steel strategically placed against her lower back as her stalker leaned in to lightly nuzzle the back of her neck.

"I don't want to have to hurt you - or that nice lady behind the counter, for that matter," he whispered to her. "So, we're going to put on a little show for her. We're gonna walk out of here together calmly, like two people who love each other. Sound good?"

Love each other? Seriously?

Struck dumb, Sophie could only nod her consent.

He kissed her earlobe as his grip moved from around her wrist downward so that they were holding hands, and she realized the reason for it. To anyone else, they would appear to be a mismatched May-December romance rather than victim and kidnapper.

"Good girl. Come along, then. And sell it, Sophie," he hissed. "Make it believable. Your audience's life depends on it."

The steel pressed against her back faded and he gripped her hand tightly as he steered her forward.

"Good night," she said gaily and smiled at the oblivious cashier as they passed the counter and headed out the door.

Once outside, Sophie started to move toward her little car and was subtly yanked backward to rest up against his torso.

"No, my pet," he breathed in her ear again as he wrapped his left arm around her waist, then let go of her hand. "I think it's best if you ride with me."

"I don't think so," she snarled, and he sighed and tightened his vicelike hold on her body.

"I was afraid you might resist me. Good thing I thought of a way to fix that," he muttered.

Sophie felt a pinprick and started to struggle, but it was too late. Moments later her vision began to swim. She barely registered being scooped up and placed in the passenger seat of the SUV as whatever she'd been injected with plummeted her into sleep.

An exhausted Susan arrived home just before nine o'clock. She'd wasted the bulk of her day chasing down a juicy anonymous tip that turned out to be a complete fabrication.

Wincing at the intense headache that had formed just behind her eyes, she glanced over at the cell phone she'd left on its charger and noticed one missed call from a number she did not recognize, and one new voice message.

"That is gonna have to keep until tomorrow, whatever it is," she mumbled.

Susan rubbed her temples as she made her way to her bathroom and swallowed two Excedrin before she climbed gratefully into her bed.

Chapter Fifteen

Esteban Cortinas walked out onto the second-floor veranda of his expansive home in Reynosa, Mexico with the day's first cup of coffee in hand. Sitting and greeting the sunrise in this manner was a ritual he'd long favored to ease into his day – particularly when meetings were scheduled by his father at ridiculously early hours – because the pre-dawn stillness gave him a chance to clear the cobwebs from his mind.

But it wasn't lost on him that his subtle practice of gradually coming to full alertness was now completely at odds with the two massive lines of coke he relied on to jump-start his system each morning.

His lips curled downward at that bit of irony before he pursed them to blow softly across the surface of his drink and cool it just a bit. Then he sat and sipped, adding in richly brewed caffeine to underpin his chemically induced adrenaline rush, and frowned as his cell phone's ringtone disturbed his purposefully quiet routine.

"Yes?" he snapped once he had lifted the device to his ear.

The individual on the other end of the call spoke rapidly, and as Estoban listened a slow, steady smile crept its way across his lips.

"And where does this agent reside?" Estoban asked, then listened further.

"Interesting," he finally purred in approval. "I give you leave to act upon this information. Nothing violent, however – at least, not *yet*. Let's see if a warning is sufficient to motivate him and his team members to cooperate."

He ended the call and returned to his morning ritual with satisfaction as his servant approached with his breakfast.

In Fort Worth, a still-waking Lizzie sat on the edge of her bed and put her socks and boots on an hour and ten minutes earlier than she normally did.

"You're going to be careful, right?" Donny asked from the doorway before he strode over to her and handed her a travel mug of coffee.

"Always," she replied, then breathed in the aroma of the beverage he'd brought her and grinned at him. "It's a simple reconnaissance mission today, nothing more. Go in, look around as much as I can without being obvious about it, and leave again."

"All right. I've got some client meetings scheduled today, but I should be home by three," he told her, and she nodded before she kissed him goodbye and left for work, clutching the portable mug that contained her morning nectar.

Meanwhile, in Corpus Christi a bleary-eyed Susan woke suddenly at ten minutes past six. She sat upright and yawned and stretched before she threw back the covers, then padded on bare feet into the kitchen to start the coffeepot before she retreated to the shower.

Twenty minutes later she was wide awake, toweled dry, dressed, and ready to officially start her day. Susan returned to the kitchen and poured herself an oversized cup of her freshly brewed coffee, then grabbed her cell phone and a little pad and pen to take with her to her kitchen table.

After taking a long sip from it, she set her mug down. Susan pulled up her voicemail app on her phone and clicked the 'new messages' icon, then picked up the pen so that if needed she could make notes about the new message she'd received. As an investigative reporter, Susan had learned early in her career that unsolicited calls from strange numbers sometimes resulted in superb story leads.

Well, it's usually either a lead, or the 'we've been trying to reach you about your car warranty' people, she thought to herself wryly, then pressed the button to hear the message.

But she soon realized that this was not the anonymous tip she had expected it to be, and as she listened to the voicemail for the first time, her jaw hung open in disbelief.

She immediately played Sophie's message to her again, this time on speaker, and her little sister's ominous words wove themselves around both the room and her psyche like a thick, cloying cloud of doom.

What? Surely this is some sort of joke...

She listened to it a third time, the knot of clutching fear in her abdomen growing with each syllable Sophie had uttered.

Susan snatched up her phone and immediately dialed Sophie's number, then listened, panic settling into her chest, as the call rang and rang.

The instant she was able to leave a message, Susan waded right in.

"I got your message, Soph. If that was a prank call, it was not a funny one. Call me back."

She hung up, counted to one hundred, and called again, only to get the same result.

This time, the message she left was more urgent.

"Sophie, you're scaring me. Please call me back."

She placed her phone on the kitchen table with a shaky hand and forced herself to wait. As she did, she rationalized the situation.

She's not a morning person, that's all. She's probably not even awake yet. She'll call me back and explain that her message was a joke, and we'll laugh about it. You just wait and see.

But twenty minutes elapsed, and Susan's phone didn't ring.

Finally, she called Sophie a third time. But this time, it went straight to voicemail, like someone on the other end had powered down the phone.

Susan stood and paced, her instinct to hop in her car and go look for Sophie growing by leaps and bounds with every lap she made around her kitchen.

Wait, the voice of reason in her head commanded. *She didn't call you from her cell phone last night, remember? Why don't you try calling her back at* that *number?*

Hope renewed, Susan navigated to missed calls, pulled up the unfamiliar number, and pressed 'send' to return the call.

And she listened and waited and prayed as she endured seven rings before the call disconnected.

Close to tears, she backed up one screen, and dialed a different number.

"Can you come over? I need you, Trevor," she said the moment he answered. "Please hurry."

As previously scheduled, Nathan's team gathered in the basement level of the parking garage where a talented FBI mechanic was putting the finishing cosmetic touches on Lizzie's loaner car.

Lizzie, Nathan, Ben, and Annie stood and watched as at last the tech drove it toward them and parked.

"That is one ugly car," Ben remarked. "But you told them we needed a junker, Nathan. It's obvious they took you at your word."

"Is this thing even street legal?" Lizzie asked as she slowly walked around the sad looking two door hatchback, making mental notes of every ding and dent in the car's exterior. "Is it even going to get me over there in one piece?"

The tech, hearing her questions, looked at the quartet and grinned.

"She's ugly as hell but completely functional, I assure you," he answered. "The only thing not road-worthy about her are the tires, but we put those on last night so that you'd legitimately have something for the garage to work on."

"If they ask, you can tell them it's the very first car you ever bought, and you love it and you never want to part with it," Annie chimed in helpfully.

"That could work. This thing's what, twenty years old?"

"Twenty-two, actually," the tech replied. "In eight more years, it will be considered a classic."

"Classic piece of junk, maybe," Hank Myers quipped as he strolled up to join them. "That thing is *hideous*."

"Agreed. But if it helps us catch Cortinas..." Nathan said softly, and Hank nodded in solemn agreement.

"If this little car helps us bring that asshole down, I'll personally make sure it gets fully restored to mint condition," Hank announced.

Nathan grinned, then turned to Lizzie.

"Okay, let's go over your approach right quick."

"Sure," she replied. "What I'd planned on was – "

Her cell phone ringing interrupted the strategic planning, and Lizzie retrieved it from the clip at her waist, looked at the display, and frowned.

"It's Renee," she said, her brows knitted in confusion. "She hardly ever calls me. I'd better take this."

She stepped away to answer the call as the rest of the team continued talking about the car.

Moments later Nathan glanced in Lizzie's direction and noticed that her face had lost all color. Hank noticed it too, and he paused mid-sentence to walk over to where the seasoned, usually unflappable agent had dropped to her knees, with the phone still up to her ear. Nathan, Ben, and Annie followed him and hustled to close the distance quickly to their teammate.

She uttered a stilted "I'm on my way" before she slowly hung up the phone, and sharp, harsh sobs wrested their way free of Lizzie's body. She lifted her head to reveal a shocked, pale face to her co-workers, and Nathan squatted down beside her and put a hand on her shoulder.

"Lizzie. What's wrong?"

She hung her head again as the tears rained down in a deluge that robbed her of her ability to speak.

"It's Tank," she finally managed to whisper. "Tank... he's gone, Nathan. *He's gone.*"

Annie knelt and wrapped her arms around a devastated Lizzie to try to comfort her as Nathan stood upright again and stepped off to the side to dial Donny's number.

Nathan closed his eyes and waited for the call to connect as Lizzie's sobs echoed eerily through the large underground space.

"Donny, you need to come to the office as soon as possible," he murmured gently the moment her husband answered. "Lizzie's old partner's been killed. She just got word."

Once he'd finished the phone call, Nathan glanced over and caught Annie's eye.

"He's on his way. Let's get her upstairs," he suggested, and Annie nodded.

"Come on, Liz, come with me," Annie whispered as she helped Lizzie to her feet, then wrapped an arm around her shoulders and led her to the elevator.

Chapter Sixteen

THE WORRY WAS SHINING in his eyes like a beacon when Trevor arrived at Susan's apartment.

"What's wrong?" he asked the moment she opened the door.

"You need to hear this," she said in a panicked staccato, and tugged on his hand to lead him to the kitchen table.

He sat in the chair next to her and she played Sophie's message for him.

"What the hell?"

"I know, right? And she's not picking up when I call her. Matter of fact, the third time I tried it went straight to voicemail and didn't even ring at all," Susan exclaimed, then scrubbed her face with her hands. "Then I tried to call that strange number back. I'm worried sick."

"What strange number?"

"She didn't leave me that message from her cell phone. She called me from another number."

"And did you try calling that one?" Trevor asked.

Susan growled at him.

"*I just told you that I did,* Trevor. And it rang seven times and disconnected."

"Okay, okay, sorry," he said as he patted her shoulder. "I know you're concerned. So am I. But we have nothing to go on yet, Susan. Knowing what is in the box she says she sent you would really help, but we don't even know for sure when it's coming, do we? I mean, 'overnight' doesn't necessarily mean first thing in the morning. It might not get here until sometime this afternoon."

Susan placed her elbows on the table and leaned forward to rest her face in her hands.

"I know," she said, her muffled voice trembling. "Nothing we can do but wait until it gets here. And hope like hell that in the meantime, she calls me back."

"Well, there might be *one* thing we can do," he told her. "Let's run a reverse search and see if we can't find out who that other number belongs to. If nothing else, we should be able to find out the general location, and maybe if we're lucky we will be able to determine whether or not it's a cell phone or a landline."

"I should have thought of that," Susan said bitterly, then got up and went to retrieve her laptop.

"Have you eaten anything?" Trevor called out to her.

"No. I'm not hungry," she answered as she returned to the kitchen table, sat down, and fired up her computer.

But her stomach rumbling contradicted her answer.

"I take it from that sound that's a yes," he said. "I'm going to make us some breakfast, and after that, let's round table about this some more."

———

Meanwhile, in the FBI's Dallas office, Nathan finished filling him in about the devastating news Lizzie had received, then sighed and looked over at his boss.

"I take it they were close?"

"He and his wife asked Lizzie to be their child's godmother, if that answers your question."

"It does," the director replied, his eyes filled with sympathy. "Please pass along my sincere condolences to Agent Zimmerman."

"I will, sir. And thanks."

There was a brief, respectful pause before the director leaned back and steepled his hands.

"Now, about that visit to the garage," he said. "What's your next move? Do we need to postpone it?"

"No, we don't. Annie's volunteered to go today instead."

"Good. And how soon can you loop Rick in? The electronics warrant arrived about fifteen minutes ago."

"That's my next order of business after I check on Lizzie. Donny should be here just anytime now."

Lizzie sat in the breakroom on the eighth floor, staring vacantly into the coffee mug that someone had set down in front of her. The initial wave of shock that had flattened her in the garage was beginning to ebb just a little, but as it retreated a raw, soul-deep grief took another step forward.

This isn't real. It can't be. Any minute Tank's gonna call me...

But in her core, she knew, and the tears welled up again as she replayed Renee's words in her mind.

He was supposed to be off shift at midnight, but they asked him to join a raid team at the last minute, and you know Tank, he is always willing to help back up his teammates. But it went wrong, Lizzie, it just... went wrong. They didn't know until it was too late that they'd walked into an ambush...

A large, warm hand gently closed itself around hers, and she slowly lifted her head.

"Hey there," Hank Myers said softly. "I'm so sorry, Lizzie. I'm so damn sorry. Anything I can do for you?"

"He was supposed to be done working at midnight," she blurted out. "That's what Renee said. But he volunteered to be part of a team to do a raid, and he didn't come back. He didn't come back, Hank. I always say that Tank has been one of my best friends for over fifteen years. But that's not true. He's so much more. He's the brother I never had. We met at the police academy and that was it, done, instant friends. We've always just... *been*, you know? It's hard to even remember a time when he *hasn't* been in my life."

She paused and took in a shaky, shuddering breath, and he laid his other hand over the one he was already holding and gently squeezed in silent support.

"And now... he's just... *gone*, and I don't understand it. This can't be real," Lizzie finished on the barest whisper.

A noise in the hallway caused her to look up, and she yanked her hand out of Hank's, shoved her chair backward, skirted the table, and flung herself into Donny's arms.

As he held and comforted his crying wife, Donny looked over her shoulder and locked eyes with Hank. He'd been standing in the doorway listening to Lizzie speak, and he'd noticed the tall blond DEA man touching her, holding her left hand with both of his.

Not sure what he's up to, but now's not the time, Donny thought grimly. *But we will be having a discussion later. He can count on that.*

The intensity of his uncharacteristic – and stark – jealousy startled him.

Stop that right now. She needs you.

With effort, Donny purposefully shoved it back down for closer inspection at a later, more appropriate time. He broke eye contact with Agent Myers and retrained his focus on the usually strong, resilient woman he'd married who was falling apart with grief at the loss of one of her closest friends.

"I'm here, baby," he murmured against her hair. "I've got you."

A single but powerful thought crept through Hank's mind as he watched the display unfolding in front of him.

I wish Lizzie needed me like that...

His gaze tracked upward from Lizzie's back to Donny's face, and he almost raised an eyebrow at the gleam of silent but threatening jealousy he could see in the man's eyes.

Hank watched it flare, then disappear as Donny abruptly shifted his focus back to Lizzie.

Can't say I blame him, though. If she was mine, I'd be a little over-protective, too...

And as Donny spoke to her, Hank recognized the subtly pointed and carefully inflected barb launched his direction.

"I've got you."

Trevor slid a plate in front of Susan that contained bacon, eggs, and biscuits, then took his seat again and picked up his fork to dive into his own meal.

"Thanks, babe," she said.

"You're welcome. Any luck with the search?"

Susan frowned as she worked through her first bite of eggs.

"Yes, and no," she replied once she'd swallowed. "It's a landline somewhere in Jacksboro, Texas. Beyond that, the trail ends."

She looked over at Trevor and sighed.

"We're back to waiting on this mysterious box to arrive."

Annie tucked some stray strands of her naturally dark hair up into hiding, then turned to look at Ben.

"How do I look?" Annie asked once she'd adjusted the blond wig she'd put on for her mission.

"Beautiful, as always," Ben said sincerely. "But I like you better as a brunette, honestly."

"Me too," she quipped, and turned back to the mirror.

"So," Ben began, and shoved his hands into his front pockets, "do you think you're going to have to flirt to find stuff out?"

She glanced over at him.

"Possibly. But we need to bust these guys, Ben. If a little flirty behavior gets the job done, well..."

The tic in Ben's jaw was obvious.

"Don't go all caveman on me," she scolded.

"I'm not," he snapped.

"Good," she retorted. "Because that would be juvenile and stupid – and I won't put up with it. I am a federal agent, Ben, just like you are, and if I need to play a role to solve a case, then that's what I'm gonna do. Understood?"

"Fine," she heard him mutter before he walked away.

Annie looked at her reflection, then rolled her eyes.

"Rick, how are you?" Nathan asked when the retired Navy cryptologist answered the phone.

"I'm doing well, thanks. I take it you need my help with something."

"Can't I just call to see how you are?"

Rick chuckled.

"Before eight a.m.? Not likely, brother-in-law of mine. Whatcha got?"

Nathan read him in.

"Can you help?"

"Not only can I help, I would be *delighted* to play a part in shutting that operation down completely."

"Thanks. Can you be here in an hour?"

"Yep."

"One more thing, Rick. I don't know if Lizzie's called Faith about this yet or not. My guess is probably not. But she's going to need our support. Can you put Faith on the phone right quick?"

"Why?" Rick asked, alarm creeping into his tone. "What's going on?"

"Her old partner was killed in the line of duty early this morning."

"Oh, my God. Yes, hang on just a second."

A few moments later, Nathan's older sister was on the line.

"Hey, baby brother. Rick said you need to talk to me?"

"Yeah. Lizzie got word about a half-hour ago that David died."

"David... you mean *Tank*?"

"Sorry. Yes."

A shocked gasp was followed by "Oh, *no*! Is she with you?"

"She's in the breakroom, last I knew. I was just about to go check on her again. I already called Donny, and he's on his way."

"Take me to her, Nathan. I wanna talk to her."

When Nathan arrived at the breakroom's doorway, he tapped on Donny's shoulder.

"Sorry," Donny murmured and took two steps to the right with Lizzie still in his arms so that Nathan could enter the room.

"It's okay. Faith is on the phone for Lizzie," Nathan announced, then held out his cell phone.

Lizzie grabbed it and immediately began to cry harder as she wailed, "He's gone, Faith. Tank's gone."

Donny's attention was on his wife, still standing in front of him. But Nathan's shifted to Hank Myers, who was still sitting at the small square table with a neutral expression.

He raised one eyebrow, and Hank responded with a small head

shake that Nathan interpreted as *'not now'*, so he turned back to face Lizzie.

"Are you sure? All right. Yes. I love you too, girl," Lizzie said, then handed the phone back to Nathan.

"Faith is coming to Houston with us," she told Donny as she wiped her eyes with the tissue Nathan handed her. "She's going to meet us at our house."

"Okay. Let's get moving, then," Donny replied gently.

"Nathan, I don't know how long..." Lizzie started to say, but Nathan waived her off.

"Take the time you need, Liz," he told her softly. "Don't worry about it. Please."

She nodded, then sniffled.

"Okay," she managed, her voice shaky. "Okay."

When it reached the basement level, Annie stepped off the elevator and made her way over to the tech.

"I'm ready," she said, and held out her hand for the keys to the hatchback.

The tech did a double take.

"Wow. You look... different," he said as he tossed her the keys. "You have any backup? I don't think you should go alone."

"She's not going alone," Annie heard a determined Ben say from behind her. "I'll be there."

She whirled to face him and quickly closed the distance.

"If you think I'm going to indulge your being jealous while I am undercover you are sadly mistaken," she hissed.

"The standing order is, no one goes into the field alone," he retorted as he folded his arms across his chest. "And that includes you, undercover or not. So, I will be there, Annie, whether you *like it,* or not."

He stepped around her and addressed the tech, who had observed the entire exchange with a bemused smirk.

"Got mine ready?"

The tech nodded.

"Yep, it's just over there," he answered, pointing to the Ford F150. "And it's about two thousand miles overdue for an oil change. That should buy you a good half-hour, at least, to hang out and look around."

"Thank you," he told him as the man handed over the keys to the truck.

Ben turned back to Annie only long enough to say, "See you there," before he walked away from her.

Chapter Seventeen

FAITH WAS PARKED at the curb and waiting for them by the time Lizzie and Donny got home.

She immediately got out of her vehicle, walked to the passenger side of Donny's SUV, and opened the door to scoop Lizzie up in a fierce hug the moment Lizzie stepped out of the car.

"I'm so sorry, sweetheart," she murmured as Lizzie clung to her. "And Rick said to tell you he loves you and he's thinking of you."

After a long embrace Lizzie stepped back.

"Thanks, Faith. I'm glad you're here," she said as she wiped her tears away with a tissue, then looked at her husband and best friend as they stood side-by-side in front of her.

"Now, we need to get moving," she announced, her voice a little steadier. "I know that Houston PD probably sent someone over to their house, but as far as family goes, Renee's all alone right now. Her and Tank's people all live in Seattle, and it could be tonight before any of them can get down there. We need to leave within the next twenty minutes."

"I've already packed a bag for me," Donny said. "I didn't know what you'd want to take."

"I'll be right back, then."

And with that, Lizzie pivoted and strode toward her house to go pack a suitcase as Donny and Faith went to Faith's car to move her bag over to the back of Donny's SUV.

Annie arrived at the little garage on Fort Worth's south side before Ben did. She pulled into one of the parking spaces facing the street, then took a moment to shore up her frayed nerves. Seeing Lizzie so distraught earlier had rattled Annie to the core.

But now she needed to focus and do the job.

"You got this," she murmured as she looked at herself in the rearview mirror. "You can do this."

Despite Ben's misguided impression that she was looking forward to this, Annie wasn't comfortable with the idea of using her feminine wiles to find out what she needed to know. The previous time she'd gone undercover had been much different - a specific trap for a specific predator – and had happened from a distance, not up close and personal.

Now she was literally about to walk into the lion's den – a place that her gut was screaming was a fellow agent's murder scene. Annie felt exposed, naked, and she closed her eyes and took a deep breath to center herself.

"Showtime," she whispered, and opened her car door.

From his vantage point across the busy street, Ben watched as Annie mumbled something to herself, then closed her eyes and hesitated before opening them again and getting out of the car.

She's really nervous, he realized, and wished like hell that he had some way to subtly communicate with her to let her know he believed in her ability...

"Duh, stupid," he mumbled, chastising himself as he reached for his phone and fired off a quick text, then waited.

And grinned as he watched her pull out her phone and skim the message, then put the phone back in her purse – and walk toward the customer entrance with her shoulders back, her head high, and an exaggerated sway of her hips specifically designed to attract attention.

"Atta girl," Ben murmured. "Give 'em hell."

The moment Rick arrived at the office Nathan ushered him to the small conference room.

"Anything you need?"

"Nope, just space to work," Rick replied, and grinned as he unpacked and set up two laptops side by side on the table. "With luck, I'll be in within the hour."

"I'll leave you to it, then. You know where to find me."

Nathan started to walk out of the room, then paused, one hand on the doorknob.

"Are you still sure about the whole '*I don't want to officially join the team*' thing?"

Rick chuckled.

"I'm still sure, yes."

Nathan shrugged.

"Hey, it was worth a shot."

"That's the spirit. But feel free to keep trying. You never know, I might just surprise you and change my answer one day," Rick answered with a mischievous twinkle in his eyes.

"Tease," Nathan shot back, then walked into the hall, Rick's roar of laughter echoing behind him.

As she expected, the moment Annie stepped through the doorway her discomfort began. One man behind the counter – the manager or owner, she assumed - and another who was wiping his hands with a rag paused their conversation mid-stride to turn and openly ogle the newcomer.

"Good morning!" she said brightly, smiled, and tried her best to ignore the fact that she was being eyeballed like a piece of meat, particularly by the guy behind the counter. The sickening leer he wore as his greedy eyes roamed over her body made her flesh crawl.

Stay in character, Annie...

"So, like, I really need tires, and my friend was telling me about this place and a really nice guy that, like, helped her with her car? I think she said his name was Cruz, or something like that?"

Although she didn't let it show, Annie noticed that the man with the rag flinched as if he'd been struck, and his face paled - and Annie *also* noticed that the moment she'd mentioned Cruz by name, all the creepy flirty vibes radiating from both men ceased.

The man behind the counter shot his co-worker an ominous glare before he stepped around the end of the waist-high setup and walked over to her.

"I'm afraid Cruz quit recently," he murmured, "but Ramon here can definitely help you with tires."

The manager then turned and fired off a rapid string of Spanish. Annie couldn't understand it at all, but the tone and forcefulness with which he spoke led her to believe that whatever he was saying wasn't happy – or good.

The man with the rag replied 'Sí,' in a slightly shaking tone before he tore his gaze away from his boss to look at her.

The mechanic pasted on a smile, but Annie could clearly see that it was a half-hearted one, and he was still quite pale.

He looks like he's seen a ghost, Annie thought to herself. *Ramon here might be the weak link. Maybe we can use that to our advantage...*

"Come with me, please, miss, and let's take a look," Ramon told her, and gestured with a trembling hand toward the door that she'd just come in through.

She led him back over to her car and Ramon had just squatted down beside her front passenger tire when Ben's F150 pulled into the lot. He parked the truck five spaces away from Annie's hatchback, then hopped out and acted like just another customer as he seemingly ignored everything around him and walked toward the entrance of the building.

By the time Ben was at the garage's counter explaining his need for an oil change, Lizzie, Donny, and Faith were loaded up in Donny's SUV and had just backed out of the driveway to start the four-hour drive to the Lydealea home.

"I know you may not be hungry, Liz, but you need to try to eat something," Donny chided softly, and met her gaze in the rear-view mirror since Lizzie had opted to sit in the back seat with Faith so that they could talk.

Lizzie sighed.

"Yeah, I'm definitely not hungry. Food's the last thing on my mind right now. But you're right. Let's hit a drive-through on the way out. I need more coffee, too."

"You got it."

"I love you."

His eyes sparkled with affection as he answered, "I love you too."

Lizzie picked up her cell phone and dialed.

"Hey, Renee," she said. "We're on our way. We should be there by one at the latest."

After a few more minutes, the call ended, and Lizzie leaned back and sighed again, then reached for Faith's hand.

"So. Tell me what's going on at the bookstore, at your job. Distract me, Faith. Please. I need a distraction."

The box that Sophie mailed to Susan arrived around eleven a.m., and a frantic Susan signed for the package, then hurriedly shut her apartment door, and carried the box over to her kitchen table.

"Wait," Trevor cautioned as she started to rip into the packaging. "Do you have any gloves?"

She blinked rapidly.

"Huh?"

"*Gloves*," he repeated. "So that we don't get our prints on anything."

"I don't think so," Susan admitted.

"What about any bags? Like a plastic grocery bag. Anything we can put over our hands but still have some dexterity."

"Um, okay."

Feeling foolish, Susan waited until both she and Trevor were wearing plastic bags over their hands, then carefully ran a sharp knife along the top seam of the box to cut apart the packing tape.

She eased the box open and looked inside, then looked up at Trevor.

"Bagged bottles and a flash drive? What the hell?"

"I think you'd better start with those folded pages," he suggested. "Something tells me that reading those first will explain a lot."

Susan eased the papers out of their resting place, unfolded them all and set them on the table.

"This is Sophie's writing," she remarked as she looked over the four notebook pages, then turned her attention to the single smaller-sized tri-folded paper.

"But *that* is not."

"Look, she numbered them," Trevor pointed out.

"That single page has 'number two' on it, and this fourth page that you said was in her handwriting is marked 'number three'. She gave us a reading order. Smart cookie."

Susan quickly scanned Sophie's messages to her, starting with the first page of the three-page set. She blanched, shuddered, and picked up the oddball paper. Once she'd read it in its entirety, she continued in the three-page set until she suddenly snatched up the single page of names and dates, then finished out the long letter.

She looked up at Trevor, tears streaming, and thrust him the pages, then stood up and began to pace.

"She's in trouble. Read these and see for yourself. She's in really big trouble, Trevor, and we *have* to find her."

Trevor read the pages in the designated order, then met Susan's gaze.

"I'm thinking that we're going to need to call the FBI about all this, Susan," he said grimly. "The local police here won't be able to help us. They can't do anything because it's out of their jurisdiction, so I don't think there is any point in even reaching out to them. But, let me make a call to one of my contacts and get some solid advice on how to proceed here before we do anything. Okay?"

He rose from his chair and wrapped his arms around her as she began to sob.

"We'll find her, honey," he murmured against her hair as Susan touched her forehead to his chest. "I know we will."

She surged to consciousness in a blind panic then blinked rapidly, wincing at the pain in her head as she looked around and tried her best to figure out where she was.

Wooden ceiling, wooden walls, wooden door, no windows. But everything looks super old, not at all like the cabins at Lighte's Landing. And it smells damp and musty in here.

None of this is familiar...

Sophie started to try and sit upright and realized that she couldn't. Her arms had been stretched out to either side and then immobilized, her wrists bound to the sturdy steel bedframe with handcuffs.

What the hell?

A squeak of old wooden floorboards followed by ancient metal hinges creaking in protest as the door swung open let her know she wasn't alone.

A roiling fear crept its way up and lodged itself in her throat.

"Good, you're awake. I was beginning to worry. Are you hungry, sweetness? I brought you some lunch. You slept so long you missed dinner *and* breakfast."

Sophie glared at her captor from the bed she'd been handcuffed to but did not speak.

"Come on, darlin. You need to eat. I need you to keep up your strength," he purred.

"Screw you," she spat out in a venom-filled voice.

He sat beside her on the bed, then reached out and caressed her cheek as his gaze traveled hungrily up and down her body.

"In due time, love. In due time, I promise you. But not quite yet."

Chapter Eighteen

Trevor hung up the phone and looked at Susan.

"He said the Dallas branch office is the one we need to talk to," he explained to her. "It's the regional office that covers most of north Texas."

Susan chewed her lip as she mulled over their choices.

"Do we have to call?"

"Well, yeah, if we want them to help us find Sophie," Trevor answered.

"No, I mean, I *know* we need their help. But why waste time on a phone call when you and I both know they are going to want to take a closer look at what is in the box? What time is it?"

"Almost noon."

Susan's jaw set with conviction.

"Look up the address, and let's go. If we leave now, we can be there by six."

"Let me make sure I have this right. You want to drive to Dallas and just show up on the FBI's doorstep unannounced," Trevor confirmed aloud.

"I want to find Sophie. If that means camping out in their lobby until they agree to help me, then so be it," she said firmly. "Besides, it's the FBI for crying out loud. It's not like they won't be open past five. They're not a bank, Trevor."

"How about this. Let's call them, and at least talk to someone and let them know we're on the way, all right?"

Susan huffed.

"Fine. But we're still going."

At the garage in Fort Worth, Annie had somehow managed more than once to refrain from rolling her eyes.

Ramon's spooked demeanor had gradually shifted, and as it did, he'd reverted to his original reaction to her – leering, with a generous helping of some of the lamest come-ons and flirty remarks she'd ever heard.

Inwardly, she cringed, but Annie never missed a beat as she chatted, giggled, and flirted right back.

By the time the fourth extremely overpriced new tire had been installed on her car, she'd played a hunch and agreed to a dinner date with Ramon on Saturday night.

Hopefully Rick can get into their system quickly and find something useful, she thought in desperation. *Because I would love to meet this idiot as scheduled – and take him into custody.*

She finally managed to get away from him when she got back in her car. Annie watched in her rear-view mirror as Ramon sauntered back through the open bay door. Once he had disappeared into the garage, she sighed in relief.

"Glad that's over," she muttered under her breath as she started her decoy car and left.

Annie was halfway back to her office before it hit her.

Crap. I am going to have to tell Ben about setting up that date, she realized with a frown.

That conversation ought to be loads *of fun...*

"How's it going?" Nathan asked the moment he stepped into the small conference room.

"Child's play. Their so-called 'firewall' was complete crap. I was in within the first ten minutes. So, I have been downloading all their stored footage. There's roughly three months' worth, at least," Rick revealed with a satisfied smile. "They're extremely lazy about their setup, so, your team will have a *lot* of past videos to sift through. But I also set up a direct feed. A copy of any new footage will automatically route here, not to mention that you can always watch in real time anytime if you need."

"Very nice," Nathan murmured in approval. "Very nice indeed."

"Thanks. The downloads should be complete in two or three hours, give or take. Anything else you need me to do while I am here?"

Nathan scratched his chin as he pondered the question.

"Not that I can think of right now," he answered.

"Well, in that case, how about we grab some lunch?" Rick suggested. "We don't have to be here for the downloads to keep going."

"Sure, sounds good."

"But *you're* buying," Rick added.

Nathan grinned at his brother-in-law.

"Yeah, I kind of figured that. Let's go."

They crossed paths with Annie in the garage as she was parking the hatchback.

"How did things go?" Nathan asked when she stepped out of the car.

"Pretty well," she told him as she took off the wig, then pulled a small hairbrush out of her purse and worked her natural hair up into a ponytail.

"There. *Much* better. That wig gets itchy after a while," she announced.

"We're headed to lunch. Why don't you two come with us, and you can both fill us in on what you found out?"

Confused, Annie looked in the direction Nathan's eyes were focused on – over her shoulder – and saw Ben approaching.

"Count me in, too," Agent Myers drawled as he stepped over to the group.

"Um, sure," Annie answered, and held up the wig. "Just let me go give this back right quick."

Oh goody, a full audience, Annie thought as the elevator door closed and shut off her line of sight to the others. *But that might work in my favor. Hopefully Ben will freak out a little less about the whole date thing since Rick and Nathan and Hank will all be sitting right there.*

Once they had settled in around the table in the corner of the restaurant, Nathan looked at their surroundings to ensure no other patrons were seated within earshot, then quietly kicked off the discussion.

"Rick got into their setup really quickly, and it's just as we suspected, Hank. They haven't deleted any footage in a long time."

"Good to hear," the DEA man remarked before he took a sip of his iced tea.

"You say that now, but everything I'm downloading is going to take a while to review," Rick pointed out. "There's at least three months' worth."

"It is what it is," Hank told him. "If wading through all that helps us nail these guys and find Cruz, then I'm happy to do it."

Nathan turned his head and looked at Annie.

"So, fill us in."

The three others at the table also gazed at her, waiting, and Annie hesitated.

"Well," she began slowly, "at first it started off just like I thought it might. I walked in and right off the bat the guy behind the counter was... creepy."

"That would be Miguel, the owner," Ben interjected. "And yeah, he definitely came across as a creeper."

"So, what I did was, I walked in and did the whole ditzy routine and asked about tires. Told them that a girlfriend of mine recommended that I come there and deal with a guy named Cruz. And immediately, they both started acting way, way different."

Nathan's eyebrow raised.

"Both of them?"

"Yeah. Miguel, and Ramon, the mechanic."

"Then there's three of them there, at least," Ben interjected again. "The guy that did my oil change was named Javier."

"What do you mean, they started acting differently?" Nathan pressed after casting a sideways glare at Ben that Annie interpreted to mean '*stop interrupting.*'

"The minute I mentioned Cruz, things got really tense, and then Miguel looked at Ramon and rattled off a bunch of Spanish. No idea what he said but I can tell you that whatever it was, I do not think it was good. But Ramon's reaction to what *I* said was interesting, to say the least."

"How so?" Hank asked.

"He went white as a sheet when he heard Cruz's name. And he seemed genuinely frightened, almost ready to bolt out of there."

"They know what happened to Cruz," Hank surmised, his jaw clenched so tight that a tic had formed. "They either witnessed it, or they had a hand in it. Or both."

"I believe so, yes. And Ramon is the weak link of the group, based on the '*don't say a word*' look Miguel gave him before he spoke Spanish. Which is why I really, *really* hope that all the videos Rick found yield some super compelling evidence."

She paused, took a deep breath, glanced over at Ben, then shared the rest of her story.

"Because if we can gather enough evidence between now and Saturday night, we can take Ramon into custody when I meet him for our date."

Another glance in Ben's direction confirmed that regardless of the presence of others, Annie's big reveal did not go over well at all with him.

Ben started to sputter but Nathan held up a hand to silence him.

"Stop, Ben. Just stop," he directed sharply, then turned his attention back to Annie.

"You know, Annie, that's clever thinking. Get him away from the garage, where he is more relaxed and unsuspecting. It's a good move."

"I just thought that if we can lure him offsite, away from Miguel and whoever else, he'll be easier to deal with," she explained. "More trusting. It also gives us the ability to grab him without anyone at the garage being the wiser."

When Nathan nodded his encouragement, she continued.

"And my gut says that if we play this right, we can get him to flip on the others. It wouldn't do anything but bolster our case – *especially* if we have corroborating video that proves out his testimony."

She shrugged, intensely aware of the silent anger coming off Ben in waves.

"That was my line of thought, anyway," she finished, and looked around the table at her peers.

Three faces looked back at her with approving smiles, while the fourth – the one she loved – had no discernible expression at all.

Conversation lapsed as the five finished their meals, and the ride back to the office was eerily silent.

Nathan parked in his usual space, then cleared his throat and gently said, "Ben, I'd like a word, please."

Once everyone had exited the vehicle, the others walked toward the elevator, and Nathan paused for several beats until he was sure that he and Ben were alone.

Ben started to speak but Nathan overrode him.

"*No.* I'm going to talk and you're going to listen."

Ben stood still, hands clasped together in front of him, and stared at his boss.

"I'm not sure what's gotten into you lately, but you need to knock it off," Nathan said evenly as he maintained eye contact. "I've not called you two out on dating because there's no hard rule against it and up until now, it hasn't interfered with the job. But if you keep undermining Annie's work as an agent, then I can - and will - transfer you off my team without a moment's hesitation. Is that clear?"

"Nathan, I..."

"Is that clear, Ben? Yes or no."

"Yes, it's clear."

"Good. You'd *never* have interrupted me or Lizzie the way you did Annie earlier. It was extremely unprofessional behavior, Ben, and quite frankly I expected better from you."

"May I speak freely for a moment?"

Nathan gestured for him to go ahead.

"I'm in love with her, Nathan. And it's making me crazy, and I just keep screwing things up between us. I don't mean to. I just want her to be safe."

"I get that, Ben. But you need to get that stuff squared away. You think you are being protective, but she will see it as controlling - and knowing Annie, she will only put up with that for so long. If you want to keep her in your life, then you need to loosen up and show some trust and stop trying to protect her all the time. Because in case you have not noticed, she is an excellent agent – and she is *also* a strong, intelligent woman. Believe me, she can handle herself."

Nathan took a step forward and laid a hand on Ben's shoulder.

"Trust me when I tell you that I'm speaking from experience here. My wife Bella is one of the strongest women I have ever met. And when we first got together, I really had to fight to get a handle on the exact same things that you are struggling with right now. If you want Annie in your life, you need to respect her abilities – and her boundaries – and give her some space to breathe. Otherwise, it will never work. She'll end up walking away from you."

With that, Nathan walked over to the elevator and pressed the 'up' button to travel to the eighth floor, leaving a chastised Ben standing by himself in the parking garage with a lot to think about.

It was past their habitual lunchtime, but an increasingly worried Claire still sat in the dining room of Lighte's Landing's main building and waited for her young friend to arrive.

"Something's happened to her, I just *know* it," she finally muttered under her breath when over an hour had come and gone with no sign of – or word from - Sophie.

Concerned but determined, Claire slowly rose from her chair and went to look for the one person who might know something – Brother Remiel.

Just before one p.m., a solemn Lizzie, Faith and Donny pulled up to the curb outside Tank and Renee Lydealea's house. Donny parked right behind one of several Houston Police Department cruisers that lined both sides of the quiet suburban street.

They rallied so she would not be alone, Lizzie thought, and was grateful that Tank's teammates had gathered to show Renee their support.

She unbuckled her seat belt, climbed out of the car, and stood for a moment staring up the driveway at the house.

I would give anything to hear that big booming voice and be wrapped up in that big bear hug of his right now...

Lizzie felt rather than saw her best friend and her husband take up station on either side of her, and she closed her eyes as each one reached out and held one of her hands in theirs.

"I'm glad you're with me," she whispered, and squeezed each warm hand gently.

She took one last deep, shuddering breath as she squared her shoulders and willed herself to be strong for Tank's wife and infant son before she opened her eyes, softly said, "Let's go check on Renee and Tucker," and led the way up to the front door.

Chapter Nineteen

By the time Ben got upstairs, most of the task force had already assembled in the conference room.

"Do you mind if I sit here?" Ben quietly asked Annie as he stood behind the open chair next to hers.

"Knock yourself out," came the chilled reply, and a rebuffed Ben meekly sat down.

"We have about three months' worth of footage to sift through," Nathan announced. "And we really need to find something useful in the next three days to give us some leverage when we make contact again on Saturday with one of the suspects."

Hank waved his hand to get Nathan's attention.

"Should we work backward? Start with the most recent videos?"

"Let's do this," Nathan suggested. "Who's got Cruz's file notes?"

Evans held up a folder.

"Take another look through that thing. Maybe there's some sort of pivot point that we can use to help narrow things down."

"That's easy," Evans responded. "Cruz sent in a coded message letting the director know that he'd been asked to start working

Sundays. But here's the thing – according to everything we've researched about the place, that garage is *closed* on Sundays."

"Okay. That's good. So, here's what we do, then. Don't bother at all right now with any videos older than..." Nathan trailed off and looked over at Evans.

"When exactly did Cruz send that message?"

"Um.... here we go. Friday the third at six-twenty-two p.m."

"Okay. Focus on recordings *since* then. The DEA's already reviewing other videos from Cruz's medallion to build out their case against the cartel."

"Speaking of that. Nathan, we also know the exact day and time that Cruz's camera feed went offline," Rick gently reminded him. "I would say that for maximum results in the least amount of time, you should focus on the recordings *between* those two precise timestamps."

He paused.

"And, based on what Evans just shared, you might *also* consider making Sunday recordings a priority within that smaller group, since it sounds like that is probably when the most smuggling activity takes place. Those should be the videos that the DEA can use to corroborate the medallion recordings."

"Good point," Nathan observed.

"So, to sum up - any video older than Friday the third can be disregarded completely by this team. As a matter of fact, Rick, let's go ahead and forward all those recordings to the DEA and let *them* sift through them all," Nathan announced.

He glanced at each team member and could see questions beginning to form, so, Nathan preempted them.

"Don't forget, *our* primary task here is twofold: confirming what happened to Agent Delgado and catching the men responsible for it. If in our efforts we find additional evidence to help strengthen the DEA's case, then great. But that is *not* our main goal here."

Another sweep around the table confirmed any possible questions had been put to rest with his last statements.

A light tap on the door preceded an FBI computer tech pushing a multimedia cart loaded with eight slender laptops and eight high-definition headphone sets.

"Excellent timing, Jason," Nathan said as a means of greeting the newcomer, and the man grinned.

"We try. Okay, gang, these are all configured the same way," the tech explained as he maneuvered the cart to rest up against one end of the table. "Take one and pass it down. I'll stick around long enough to make sure that everyone can get logged in, then leave you to it."

"And once you're all in, I'll lead you to where I stored the videos on the server," Rick chimed in. "I've set it up so that only task force team members and the Director have access."

"Agent Thomas, I'm so sorry to interrupt, but you have a call holding on line one," the unit secretary said abruptly from the doorway.

"Thanks, Diane. Give me sixty seconds, then transfer it to my extension."

To the task force Nathan said, "Keep going, guys, I'll be right back," before he hurried down the hall to his office.

Nathan had just walked into his office from the hallway when his phone began to ring. He swiftly rounded the side of his desk to answer it.

"Nathan Thomas," he said briskly.

"Um, hi. This is going to sound really strange, but, I really need your help," a woman's voice said.

Nathan's eyebrows raised as he cradled the handset between his shoulder and his ear and grabbed his pen and notepad.

"Okay, sure, happy to help if I'm able. Can you tell me your name?"

"Susan Lawford."

"Nice to meet you, Ms. Lawford. So, what seems to be the problem?"

The longer Susan spoke, the more notes Nathan took, and at last he said, "I am *definitely* going to need to examine the package you were sent. When can you be here?"

"We're on the way now, actually. But we're driving up from Corpus Christi, so it will be around six o'clock before we get there."

"We?"

"Trevor Andersen is with me. He's my boyfriend. He's the one that suggested I call ahead and talk to you."

"Ms. Lawford, I'm glad you did. And I will wait at the office for you," he assured her. "You two drive safely, and I will see you this evening."

Nathan hung up, pulled out his cell phone, and called Bella as he left his office again to go update his team.

"I have a feeling it's going to be a late night for me, honey. But I'll call when I'm able to head home."

"Okay, then," he summarized when he rejoined his task force. "There's been a development, and since Lizzie's out I'm pulling in Agents Womack and Calloway to help us. They'll be here in just a moment, and I've asked Jason to bring in more laptops, as well."

"Two? Why two?" Hank asked.

"Because long story short, I now have a couple driving up from Corpus Christi to meet with me this evening. I have a feeling I'm going to need to switch my focus over to that for the next couple of days at least."

"Let me know if you'd like my help on that case, too," Rick said earnestly. "You know I'm not just an IT guy, Nathan. I also happen to do well with research. Besides, Faith went with Lizzie to Houston and Micah's minding the bookstore, so, I've got the time to spare right now."

"Done. You're in," Nathan told him. "And thanks."

Nathan looked up and nodded in approval as the two agents from night shift that he'd hand-selected to join the group walked into the room, followed by Jason with the extra laptops and headsets.

Nathan paused only long enough to introduce new team members Womack and Calloway to the four DEA agents before he got down to business.

"Everyone have their assigned videos?"

"Yep, ready to get started," Rick confirmed.

"Great. Let's get rolling – and remember, we need as much as we can find by Friday night at the latest. Both directors have already signed off on any overtime."

With that, Nathan stepped out into the hall again to handle two more pieces of business.

The first was a call to the security desk on the first floor.

"This is Agent Thomas," he announced. "I have some visitors en route. Susan Lawford and Trevor Andersen should be here around six p.m. tonight. Can you please call my cell phone when they arrive so that I can escort them up?"

That accomplished, he made his way to the unit secretary's desk and asked Diane to order in dinner for his team. Then he returned to the conference room.

"Where do I need to start?" he asked as he took his place among them in front of one of the laptops.

"I've queued your first file up for you already," Rick answered. "And when you're reviewing these, if you find something useful, jot down the file name and timestamp. That will make it easier later when we compile footage for the case."

Nathan gave Rick a thumbs-up as he slipped on his headphones, pressed 'play', and leaned back in his chair.

It was a half-hour before Claire found Remiel. She met him as he strolled casually up the path that wound between the cabins.

"Good afternoon, Sister Claire," he called out in a cheery voice.

"Have you seen Sophie?" she blurted out in response.

His brow furrowed.

"No. Why?"

"I haven't either. Not since yesterday."

Remiel paused his stride.

"Come to think of it, the last time I saw her was when the two of you came to the main building and got some food."

"Yes," Claire confirmed. "But that was almost twenty-four hours ago. Her car's not at her cabin, and no one answers when I knock on the door. Her cell phone goes straight to voicemail, too."

"Come with me," Remiel directed, and they quickly closed the distance to Sophie's cabin.

Remiel used his master key to let them both in. Claire raced to the bedroom, then the bathroom, before she returned to stand by him with a disappointed look on her face.

"Her bed is made. It's almost like she didn't sleep here overnight," Claire announced.

"And perhaps she did, and she just got up early. Try not to worry, Claire. It will drive you crazy, trust me. And you know how much she loves her books," he said gently as he pointed to the almost overflowing shelves, "and they're all still here. So, whatever's going on, she hasn't left completely."

He turned his gaze to the worried woman standing beside him.

"I'm sure she's fine, Claire. Maybe she just went into town to get some space for a while. While she's usually sunny and cheerful, you and I also know Paul's death hit her pretty hard. All we can do is be there for her – and sometimes, that means giving people the room they need to deal with what's happened."

They exited the cabin and Remiel secured the door again.

"You know I'm available to talk to, right?" he asked her.

Claire nodded.

"I'm probably just being overprotective. I'm sure she'll show up anytime now."

He patted her on the shoulder.

"See you later, Sister Claire."

But as she watched Remiel walk away, a thin ribbon of doubt began to weave itself through her mind, and her eyes widened with realization.

Oh, my God.... What if Remiel's one of the people mentioned in that mysterious note that Sophie got?

By mutual consent the task force members took a short break at the two-hour mark.

"We just got started on this and already I feel like I could mount and dismount a tire with my eyes closed," Hank remarked as he and Nathan traveled down the hall for more coffee.

"I myself am surprised at the quality of the video," Nathan confessed. "I thought for sure we'd be suffering through lots of hazy, grainy footage. Glad to see I was wrong."

"Excellent audio, too," Hank mentioned, and his grin faded into a solemn, haunted look as he turned to Nathan. "And you know what that means."

Nathan laid a hand on Hank's shoulder.

"When we find that footage, you don't *have* to be the one to watch it, Hank. You know as well as I do that you can't unsee something like that. It will stay with you forever. No one will think any less of you if you opt out. You don't have to put yourself through that."

Hank sighed.

"I do, actually. Because I know down to my core that if our roles were reversed Cruz would do the same for me. He wouldn't let anything at all stop him from finding out what happened to me."

He looked at the floor and set his jaw with a grim determination.

"That's why I asked Rick to assign the twenty-four hours leading up to Cruz's medallion camera going offline to me," Hank muttered. "If Cruz was killed in that building, it's not a question of *if* I see it, Nathan. Only *when*."

———

The vibrating buzz of his cell phone on his hip had Nathan jerking involuntarily two hours later. He paused the clip he was watching and removed his headphones, then stepped out into the hallway to answer the call.

"Good, thanks. I'll be right down," he told the man at the security desk in the building's lobby.

Nathan poked his head back in the conference room to get Rick and Hank's attention, then waited until both removed their headsets so that they could hear him.

"They're here," he said. "I'm heading down to meet them."

"Should I come with you, or stay here?" Rick asked.

"Join me," Nathan answered. "There may be some things that I can pass off to you right away."

"We've got this covered in here," Hank confirmed. "Do what you've gotta do."

———

"Ms. Lawford, Mr. Andersen, it's so nice to meet you both. I'm Agent Thomas, and this is Rick Conner, a consultant with the Bureau. If you'll just let Roger run that box through the scanner, please," Nathan instructed when he and Rick arrived in the lobby. "It's standard procedure."

Susan cast a sideways glance at Trevor, then dutifully handed over the box she'd been clutching to her chest to the gloved security guard.

A few moments later, once it had been confirmed that the small package didn't contain any explosives or bioweapons, Roger handed the box off to Nathan, who had also donned gloves.

"Right this way, please."

They stopped at the floor where the lab was located.

"Hold here for just a moment," Nathan politely directed, and walked into the lab.

"Hey, guys," he said. "I have a priority for you to work. But I need photocopies of the pages in this box before I leave you to it."

"Sure thing, Nathan," the lead tech said, and quickly retrieved the pages and made photocopies, then handed the copies over. "We'll get right on this."

Nathan rejoined his guests and Rick at the elevator.

"Let's head up to my office and talk."

Once they were settled in Nathan's office, he looked at Susan.

"I know we talked on the phone earlier, but, let's take it from the top," he said as he grabbed a fresh legal-sized notepad. "Whenever you're ready."

Susan began the story with Sophie's excited call to her about the interview and walked them through all the correspondence with her sister since then.

"And then last night, she left me this message," Susan said, and swallowed hard as she retrieved her phone from her purse, set it on the desk, pressed the speaker button, and then pressed 'play'.

As Sophie's voice filled the room, Susan reached over for Trevor's hand.

"I think I've stumbled onto something here. I just overnighted you a box. If my gut is right, what's happening is horrible and it's big, Susan, really big. I can't talk much longer right now, but I'll call you back later and by then I should have even more evidence to blow this thing wide open."

There was a pause before the message continued.

"One last thing. I think someone is following me. If you don't hear back from me in two days, I want you to reach out to Claire, understand? Come up to Jack County and go to the farmer's market

that happens every Friday and find Claire and talk to her. I love you, sis."

"Can you forward me that message?" Nathan asked after a brief silence.

"Yes, sure," she replied.

"Thanks. What happened after that?"

"I didn't get this message until this morning," Susan admitted. "I saw I'd missed a call, but I didn't recognize the number and I was exhausted, so I didn't listen to it until today."

Her face crumpled with guilt.

"If I had listened to it last night... maybe..."

"Don't do that to yourself, honey," Trevor immediately murmured as he put an arm around her shoulders. "Don't go there."

"And what number did she call you from?"

Susan showed Nathan, and he wrote it down on a smaller pad, tore the page off, and handed it over to Rick.

"I'm pretty good at finding information," Rick assured her when Susan's look turned to one of confusion. "I will be able to get to within ten feet of this phone's location if it's a land line."

"Okay, so, this morning, you got up, and you listened to the message. Then what?"

"I tried to call her, several times. The phone just rang several times before voicemail kicked in – until the last time. That time it went *straight* to voicemail. Then I tried to call her back at that strange number. Seven rings, and then a dial tone."

She shrugged as the tears began to well up.

"Then I called Trevor. And after that, we waited for the box to arrive, and once it did and we saw what was inside...well, read the pages, Agent Thomas, and you'll see for yourself. Sophie's in big, big trouble."

Chapter Twenty

Nᴀᴛʜᴀɴ ᴛᴏᴏᴋ a few minutes to do just that, and once he was finished, he silently passed them off to Rick for perusal.

When his brother-in-law's eyebrow raised slightly as he read, Nathan knew for sure that he and Rick had formed the exact same opinion.

Susan Lawford's hunch was spot on. Sophie Drimmel had potentially stumbled right into the middle of a massive – and deadly - hornet's nest.

"Can you give us just a moment, please? We'll be right back," he told them, and indicated to Rick to join him in the hall.

They spoke in hushed tones the moment that Nathan's office door was firmly closed behind them.

"Rick, we need to know the origin of the last call Sophie made - and I need you to get copies of those ten death certificates as soon as possible."

"Agreed. It sure feels like some seriously foul stuff is happening out at Lighte's Landing. I'm going to need to make myself another copy of that list of names so I can get started."

"And I'm going to put out a 'missing/endangered person' bulletin for Sophie, and then start digging into Lighte's Landing and everyone she mentioned in that letter," Nathan revealed. "Maybe we'll catch a break here."

They stepped back into Nathan's office, where Susan and Trevor watched them expectantly.

"Ms. Lawford, Mr. Andersen," Nathan began, and Susan shook her head.

"Please. It's Susan and Trevor."

Nathan smiled.

"Susan, Trevor. I need to get more specifics about Sophie personally – height, weight, age, hair color, eye color, and so on. A recent picture would be extremely helpful. And if you know the type of car she drives, that information would be useful, too."

He indicated Rick with his left hand.

"Rick is going to make more copies of the letters, and he's going to trace that unknown phone number and some of the other data points that Sophie provided. I promise that we will keep you informed throughout the investigation, and that we will do everything in our power to find Sophie. But I must insist for your own safety that the two of you either remain here in Dallas or go home. Do *not* go out to Jack County. Let us do the work on this."

Susan went from passive to belligerent in a nanosecond as she leapt to her feet.

"If you think I am going to just sit around and wait while my baby sister is out there somewhere with God knows what happening to her right now, then you've lost your damn mind!" she snarled.

It was Trevor who pulled her back, both emotionally and physically, from the brink. He wrapped his arms around her and spoke gently into her ear.

"Susan, I need you to breathe right now. Yelling at Agent Thomas won't help Sophie. They know what they're doing. We need to stay out of the way and let them do it, Susan."

The fire in her temperament abruptly deserted her, and Susan's body sagged in Trevor's arms.

"I know. I'm sorry. I just…"

"It's all right, Susan. I totally get it – she's your kid sister, and you'd do anything to keep her safe. But the last thing this situation needs is the two of *you* in harm's way, as well. I need you to trust me, and to let us handle it. Please," Nathan said earnestly, then held her gaze until she closed her eyes, sighed once, and nodded.

"All right, Agent Thomas. I trust you. We'll stay here."

By the time Susan Lawford and Trevor Andersen left the building a half-hour later, Nathan had not only vital statistics for Sophie, but two pictures of her, as well. He set up the parameters of the missing persons bulletin, added in her photographs and the details of her 2005 Honda – including the vanity plate number – and uploaded it all into the nationwide alert database.

Two minutes later his desk phone rang. It was the lab.

"Hey, Nathan. I've scanned the flash drive's contents for any malware or viruses. They're clean. I made you copies of its contents. Do you want me to email them to you, or do you want the flash drive?"

"Email's fine, thanks."

He walked around the side of his desk to the medium-sized whiteboard on the wall and started lining out the known facts of what he'd dubbed 'the Lighte's Landing case' in his head: possible victim names and death dates, the information mentioned in Sophie's note about Brittany's mysterious and sudden disappearance, and the basic data for Sophie herself.

Nathan had just tacked up Sophie's pictures when a rap on his doorframe caught his attention.

"Food's here," Ben told him, then did a double take when he glanced over at Nathan's whiteboard.

"Why is she on your whiteboard? How do you already know about her?" he asked.

"What do you mean?"

"*Her*," Ben repeated, and pointed at Sophie's pictures for emphasis. "Half of us started with the newest footage, and the rest of us got assigned the oldest. Rick gave me the footage from Friday the third. I'm almost done watching it, and I swear she looks *just like* the blonde customer that interacted with Cruz at the garage that afternoon."

Nathan reached out and grabbed the pictures and then the legal pad filled with his notes.

"Show me this video."

They retreated to the conference room, and Ben led Nathan over to the laptop he'd been using.

"That one," Ben said, and pointed at an open video file on the screen. "You should only have to back up about twenty minutes or so, boss. That should be about right. She shows up on the footage at around five p.m. I'm going to go grab a plate of food right quick while you're checking it out."

Nathan moved down the table long enough to grab the headphones he'd been using previously, then settled in at Ben's station and watched in disbelief as his two current cases seemed to collide head-on.

He paused the video when the little car's license plate was clearly visible, then skimmed his notes.

Yep, that's her car, all right, he confirmed via comparison of the picture on the screen to the vanity license plate Susan had mentioned.

But since the video was taken from an exterior camera on the building, the audio was lacking in quality – way too much extraneous noise from the busy street easily drowned out the conversation between Sophie and the undercover agent.

A puzzled Nathan leaned back in his chair.

What the hell was Sophie Drimmel doing at a known *cartel-controlled business?*

He cleared his throat.

"May I have everyone's attention, please," Nathan said, and waited until each task force member was looking in his direction.

"It seems that a young woman named Sophie Drimmel appeared in the security video on Friday the third. She also has gone missing. That's the case that my two guests brought to my attention earlier this evening. As you continue to review footage, I'd like to ask each of you to let me know *immediately* if she appears in any further videos. Please take a moment to come look at the still shots I'm about to leave up on Ben's screen, so that you will know what both she and her car look like."

"Let me take a look at the footage," Wilford offered. "I might be able to help you pinpoint what's going on."

Nathan left the chair so that Wilford could take his turn watching the video. As he waited for feedback, Nathan walked over to the long credenza along the south wall where someone had laid out the Chinese food he'd ordered and filled his own plate on autopilot as his mind grappled with this new tidbit.

Twenty minutes later Agent Wilford was able to set his mind at ease.

"I watched their interaction, Nathan. I don't think she's a regular customer there if that's what you were thinking."

"What makes you say that?"

"Cruz was replacing a serpentine belt on her car. That's not an everyday purchase, Nathan. If I had to guess, hers came off while she was driving down the road, and this garage was the one closest to where it happened. She wouldn't have had much choice in where to stop – the way that her car's engine is configured, she would not have been able to go very far at all without that belt."

Wilford took a small sip of water, then kept going.

"Not only that, but, did you notice the anxious look on her face when she got out of the car? She was rattled. This was an emergency stop, not planned at all. I think it's safe to say this was a weird coincidence and nothing more."

"Thanks for checking it out," Nathan said, and heaved a silent sigh of relief.

"No problem. I'm just glad to know my summers spent wrenching on cars are finally paying off," Wilford replied with a grin, and went back for a second helping of lo mein before returning to his own seat and his own set of videos to wade through.

Susan and Trevor checked into a hotel not far from the FBI's Dallas office and lugged their bags up to their room on the fifth floor.

"I still don't feel right about not looking for Sophie myself," she grumbled as she unpacked her toiletries.

He closed the distance between them to lean against the bathroom's open doorway.

"I know. But it really is for the best, Susan. Agent Thomas strikes me as extremely capable. We just need to trust that he'll find Sophie and get her to safety."

He paused, watching her.

"In the meantime – where would you like to go to dinner? You must be hungry."

By nine-forty p.m., over half the team members were beginning to yawn.

"How much have we gotten through?" Hank asked Rick.

"About thirty hours' worth, give or take," came the answer.

"Did we get some good clear pictures of everyone that works at the garage?" Nathan inquired.

"Sort of," Ben piped up. "All the footage so far of Javier, the guy that did my oil change, isn't very helpful."

"Why is that?"

"He has a full beard and wears a ball cap all the time. No real clear shots of his face," Ben explained. "But I think we were able to get good pictures of Miguel, the manager, and that Ramon guy. Right, Rick?"

Annie, seated next to Ben, tensed slightly at the mention of Ramon, but only Nathan noticed it – everyone else had looked over at Rick, who was nodding his head to confirm the answer to the pictures question.

"At this rate, we could be through reviewing all the Sunday videos in our timeframe by sometime Friday night, it sounds like," Nathan mused.

"Yes, we can," Rick confirmed. "And that's a good pace. Sitting and staring at a screen for hours on end is more physically taxing than people think. We have about ninety hours left to get through the first data set. Spreading those out among the team is an excellent idea. Means that each person only needs to spend another nine to eleven hours of screen time to get what you guys need by Saturday."

Womack and Calloway raised their hands.

"I'd like to keep going, boss," Grace Womack announced with a smile. "Keep in mind, we're not morning glories like you all are. We're usually just getting rolling this time of night."

"She's right, Nathan," Calloway chimed in. "We can keep going. We're solid until three or four a.m. at least."

"Fair enough – but keep taking little breaks, don't try to marathon through. Ben, Annie, Rick, wrap up and get going. Back here at six a.m. please."

Nathan's day-shift team members began to shut down their laptops. Meanwhile, Hank looked at the DEA agents under his command.

"How are you guys feeling?"

"We all can be back at six, no problem," Baker said, and his teammates all nodded their agreement.

―――――

Tension hung heavy in the air as Ben and Annie rode the elevator down to the garage.

"About earlier today..." Ben started to say but Annie cut him off.

"I'm not doing this with you right now, Ben. I'm just not," she retorted as she stared straight ahead at the elevator doors. "It's been a very long and trying day, and I am exhausted. We're going to go home, and we are going to sleep. That's non-negotiable."

She exited the moment the doors opened wide enough for her to fit through, and Ben followed behind her, unwilling to say anything else that might provoke her anger even further.

The ride back to Ben's apartment was uneasy. Once they'd reached their destination, Ben unlocked the door then stood aside for her to enter.

Annie immediately moved to their bedroom and grabbed a change of clothes, a blanket, her pillow, and her phone charger.

"See you in the morning," she said bluntly as she moved past a chastened Ben in the hallway and returned out to the living room to stretch out on the couch for the night.

―――――

A weary Nathan arrived home and walked through his front door a little before eleven p.m. to find Bella still awake and waiting for him in the living room.

"Long day, huh," she observed as she used the remote to turn off the TV, then stood and shuffled over to hug him.

"Yeah. And, I need to go in early, so tomorrow will be, too," he replied as he rested his chin on the top of her head, closed his eyes, and just held her for a moment.

"Did you grab something to eat, at least?"

He chuckled.

"Yes, ma'am. As a matter of fact, I made sure the whole team had dinner."

"Good. So, how about a soak, then sleep?" Bella asked, her cheek pressed against his chest.

"Just what I need. Lead the way."

Chapter Twenty-One

By the time the rest of the team rejoined Womack and Calloway at six a.m. Thursday morning, there'd been some progress made.

"What we watched last night is pure gold, I'm telling you," a tired Grace Womack told Nathan once she'd motioned him, Hank, and Rick over.

"We've got two different Sundays so far that show *a lot* of activity all day long – specifically, drugs being transferred from one car chassis to another. The quality of the video is top-notch. More than enough for warrants, for sure."

She pointed to her screen.

"I tried to rename those two files for easier identification," she continued, "but my user access wouldn't allow for it. Somebody should put some subfolders in here or something, so that we can more readily find the ones we've already looked at and are keeping."

"I can do that," Rick replied as he sat down at his computer. "Give me just a moment."

Thirty seconds of rapid typing later, he said, "Try it now."

She smiled when she was able to successfully place the two files into the new folder.

"Thanks. What time do you want us back here, Nathan?"

"Four p.m. Good work, you two. Go get some rest."

Hank Myers reluctantly took his seat.

His meager sleep overnight had been heavily laced with dreams, not one of them pleasant. As a result, he already had a headache forming at the base of his skull, and he had a gut feeling that a day's worth of computer time would only increase that pain.

Not to mention that depending on which video pops up today, there won't just be physical pain to deal with, he thought sourly.

He frowned, took another sip of coffee, booted up his laptop, and braced himself for what lay in wait for him in his assigned files.

Just across the table from where Hank had set up, Ben and Annie sat, side-by-side in physical distance but oceans apart emotionally.

She'd not said a word to him all morning.

Ben fought back a snarl as he shoved the headset down and over his ears and prepared to dive headfirst into the day's distraction from what he felt was now most likely his doomed relationship.

Worst part is, it's my own damn fault, a little voice in the back of his mind proclaimed, and Ben clicked the 'play' icon a little harder than necessary.

Once he'd touched base with his team, Nathan Thomas strode down the hall to the kitchen to get some coffee, then headed to his office and shut the door. He carefully re-tacked Sophie's pictures up on his whiteboard before he sat at his desk and fired up his computer.

"Let's see what we can find out," he murmured to himself, and opened the folder with all his notes so far about Sophie Drimmel and the strange events out at Lighte's Landing.

He flipped his legal pad to a fresh page, then picked up Sophie's letter and began to scan the contents.

Lighte's Landing became the first entry on the pristine paper.

He skipped down fifteen lines, then wrote, *Remiel Lighte.*

"Good to start with," he said, and opened a browser window on his computer.

Back in the conference room, Rick Conner pulled double duty in the form of side-by-side laptops.

One was solely for displaying and running videos from the South Fort Worth garage. The other was dedicated to finding out more information pertaining to the Sophie Drimmel case.

He'd left searches running overnight for the phone number and for the alleged victims' names. While the search for death certificates had not yet returned any results, his other search – trying to pin down the phone number's origin – had already struck gold.

He copied those results into an email and sent it to Nathan before he switched gears and opened the next security video that he'd assigned himself.

To try to gain more year-round business, the little ice cream shop on Jacksboro's town square had started serving breakfast and lunch, as well.

The shop owner was already irritated when he walked up to the front door of his business at seven a.m.; he'd slept right through his alarm, and as a result, he was running over an hour behind schedule.

And then, he noticed it.

The crappy little four-door Honda still sat where he'd last seen it after closing the previous night – and the night before that. And it was still taking up prime real estate – one of only five precious parking spots the optimal distance from his shop's one and only door.

"Ridiculous," he grumbled as he took out his keys to unlock his establishment, bound and determined to rid himself of the unsightly impediment.

If it's not gone by lunchtime, I'm having it towed. That'll teach 'em.

By eleven a.m. Rick was sitting in one of the visitors' chairs in Nathan's office.

"We're going to need to go a different route on the death certificates," he informed him. "I've tried everything I can think of, short of hacking the State's database. The only way to find out for sure if they exist is to make a formal request. They'll give them to you since you have an open and active investigation going on."

"I'll let the director know. I think he has a point of contact down in Austin for things like this," Nathan answered, and reached for his desk phone.

A few minutes later, he hung up and grinned at Rick.

"The director said to forward him the list and carbon copy me on it, and he'll formally request the documents personally. With a little luck, we can have them in hand by Monday."

Out in Jacksboro Mr. Gillespie, the owner of the ice cream shop, watched with satisfaction as the little Honda that had taken up a valuable parking spot in front of his business for almost two whole days was hooked up to a tow truck.

But a police cruiser arriving onsite stopped the process in its tracks.

"Stop. You can't tow that car. Unhook it," the officer directed the moment he stepped up onto the curb.

The belligerent shop owner fisted his hands on his hips.

"Why on earth not? It hasn't moved at all, and I have a right to...".

"Because there's an FBI bulletin out involving this car, that's why. It needs to be processed before it can be moved," the officer interrupted before he turned his attention back to the tow truck driver.

"Unhook the chains. *Now.*"

Then he pressed the 'mike' key on his walkie-talkie.

"Dispatch, I need the processing team to come to my location, and we need to contact the FBI. I'm looking at the car mentioned in their missing persons notice."

"Missing person?" a pale Mr. Gillespie parroted.

The policeman turned and levelled his gaze at the man.

"Yes. A missing person. A young woman, to be exact. How long has this car been here?"

Mr. Gillespie's eyes widened with concern and surprise, and his entire demeanor shifted to one of helpfulness.

"Well, now, let's see," he thought aloud. "I know it was parked there two nights ago. Mabel had to leave early, and I had to come up here to close the shop for the night. I don't remember seeing it before then."

"You've got security cameras in your shop, right?"

"Of course."

"May we look at the footage?"

"Of course, officer. And I can get Mabel up here, too, if you want to talk to her as well. Whatever I can do to help you guys find that young lady."

The officer keyed his mike again.

"Dispatch, send me a computer tech, as well."

Rick had only been back in his chair in the conference room for a half-hour when Nathan sought him out.

"I just got a call from the Jacksboro, Texas police department. They found Sophie's car," Nathan revealed. "It was about to be towed. They're processing it for us and will overnight any evidence collected to our lab here for analysis."

"Where was it?"

"Parked in front of an ice cream shop on the town square. That's about twenty minutes from Lighte's Landing."

Rick tilted his head.

"*Gillespie's*, right? You do realize that's the same location as that mysterious phone number. You thinking road trip? That's only about a ninety-minute drive from here."

"I *do* realize that's the same location - which is why I let them know that they also need to send me any security footage available from the shop and the surrounding area for the last three days. As far as going out there, we can't. Not yet, anyway," Nathan answered. "We really need a confirmed status on those death certificates and some results back from the lab on that package before we can move forward."

Out at Lighte's Landing, Claire's initial concern for Sophie had increased a thousand-fold after enduring another day with no word from the young woman she'd grown so fond of. She paced back and forth across the living and dining area of her tiny cabin, desperately trying to figure out what to do next.

And then a light bulb went off.

It's been well over twenty-four hours. I can try to file a missing person's report, at least, she assured herself as she snatched up her purse and her keys.

Luckily for Claire, the predator responsible for Sophie's going off-grid wasn't around to view the constantly rolling camera footage as she climbed into her car to head into town.

Twenty-two minutes later she made sure her car was locked before she walked up to and through the double doors that served as the main entrance of the Jacksboro Police Department.

"Good afternoon, sir," she said when she approached the armed officer seated at the reception desk in the lobby. "My name is Claire King, and I need to report someone missing, please."

"Have a seat just over there, please, Ms. King. Someone will be right with you," he responded, and swept his arm out to indicate a short row of chairs along the far wall.

The moment had arrived that he'd dreaded with every fiber of his being.

Hank Myers abruptly clicked 'pause', and it took all his willpower to stay seated and not bolt out of the conference room.

He'd just watched Javier and Ramon manhandle an obviously unconscious, hooded man into the center of the camera's frame and then drop him like a rag doll onto the concrete floor at Miguel's behest.

He closed his eyes and took several deep breaths to try to steady his horrifically racing pulse.

You can do this. You must *do this.*

Hank felt someone watching him. Another deep breath later, he opened his eyes, and his gaze flitted upward to lock with Annie's.

Her dark brown eyes radiated concern for him from across the table.

She knows. Somehow, she knows...

You okay? she mouthed.

He slowly shook his head no, and watched her eyes widen, then start to glisten as her right hand moved up to cover her trembling lower lip.

He dropped his gaze downward again.

With a far from steady hand, he clicked his mouse again to set the playback of fellow agent and best friend Cruz Delgado's violent death into motion on his screen.

Chapter Twenty-Two

Nathan was just about to head out for a quick lunch when his desk phone rang.

"I have a Detective MacKinnon with the Jacksboro Police Department holding on line three for you," Diane told him.

"Thanks," Nathan answered, and pressed the corresponding button on his keypad.

"This is Agent Thomas. How may I help you?"

"Well," the detective began, "I just had a visitor here that came in to file a missing persons report. But when she told me who she's concerned about, I realized you've already got an active one going on for that same individual."

"Sophie Drimmel?"

"Yep. Ms. King– "

Nathan played a hunch.

"Ms. King's first name wouldn't happen to be Claire, would it?"

"As a matter of fact, it is."

Nathan scrambled to open his file folder and pull out the copy of Sophie's letter.

"Might I be able to speak to her?"

"She just left, I'm afraid. But she left me her contact information. I'm happy to forward you that. I imagine you'd like to interview her."

"At some point I would, yes. Did she mention when it was she last saw Sophie?"

Nathan heard a rustle of paper in the background.

"Ms. King stated that the last time she saw Sophie was around three p.m. two days, ago. Sophie spent some time with Ms. King in her cabin, then stated she was going to the cemetery on the property to take pictures of headstones."

"Did she say why?"

"Ms. King's boyfriend, a Paul Bingman, just died, and she and Sophie were asked if they'd like to select the headstone. So, Sophie suggested taking pictures of the existing stones out there to get some design ideas."

"What happened after that?"

"She said Sophie said, 'I'll see you in the morning.' But she hasn't seen or heard from her since."

"What was her demeanor?"

"Claire King is frightened, though she took great pains to hide it," MacKinnon said with conviction. "And I could not get her to give me any other details at all. She would only say she's concerned for Sophie's safety, but she refused to elaborate as to why. Then she bolted out of here."

"What I'm about to share with you might explain why she's spooked, Detective," Nathan said, and read him in on everything that had come to light so far – Sophie's ominous voice message to Susan Lawford, the box and its contents, and the long letter outlining every one of Sophie's discoveries and theories.

Detective MacKinnon let out a low whistle when Nathan finished.

"*Wow.* Cameras in the smoke detectors? Yikes. Yes, that would certainly explain the way Ms. King was acting. But I'll be honest, Agent Thomas, I just don't think she knows about any of that at all. If she did, I honestly think she would have told me. My guess is that

Sophie purposely kept her in the dark on a lot of this to try to protect her."

"I'm inclined to agree."

"When are you coming out this way?"

"I'm still waiting on death certificates and lab results. Once those hit, I'll obtain warrants, then be heading your direction."

"Whatever help you need from us, just let me know. I will tell you that Lighte's Landing is well outside any city limits, so, you'll need to loop in the Jack County Sheriff's Department when the time comes. I have a point of contact over there that I've known for years. I'll pass along his number as well when I email you Ms. King's number."

"Much appreciated, Detective MacKinnon. And for the record, I think that Claire King would be much safer if she were *not* out at Lighte's Landing."

"After everything you just told me, I think you're absolutely right. Just say the word, and I will reach out to her and coax her back here to the station where I can protect her."

"I figure from what Sophie's voicemail said that Claire is a regular fixture at the farmer's market in that area. Push comes to shove you could reach out to her in person there. You might have to tell her about the cameras to get her cooperation, but that is preferable to her staying out at Lighte's Landing and being at risk. Whoever took Sophie already knows that her and Sophie are close, so it wouldn't surprise me at all if Claire King was already on this whack job's radar."

"Good point. I'll make a trip out to the market tomorrow and find her."

"Thanks," Nathan said. "One more thing, Detective MacKinnon. What, if anything, do you know about Remiel Lighte?"

After an additional ten minutes of conversation, Nathan hung up the phone and went down the hall to the conference room to talk to Rick.

"Want to grab a late lunch? I just had another call from Jacksboro PD, and I have some updates to share with you," he said, once Rick had paused the footage he was watching and taken off his headphones.

"Sure," Rick replied.

A feather-soft touch on Nathan's arm made him turn his head.

"I'm pretty sure Hank found the murder video," Annie murmured as quietly as she could. "And I think he's watching it now."

Nathan's eyes cut across the room, and he immediately noticed Hank's bleak expression, the tightness in his jawline, and the way his hands clenched into hard fists on either side of his laptop.

"Keep an eye on him for me, please," he told Annie. "He may not want it, but he's going to need our support."

"I'd already planned to."

The first ninety minutes of video were uneventful. The one known as Javier had removed the unconscious man's hood, and then moved out of the camera's path. Although the man's face was only partially showing in profile, Hank recognized his best friend straightaway.

At around the two-hour mark, things turned violent rather quickly. Hank braced himself when Estoban Cortinas strolled into view on the video and remarked, *'Funny, he doesn't look like a cop'*, then bent down and tapped Cruz repeatedly on the cheek.

Hank watched as Miguel brought a chair over for the cartel leader to sit down on. It was only a few moments after Cruz made his comment about the man's shoes that the barrage of kicks began.

With each blow, Hank's rage intensified, but he tried his best to keep it caged long enough to do his job.

Suddenly Cortinas stepped back, then waved his hand. Hank

saw Ramon and the mysterious Javier come forward into the camera's range again and roughly pull Cruz to his feet, then secure him to both the floor and the ceiling via chains and a hoist.

Hank ground his teeth as he witnessed Cruz's body being pulled in two different directions. He knew his friend well enough to know that by that point Cruz must have been in agony. But he *also* knew Cruz well enough to know that he would never have given his attacker the pleasure of knowing that.

He managed to get through the remainder – the killing blows, then watching them carry and dispose of his friend like Cruz was nothing more than garbage – but only barely.

Hank was about to hit 'pause' when he heard Estoban say, "*I have another task for the three of you.*"

Wonder what else *he's about to do or say on camera that I can hang him with,* Hank thought to himself, and let the video continue to play.

Ten minutes later, he paused the video and left his chair to find Nathan.

<hr>

"I need to show you something," a grim-faced Hank announced without preamble from Nathan's office doorway. "Come with me."

Nathan followed Hank back to the conference room, where the DEA agent pointed at his laptop.

"Take a seat. You're going to want to hear this for yourself," Hank assured him. "It's queued up, just press play."

Nathan slipped the headset on, started the video, and watched and listened as a smug Estoban Cortinas sat behind the desk in the garage's tiny garage office and instructed three men to ferret out Agent Jones by whatever means necessary.

He paused the footage, took the headset off, and looked over his shoulder at Hank.

"We've got a problem."

"After what I just saw them do to Cruz? I'd say you have a *huge* problem. You, and every single member of your team that had any contact at all with Jones."

"That would be all four of us on day shift," Nathan muttered. "Speaking of watching..."

Hank held up his hand.

"It was as bad as I feared it would be, let's just leave it at that."

Nathan levelled his gaze at Hank.

"You know there are resources. People you can talk to," he said gently. "Don't carry that by yourself."

"I'll be okay, especially when we're able to get him out of that tank."

"What?"

"They shoved his body in the used oil reservoir... like he was *trash*..." Hank snarled through tightly clenched teeth as the façade he was so desperately clinging to started to crack wide open.

"I need some air, Nathan, I will see you in the morning," he said abruptly, and walked swiftly out of the conference room and down the hall to the elevators.

Nathan waited several beats, then left the room and ran into Annie as she was leaving the breakroom.

He tilted his head toward the elevators.

"Follow him."

"You got it."

Nathan watched her go after Hank, then turned and made his way to the director's office.

"Sir, do you have a moment?"

"Absolutely. Come in."

Once Nathan was seated, the director steepled his hands.

"I take it you have news."

"We've watched enough footage to be able to request arrest warrants on four people – including Estoban Cortinas – for drug trafficking and murder."

"Agent Delgado's death."

"Yes, sir. Top quality video and audio that shows it all, up to and including what they did with his body afterward, from the sounds of it. I've not seen it for myself yet."

"And where is this footage now?"

"I can bring the laptop in here, if you like."

He reached over and dialed a button on his desk phone.

"Diane, hold my calls for the rest of the day, please."

"Yes, sir."

The director disconnected the call and transferred his gaze back to Nathan.

"Bring it in," he instructed, "and we'll view it together."

Hank stormed his way off the elevator when it reached the garage level. He was over halfway to his car when he heard footsteps closing in quickly behind him.

He whirled, seeing red, prepared to take a swing at whoever dared disturb him – and checked himself when he realized it was Annie.

"Hank," she said softly, and took one last step forward.

"Just... *don't*," he growled, both hands thrust out in front of him to keep her at bay. "You can't help with this. *No one can help with this.* Nothing but putting a bullet in Estoban Cortinas' brain pan will make this feel any better at all."

She nodded solemnly, her brown eyes darkening even more as she held his gaze. Finally, she spoke.

"You know where I am if you need or want to talk," she said simply.

He ran his hands over his face, then through his hair.

"Appreciate it," he croaked, his voice going tight with the emotions swirling through him. "But right now, I just can't, Annie. I'll see you tomorrow."

He turned on his heel and left her standing there.

When a dejected Annie returned upstairs, Ben met her in the hallway.

"You all right?"

"Fine. Worried about Hank, is all."

Ben raised an eyebrow despite his best efforts to rein in the sudden surge of jealousy that flowed through him.

Knock it off. You are in enough trouble with her as it is. Don't be stupid.

But he simply could not help himself.

"Why?" Ben asked in a snippy tone. "And when, exactly, did he go from 'Agent Myers' to *Hank?*"

"You're a real ass, you know that?" she growled. "He just watched the murder of his best friend, and *our boss* asked me to keep an eye on him. If you've got a problem with that, then you need to take it up with Nathan, because I am done speaking to you about it, Ben."

She turned and started to walk away, then stopped, fists clenched. She slowly turned to face him again - and finally lost her temper.

Annie closed the distance with her right arm and hand extended in front of her, and she poked him hard in the chest repeatedly with her index finger as she unloaded on him.

"Matter of fact, I'm pretty much done with this relationship completely. I have *had it* with your possessive and smothering attitude. Let's get one thing straight right here, right now – *you do not own me, Ben,* and I *refuse* to be treated like I'm your personal property. So, here is what's gonna happen. *We* are going to spend some time apart, because *I* need some space, and *you* need to get your act together."

And with that, Annie turned her back on him and stormed off.

A heavy sigh behind him caused him to look over his shoulder at a frowning Grace Womack, who stood three feet away and was pinning him with a disapproving stare and shaking her head.

"I don't believe I have *ever* seen Annie that mad before. You messed up big time," she remarked, and clucked her tongue at him as she maneuvered past him to get to the conference room.

In the director's office, Nathan glanced at his phone and saw a new text message from Annie. He scanned it, then typed a short answer and hit 'send'.

"Sorry about that, sir," he told his boss.

"No problem. You missed exactly thirty seconds of watching a man lie on a floor. Shall we continue?"

Hank Myers only stopped at one place on his way back to his hotel room – the liquor store, to purchase a bottle of scotch.

While he really did not care for it, scotch on the rocks had been Cruz's favorite drink, and Hank was determined to salute his friend right.

And if I manage to get drunk enough to sleep and not replay his death on an endless loop in my head, well, that's a bonus...

He ordered a pizza using his room's phone and poured himself three fingers of the amber liquid into a glass with ice.

He was already halfway through his second glass by the time his meal arrived.

Meanwhile, a still seething Annie was at Ben's apartment, piling her clothes into suitcases and trying to figure out where she was going to stay for the foreseeable future. She'd already sent Nathan a text explaining that she'd left a bit early but would arrive on time in the morning for her shift.

When her cell phone rang, she flinched until she realized it was Grace Womack.

"Girl. You okay?"

"No, Grace, I'm not. He's an idiot."

"Based on the little bit I witnessed earlier, I agree. You need a place to crash? I've got an extra room, and you can stay as long as you need."

"I do, actually. Thanks."

"Swing back by the office and I'll give you my spare key. Oh, and Annie? I won't tell him a thing about you staying with me if you don't want him to know where you went. Let him suffer some. From the sounds of things, he's earned it."

Annie chuckled through her anger.

"And then some, actually. I'll meet you in the garage in a half-hour to get that key. And thanks again."

"No worries, hon. I've got your back."

Annie ended the call and marched to the bathroom with another, smaller suitcase to pack up her toiletries.

The director only paused the video once Miguel, Ramon, and Javier's conversation about their new assignment was over.

"That was brutal," he murmured. "But having that footage in our possession means that we should have no problem at all obtaining warrants – and getting them expedited."

"My thoughts exactly," Nathan agreed. "And we will be able to pick up Ramon Saturday night. I'm thinking the raid on the garage needs to happen on Sunday. Based on the videos we've seen so far, most of the action involving the drugs happens on Sundays, so, it'd be good to get it all done at once."

"Have you thought about who's going to be on your raid team?"

the director asked him. "Because Annie is already putting herself at risk by meeting one of these guys offsite. To maintain her cover, she needs to *not* be involved, at all, in the raid on Sunday. And we can make Saturday night's arrest look like a traffic stop or something, so that the suspect remains unaware that she is a federal agent."

"If Lizzie's back I will put her on the team in Annie's place. I know her. She's going to want to lose herself in work for a while."

The director nodded.

"So, which videos are we forwarding to the DEA?"

"Rick has already sent the older ones over to them; they have more labor they can spare to wade through footage of other Sundays to build their case. We will forward the two we've vetted, as well, but the one you and I just watched is staying with us to build our capital murder case."

"Agreed. Speaking of, let me get the warrants request drawn up and sent over right now. I'm thinking that based on what we've uncovered to date, we will have them in hand by Saturday morning."

Ben still sat in the conference room at his laptop, headphones on and video playing, but not seeing or hearing anything at all. His mind was busy replaying everything Annie had said to him in the hallway.

He gave up the charade just before seven p.m. and closed his station down for the night, then headed home. On the way he stopped and bought a bouquet of flowers, then used the rest of his short drive time to think about what he would say to try to get Annie to realize how remorseful he felt.

He let himself in his apartment and called out her name.

No answer.

Ben strode to the bedroom, then into the bathroom. Where Annie's clothes had been hanging in the closet, large gaps now greeted him. He opened drawers, wincing when he saw that each one that he had watched her fill with her things were now empty.

She left. She really left.

Knees buckling, he sat on the edge of the bed and closed his eyes.

227

A little before midnight, Hank Myers drained his glass for the sixth time, then staggered fully clothed over to the bed, where the bad dreams he had hoped to keep at bay with alcohol started up right after he passed out.

Chapter Twenty-Three

Lizzie turned her head to look at the clock by the bed in Tank and Renee's guest room.

Four a.m.

Way too much time to think before Tank's memorial service at nine, she acknowledged, and sighed quietly.

She got out of bed, then slipped her robe on over her pajamas and went to the kitchen.

"Hey," Renee said gently from her seat at the table where she was feeding Tucker his bottle. "You can't sleep either, huh."

"Nope, not really," Lizzie said, and paused behind the chair adjacent to her friend. "Are you hungry? I can make something."

"That casserole that Sergeant Wright's wife made was pretty good. I vote we heat some of that up."

"You got it," Lizzie said, and busied her mind and her hands with making sure Tank's widow ate enough.

That had been their mission since she, Donny, and Faith had arrived two days earlier – taking the best care possible of the one that Tank had wanted to spend forever with.

Tank's brothers and Renee's mother and sister had arrived the

228

following day, but Tank's parents had been unable to make the flight down at all. A bad fall resulting in a broken hip five days previously meant that his mother was in no condition to travel, so Donny had helped Renee arrange for Tank's body to be flown to Seattle for a second, smaller memorial and then interment once the Texas ceremony ended.

And after some discussion, Renee had decided that Tucker would stay at the house with Faith during the local service.

"He's much too young," she'd informed Lizzie. "Besides, we will be flying out that afternoon. That's going to be hard enough on him as it is."

The microwave beeping brought Lizzie out of her reverie, and she checked the temperature, frowned, and added another two and a half minutes to the timer, then pressed 'start'. Once the casserole was heated all the way through, she dished some onto two plates and carried them over to the table.

"He's out," Renee said, looking down at her child who'd fallen asleep again halfway through feeding. "I'm gonna go lay him down again. I'll be right back."

She stood gracefully and walked past Lizzie to head down the hall to the nursery, leaving Lizzie alone with way too many memories and ghosts.

A few minutes later Renee reappeared and reclaimed her seat, then startled Lizzie by asking, "How are you holding up?"

"You're worried about *me*?"

Renee smiled softly, even as the sorrow crept into her eyes.

"Of course, I am. Tank *adored* you, girl, as do I, and I know you loved him like a brother."

Lizzie could only nod as the huge lump of grief formed in her throat.

"But you and I both know he would not want us to wallow in this," Renee said firmly as she placed her hand in Lizzie's. "So, we are gonna celebrate him today, and love him, and miss him, and cry because he's not here anymore. And after that, girl, we figure out a way to keep going – because he would want that for us. That does not mean that we will ever love or miss him any less. And we *will* see him again, Lizzie. I believe that with all my heart. It just might take a while, is all."

Lizzie lowered her head, thick tears building behind her closed lids, and squeezed Renee's hand.

———

Hank Myers winced and clutched at his head as the alarm clock's shrill siren stabbed through the room's silence like a stiletto blade through butter.

He opened one bleary eye and slammed an open right hand against the top of the device to silence it, then groaned as he began to feel the full effects of too much scotch the night before.

Six o'clock. Gotta get ready for work...

But the moment he managed to sit upright, Hank's head began to swim and pound, an ugly, primal beat that he felt all the way down to his toes. He launched himself out of bed as the first wave of nausea reached its peak and barely made it to the bathroom before he was violently ill.

Ten minutes later he fought the urge to crawl over to the shower on his hands and knees and forced himself to stand instead, albeit on trembling legs. He turned the water on and undressed, then shuffled his way under the steamy spray. Hank leaned against the side of the enclosure and let the jets pummel his flesh.

———

Nathan Thomas arrived at the office a little before seven a.m. and was delighted to see an urgent message from the lead lab tech.

Come see me, I have results for you.

He immediately headed for the elevator, and a few minutes later was walking into the lab.

"Morning. I hear you have some news?"

"That I do – and I ran the tests twice, just to be sure. Those bottles you gave me all showed traces of tetrahydrozoline in them."

"And what is that?"

"A chemical that is fatal if ingested over enough time and/or over a certain amount. And, I can tell you that it definitely is *not* a usual ingredient in liquid sweeteners or water additives."

"Is it hard to get a hold of?"

"Sadly, it's not restricted at all. It's common in certain health products," the man replied, and went on to explain.

Nathan's eyebrows raised.

"But that's so easy."

The tech nodded.

"Yep, which is why I am amazed that we don't see lots more of this kind of thing. Must not be common knowledge."

"Thank God for that. What about prints? Any prints at all?"

"I managed to pull some good ones from the box, the letters, the flash drive, and the bottles. One consistent set on all of it, which I presume is from the person that assembled and mailed the package, but I won't know for sure unless you're able to get me a set of prints for comparison. Whoever they are, their prints aren't on file anywhere. There were also partially smudged prints on the bottles themselves that some of the fresher prints overlapped. I can tell they're from a different person, but again, without something to compare them against, I cannot say who."

"Thanks," Nathan said. "Report coming my way?"

"You'll have my official findings by ten a.m."

As he headed back to the elevator, Nathan thought, *Progress. Now I just need something to pop regarding the death certificates.*

He parked himself at his desk and began to wade through new emails. Twenty minutes later, he had just sent off an answer to the last one when he noticed movement in his doorway.

Nathan raised his head and gazed at a bedraggled Hank Myers, whose mirrored sunglasses still obscured his eyes from close inspection.

"Morning," Nathan offered.

"Maybe after some coffee," Hank conceded. "It was a rough night last night."

"I'll come with you," Nathan replied as he stood and moved around his desk. "Lead the way."

<hr>

When Nathan got back to his office he found Annie waiting for him.

"You got a few minutes? I'd like to talk to you," she asked, and he swept the hand that wasn't holding his coffee mug out in front of him.

"Sure. Come on in."

She entered first, then stepped to the side and let him pass before she shut the door and took a seat.

"Once we get Ramon into custody, I'd like to begin working the night shift, please," Annie said without warning.

Nathan frowned and leaned back in his chair.

"What's going on, exactly?"

"I've had enough of Ben's caveman crap, to be honest, and I think it would be best if we were not on the same shift anymore."

He tilted his head and looked at her, then sighed.

"I was afraid of this," he admitted. "But, at least you're not asking for a transfer. And yes, I think the two of you working opposing shifts is an excellent idea given the circumstances. I had planned to talk to you this morning anyway, Annie. The director and I spoke about it, and we both feel that you should not be involved in Sunday's raid, for two reasons. One, you are already going to be a major player in tomorrow night's events, and two, we would like to keep the fact that you are an agent off the cartel's radar. That in and of itself means your being onsite as part of the raid team is out."

"I understand, and I agree that's the best way to go. What would you like me to do?"

"After we get Ramon into custody tomorrow night, you can take Sunday off to get adjusted to your new schedule. Come back Monday at three p.m. to start on the night shift," Nathan advised her. "Is that acceptable?"

"That's perfect, actually, thanks."

"One more thing. Do you need a place to stay?"

"That's already been arranged."

"Good. Let me know if you need anything, Annie. My door is always open."

"Thanks, Nathan. And I'm sorry if this is causing you any trouble."

"No need to apologize, Annie," he said, and smiled warmly at her as she left his office.

The smile disappeared the moment she did.

No, Annie, Nathan thought to himself, *you are not the one that could not keep personal and professional separated. This one is Ben's fault.*

He reached over and pressed the intercom button.

"Diane, have you seen Ben this morning?"

"Not yet. Want me to send him your way when he arrives?"

"Please do."

Nathan leaned back in his chair again and contemplated the ceiling.

"This is the last thing I need right now," he muttered under his breath.

A half-hour later Diane was on the line.

"He's on his way to you," she murmured.

"Thanks for the heads up."

"Come in – and shut the door behind you," Nathan directed when Ben appeared in his open doorway moments later.

Ben did as instructed, then sat.

"You're taking Saturday off. I don't want you anywhere near the operation," Nathan told him bluntly. "Your being involved could put Annie at greater risk, and I won't stand for it. Understood?"

Ben nodded meekly but did not speak.

"And you'll be back here at seven a.m. on Sunday. I need you on the raid team."

"Yes, sir."

"I need your head in the game, Ben," Nathan reminded him. "We have a lot of things happening at once and we both know that things could get ugly in a heartbeat. You are an excellent agent, but I need to know, without a doubt, that your team can depend on you – especially if things go south. And lately, I'm just not sure."

Nathan leaned forward and rested his arms on his desk.

"As far as today goes, you need to stay away from her, Ben. That's not a request."

Ben met his fierce gaze, and Nathan saw a flash of raw emotion in his eyes, but Ben remained silent on that point. His throat worked a few times before he finally managed to ask, "Is that all?"

"Yes, for now," Nathan said, and handed him a small stack of papers. "I need you to follow up on these. Home office sent them down and they have asked for our take. I started them, then had to switch gears and focus on the Sophie Drimmel case. I need these reviewed and updated with your notes by end of shift today."

"Yes, sir," Ben said woodenly.

Nathan gentled his tone.

"You know where I am if you need to talk, all right?"

"Yes, I do. And I appreciate that."

The family car arrived to pick them up at eight-fifteen, and twenty minutes later was pulling smoothly into the parking lot of the church where Tank's memorial was scheduled. Lizzie could already tell that the chapel would be filled to overflowing with police officers all wearing their best dress uniforms to pay respects to one of their own.

Renee gripped Lizzie's hand tightly as they led the family's processional from the limousine into the building. Donny escorted Renee's mother just behind them, followed by Renee's sister Carla and Tank's brothers Chuck and Stephan. Their path was flanked on either side by row upon row of Houston's finest all standing at attention.

Once inside the church, the pastor directed them to a small room off to the right of the chapel.

"We'll get started in about ten minutes," he murmured, then gracefully stepped back several paces to let the family have some space.

"I'll be right back," Lizzie told Renee before she walked into the hall and toward the restroom.

"Zim," she heard someone say, and turned to find her old section chief and his wife walking toward her.

"Chief Monnet, Marge," she said as she hugged each of them. "Glad you came down. It will mean a lot to Renee that you're here."

"Is it all right if we step in and see her for just a moment?" he asked, and Lizzie shrugged.

"I don't see why not. Go on, I'll be right back."

She hurried to the ladies' room, then rushed back to the holding room to find Renee weeping, her arms thrown around Marge.

"Would you like us to sit with you, Renee? We're happy to do that," Monnet murmured, and she nodded her consent as she stepped back and dabbed at her eyes.

"I didn't realize that Renee and your old boss knew each other," Donny said quietly to his wife.

"Yes. As a matter of fact, it was his wife that first introduced Tank and Renee," Lizzie revealed. "The Monnets have known Renee for years. Marge used to give her and Carla piano lessons."

The pastor appeared again and gently cleared his throat.

"It's time, Mrs. Lydealea," he announced, and held out his hand.

Renee took a deep breath, then straightened her shoulders, and led the small group into the chapel. As Lizzie guessed, it was standing room only inside; only the first row on the right-hand side that had been reserved for the family was unoccupied.

Once they were seated, the pastor greeted everyone, then said, "We are here today to celebrate an extraordinary human being, one that's left us much too soon."

Lizzie burst into tears, sobbing quietly into Donny's shoulder.

Out in Jacksboro, Detective MacKinnon parked his unmarked unit, then strolled over to the far end of the farmer's market. He walked casually past the displays and laughing, chatting people until at last he spotted who he was looking for.

When Claire King saw him standing in front of her booth she did a double take, and her smile faltered briefly.

"Mr. MacKinnon, how nice to see you again," she said in an overly cheery tone that made his cop senses tingle. "Could I interest you in some tomatoes? Fresh picked this morning."

Mister MacKinnon? Not Detective?

She motioned to him to follow her around the side of the display, and the moment he was close enough she whispered, "You shouldn't be here. I can't talk right now."

"Then just listen. You're in danger. You don't need to go back out... there..." he murmured, trying to honor her wishes but at the same time make her understand what was at stake.

"These look lovely, I'll take three of them," MacKinnon said a little louder as the man working the stand with Claire walked toward them. "Do you happen to have any peppers?"

"As a matter of fact, we do," Claire said enthusiastically, and MacKinnon held his breath as her companion moved away again to tend to three other customers that had just walked up to the other end of the bountiful display.

"Don't ask me how I know, I can't tell you yet," he murmured, "but your cabin out there is most likely bugged. Come back to the station, Claire. I can protect you."

From the corner of his eye, he saw the other stand worker approaching them again, so he continued with, "Well, I might as well bite the bullet and pick up a trifecta of salsa ingredients. Got any onions?"

"Boy, do we," she answered, keeping up the charade. "White, yellow, and red, take your pick. And I have two recipes that I think you'll really like. I can write them down for you if you're interested."

"Sure," he enthused, and she smiled, but it didn't quite reach her eyes.

"Be right back, let me find a notepad," Claire said gaily, and walked to the passenger side of the truck.

A few minutes later she reappeared with two slips of paper.

"Here's my salsa recipe," she said, and handed him one piece of paper that displayed exactly what she said it would.

"And here's my homemade enchilada sauce recipe," she announced, and trembled slightly when she handed over the second small paper.

He scanned it quickly, then met her gaze as he tucked both pages into the front pocket of his jeans.

"Paprika, huh? Never would have guessed. Sounds good. I'll have to make a trip to the store for some."

They walked side-by-side around to the front of the display, where Claire tallied up his total, took his twenty-dollar-bill and gave him change, then bagged up his purchase.

"Thanks for the recipes. I'll make sure I come back and let you know how they turned out," he said for the benefit of her companion.

"Please do," Claire answered, then turned her attention to the next customer at the popular stand.

Detective MacKinnon retreated to his car with his paper bag of produce and left the market. He waited until he was back at the station and parked before he re-read the second page Claire had handed to him.

While it did indeed contain her enchilada sauce recipe, there was one line she'd embedded in the instructions that stood out.

Gillespie's at six.

Detective MacKinnon exited his car and walked toward the police station's front door. As he did, he dialed Nathan Thomas's cell phone number so he could update the FBI man on the latest development.

The rest of the memorial passed in a blur, and the next thing Lizzie knew the mourners were filing past the casket to say goodbye before walking over to greet and console Renee and the other family members.

At long last, only the family remained in the chapel. Tank's pallbearers had moved to the holding room to give the ones who'd known and loved Tank the best a chance to say their final farewell.

A trembling Lizzie forced herself to finally walk up to the casket, and she stared down at one of the most important people in her life.

"Not fair," she said softly. "It's just not fair, Tank. You shouldn't be here like this."

She impulsively reached out her hand and started to touch him but drew back again. She wanted to make contact, but deep down she knew that if she did it would only bring her even more pain, more irrefutable proof that this wasn't all some sort of horrible dream.

Lizzie wavered, warring within herself. Part of her wanted to scream and run, but she felt rooted to the ground as she stared at Tank's face and willed him to somehow move again, breathe again, *live* again.

And then she felt Donny's arms wrapping around her.

She leaned into him, taking comfort and strength from his presence. They lingered for a bit in silence, until Lizzie tilted her face upward to look over her shoulder at her husband.

"I can't take any more, please get me out of here," she whispered as tears coursed down her cheeks, and Donny gently turned her away from her friend's casket and escorted her down the aisle and out into the sunshine.

Chapter Twenty-Four

It was early afternoon when Lizzie, Donny, and Faith loaded their bags into the SUV for the return drive north. Each of them hugged Renee tightly.

"Text me when you land? I want to know that you and Tucker got up to Seattle safely," Lizzie urged, and Renee nodded.

"You know I will. Love you, girl, and thanks for everything."

"I love you too."

Reluctantly, Lizzie released her and climbed into the front passenger seat of the SUV, then waved as Donny pulled away from the curb.

As the Houston trio started their drive home, the director summoned Nathan to his office in Dallas.

"You wanted to see me, sir?"

"I did. Have a seat – and wait until you hear this."

"What's going on?"

"My contact down in Austin got back to me. No death records."

"They won't hand them over?"

"Yes - but only because they cannot *find* them. The State of Texas has no record of anyone on that list, *anywhere* in its database, as having passed away. In the state's eyes, all nine of those people whose names appear on those headstones are still alive and well."

"Which has to mean that their deaths were never even reported to begin with," Nathan mused with a frown. "But why?"

"*That's* the million-dollar question. And I'm about to request a search warrant for the entire Lighte's Landing property so that you can go out there and dig around and find the answer to it. I can't tell you that the paperwork will move quickly, but I'd at least expect to get an answer back on that set by Monday sometime."

"Speaking of Lighte's Landing, Detective MacKinnon called me earlier. He made contact again with Claire King at the farmer's market this morning. She couldn't talk freely, but she was able to slip him a message. They're supposed to meet up later and he's going to put her into protective custody until this is resolved."

"Good, I'm glad to hear that. One less person in harm's way. And I will keep an eye on that warrant request."

"Please let me know as soon as it comes through, sir," Nathan said, and started to rise.

"Hold on, son, not quite yet," the director said with a chuckle. "Here you go."

And he handed Nathan a sheaf of papers.

"Arrest warrants for all four men on the video, and an additional warrant to search every square inch of that building," the director revealed. "They were approved even faster than I thought they would be due to that footage we've already got. Go line out your team and your tactics, Nathan. We'll only get one clear shot at this one, and it'd be a shame to waste it."

"We won't, I assure you," Nathan answered, his jaw set in a determined line. "We won't."

At five p.m. Nathan was standing at the whiteboard in front of his task force. It did not escape his notice that not only were Annie and Ben stationed at opposite ends of the room, but that neither even looked in the other's direction.

He cleared his throat to make sure he had everyone's full attention.

"We've gotten the warrants we needed," he announced. "So, let's talk strategy."

He glanced down at the legal pad in his hand that contained his and Hank's brainstorming for the coming events.

"Tomorrow night, we will be taking Ramon Gutierrez into custody. The team members involved in this phase of operations will be Annie, Mark Calloway, Grace Womack, and Agents Evans and Wilford."

He paused to make sure everyone understood.

"Annie is supposed to meet Mr. Gutierrez at a Fort Worth restaurant at seven-thirty. She will be wearing a wire and under constant surveillance to ensure her safety – Wilford and Womack will be posing as other restaurant patrons. The guise will be a problem involving the suspect's vehicle, and we will persuade him to step outside to confirm that his car is not the one that is illegally parked. We will seize him at that time, and the goal is to do so quickly and quietly and not attract attention to ourselves."

He turned his head and addressed Agent Wilford.

"Did we confirm the make and model of Mr. Gutierrez's car?"

"I did, and we've got an exact match ready to go," Wilford confirmed.

"Good. If all goes according to plan Annie will be able to leave the scene unimpeded, and Calloway and Evans will transport Mr. Gutierrez here."

He paused, then continued with phase two of the plan.

"No one involved in arresting Gutierrez will take part in the raid, which will happen at nine a.m. Sunday morning. That core team will consist of Agent Myers, Agent Baker, Ben, and myself. I will also bring Lizzie in if she is back in town by then, but for now, we need to plan based upon who is currently in play. The DEA has agreed to back the raid team up with up to four additional agents, and we will also have another three FBI agents that can join us if needed, so, we should have plenty of firepower."

"Now," he continued, "given that we know what these suspects are capable of, we are going in quick, quiet and armed to the teeth. Full body armor, no exceptions, and each of us need to be prepared for things to go sour quickly. Does anyone have any questions?"

Ben raised his hand.

"We know from the videos we've seen that they have an excellent camera system. What's the plan to address those?"

"Solid question. Rick will be overriding their system. He will create a loop that shows old video on playback on their onsite monitors," Nathan revealed. "They should never even see us coming."

Ben nodded once, then fell silent again.

"Any other questions?"

Hearing none, Nathan concluded with, "Raid team members, you are free to go. You can either take tomorrow off completely and rest up for Sunday, or, come in at eleven a.m. tomorrow and assist with reviewing all footage dated after the Delgado murder so that we can confirm whether his body has been removed from the premises. We will go over the finer details of our raid approach when we assemble at seven a.m. Sunday morning. Saturday team, please stay a bit longer. We need to drill down into the specifics."

Detective MacKinnon arrived at Gillespie's twenty minutes early and took a seat in the farthest booth from the door. He used the newspaper he had brought along as both a means to explain why he lingered on a busy Friday night, and a distraction from checking his watch every few moments.

He almost sighed aloud with relief when he noticed Claire King walking toward him at two minutes past six.

"I think I was followed," she said in a low tone as she approached, then subtly pointed toward the back of the shop.

"Meet you out back in ninety seconds," he murmured from behind his paper, and Claire never slowed her stride as she continued past his booth toward the restrooms.

He counted to ninety, then slid out of the booth and made it look like he was visiting the men's room before he surreptitiously slipped out the back door and into the alley, where an anxious Claire waited for him.

"How are we going to get to your car without being seen?" she asked.

"Easy," he said with a mischievous grin. "We're not going to take my car. You and I are leaving in this one right here."

He reached up into the front driver's side wheel well and retrieved the keys, then unlocked the unmarked sedan that a co-worker, who had been sitting on one of the barstools at the front counter the entire time, had so thoughtfully parked in the alleyway for him a good half-hour earlier.

Detective MacKinnon ushered Claire King into the front passenger seat, climbed behind the wheel, and drove away. Once they were outside Jacksboro's city limits he pressed a button on the steering wheel to place a call to Nathan Thomas.

Nathan had just wrapped up the discussion with his players involved in Saturday's charade when his phone rang.

"Agent Thomas," he said briskly as he made his way back to his office from the conference room.

"It's Detective MacKinnon," the caller announced, "and I am on my way to see you. I have Claire King in the car with me."

"Ms. King," Nathan said, "my name is Agent Thomas, and I am a profiler with the FBI. It is nice to be able to talk to you. Has Detective MacKinnon explained what is happening?"

"Hello, Agent Thomas. No, not yet. I only know that he felt Lighte's Landing was no longer safe for me."

"He is completely correct on that point, and I will explain everything once we are face to face, I assure you. Detective MacKinnon, what is your ETA?"

"We'll be there by seven-fifteen, give or take."

"Very well. Drive safely, and I will see you soon."

He disconnected that call, then placed a new one to Bella.

"Let me guess. It's going to be another late night for you," she said with warm humor when she answered.

"Sorry, honey, it can't be helped."

"No worries, honey, I know it comes with the territory. Just promise me that you will take a break long enough to eat a decent dinner, and I will see you when you get home, okay?"

He chuckled.

"I will call and place a delivery order right now. Will that work?"

"Yes. I love you, Nathan. Be safe."

"I will, baby. I promise. And I love you too."

He set his cell phone down and looked up to find Hank Myers grinning at him from his doorway.

"I thought you'd already left," Nathan said.

"Nope. Nowhere to go except back to the hotel, really, and that did not go well at all last night," Hank admitted. "Want some company? I can order in barbeque, my treat."

"Deal. How's your headache?"

Hank pulled a face.

"Down to a dull roar, finally. I never understood what Cruz liked so much about scotch, and my adventures last night cemented my belief that that stuff is definitely *not* my go-to beverage for sure."

Nathan's countenance turned solemn.

"I'm sorry about your friend, Hank. I really am."

The DEA man moved to occupy Nathan's right-hand visitor's

chair, ran one hand across his face and through his hair, and then purposely changed topics.

"Thanks. I need to apologize to Annie at some point," he confessed. "She followed me down to the garage yesterday to check on me and I was... a little short with her."

"I know. And I *also* know that she did not take it personally. She understood completely where your head was in that moment."

"Are you sure?"

"Annie told me herself, Hank. Trust me, the two of you are good."

Hank blew out a relieved sigh and leaned back in his chair.

"Thank God. I was hoping my behavior wasn't the cause of her being so tense today," he observed. "She seemed on edge in our meeting earlier."

"Nope. That honor goes to another," Nathan muttered darkly, and Hank shook his head.

"Let me guess, she got tired of Ben's chest-thumping BS and let him have it with both barrels."

"Off the record? Yes, and not only that, but she is *also* going to switch to working nights for a while because of it."

"Which is why you were so adamant about who was assigned to which team earlier today when we lined out the assignments," Hank drawled. "That makes so much more sense now. He supremely screwed up, huh."

"Yep. He certainly did. But enough about that. What I really want to know right now is," Nathan said as he rested his forearms on his desk, "are you gonna order the food, or not?"

Hank grinned again and pulled his cell phone out of its holster.

"I'm on it. Man, you are really bossy, Agent Thomas, you know that?"

The moment Donny pulled into the driveway of his and Lizzie's home, Faith called Rick to let her husband know that they had made it back safely.

When she finished her call she said, "Rick says to tell you that you two are welcome to join us for dinner if you like."

"I'm thinking sleep at the moment, honestly," Lizzie answered with a wan smile. "Can we take a rain check? Maybe Sunday night?"

"Absolutely. Plan on seven o'clock."

"Thanks for coming with us, Faith," Lizzie said, and hugged her, then watched her best friend grab her suitcase, climb into her own car, and drive away.

"I've got the bags, Liz, if you will unlock the door," Donny suggested, and she nodded and pulled out her keys.

Once they were inside, Donny set the suitcases down and took her in his arms.

"Come on, honey," he coaxed. "I think we both could use a nice long nap right about now."

They wandered down the hall to their room, where Lizzie paused long enough to use the bathroom, brush her teeth, and trade her traveling clothes for a tank top and shorts, then climbed gratefully into bed. She snuggled up close to Donny, laid her head on his chest, and was out.

Nathan's visitors arrived at seven-twenty-one. Detective MacKinnon was a tall, robust man that looked to be in his mid to late forties, and Claire King a petite, attractive woman that Nathan presumed was in her early fifties, at most.

He greeted them in the lobby, and after the formal introductions were out of the way he escorted them up to his eighth-floor office.

Claire King's gaze was clear and direct when she settled herself into one of his visitor's chairs and asked, "What is going on, exactly?'

"Sophie Drimmel sent her sister a box," Nathan began, and shared the highlights with his guests.

As he did so, Claire turned increasingly pale.

"Cameras?" she sputtered. "But... but that means whoever is behind all this is aware that Sophie was nosing around! I just don't see how they couldn't...."

Her voice trailed off as her eyes went wide with fear.

"*That* is why she is missing, isn't it? Whoever has been killing people out there realized that she was on to them, and they grabbed her to keep her quiet."

"I believe so, yes," Nathan murmured, and his eyes filled with sympathy as Claire's face crumpled in anguish.

"You... you have to go out there! You have to find her!"

"And I will. The only thing I am waiting on is a warrant, so that I can get my team out there to do *exactly* that."

He leaned forward.

"Sophie's voicemail to her sister mentioned *you* specifically, Ms. King," he told her. "Which is why Detective MacKinnon and I both felt you would be much, *much* safer away from Lighte's Landing. Whoever has Sophie knows how close the two of you are. And because of your relationship with her, I am willing to bet that it was just a matter of time before you disappeared, as well."

Claire closed her eyes and swallowed hard.

"Me too," she whispered. "And things have been very strange the last day or two. I felt like someone was watching everything I did and everywhere I went on the property – and based on what you just told me, they probably *have* been."

She shuddered involuntarily at the realization.

"And then this morning when Detective MacKinnon approached me at the farmer's market, I was scared spitless. I almost did not acknowledge him at all, because I didn't know if it was safe to even speak."

She opened her eyes and glanced over at the detective with a grateful smile.

"Luckily, he is much better at thinking on his feet than I am, and he was able to make it sound like just a normal conversation, enough so that I had a chance to slip him a note."

"You did supremely well," MacKinnon assured her with a wink. "Top-notch, actually. Had I not already known better, I would have been hard pressed to notice any stress in your demeanor at all. And embedding the meeting message *in* the recipe? That was a *brilliant* move, Claire."

She flushed scarlet.

"Thanks, Glen," she said before she turned her attention back to Nathan, whose neutral expression did not reveal that he had noticed the sparks of attraction arcing back and forth between his two visitors.

"What happens now?"

"Well, I'd like to ask you to remain in this area and stay away from Lighte's Landing altogether until I can solve all this and find Sophie."

She nodded.

"I can do that. But I do not have any clothes with me. I couldn't risk packing anything, couldn't take the chance that someone would notice my leaving the property with a suitcase."

"And that was another smart move on your part, Ms. King. No worries. I am going to pair you up with one of our female agents, and she can assist you with clothes and a safe place to stay. With luck, this will all resolve quickly."

"I sure hope so," Claire confessed on a deep sigh. "Because I'm worried sick for Sophie."

Me too, Nathan thought but did not express.

"I'll be right back," he informed them instead, and traveled to the conference room to ask Grace Womack to join them.

He introduced the two women and sent them off together, then turned back to the detective.

"She'll be fine. We will take good care of her," he told MacKinnon, who was still looking in the direction that Claire King had walked away.

"I know you will. Hey! I almost forgot," the man replied. "I am supposed to give you these."

MacKinnon reached into his jacket's interior pocket and pulled out four flash drives.

"Here's all the security footage that you asked us for. When I realized that I was probably going to wind up coming to see you in person, I figured why waste time trying to email it all?" he explained as he handed them over.

Chapter Twenty-Five

Lizzie woke a little after four a.m. with her stomach growling.

She stretched and reached for Donny but found only empty space to her left. Confused, she got out of bed, put on her robe, and went to look for him.

She found him in their kitchen putting together a massive sandwich.

"Good call, I'm starving," she said, and got two more pieces of bread out for herself, then stood at his side and made her own snack.

"I thought you might be up soon," he informed her, "so I started the coffeepot already."

"Sweet!" Lizzie answered, then stood on bare tiptoes to kiss him before she swiveled to move across the kitchen to retrieve two mugs.

They settled in with their food and their coffee at the kitchen table.

"You going in today?" he asked.

"Yep. You know me. I need to dive back in," she confirmed. "I wonder what I've missed."

She crossed over to the counter where Donny had plugged in her cell phone and was about to fire off a quick text to Nathan to let him know she was back in town when she noticed she had missed one from Renee.

In Seattle, was all it said, and the text was time-stamped eight-forty-nine p.m.

"Renee and Tucker got there safely last night," she told Donny as she resumed her task of sending a message to Nathan.

Then she returned to her chair to enjoy another mouthful of her sandwich.

"What about you?" she asked in between bites.

"Yep, hitting the ground running today also," Donny said. "I've got existing meetings already, plus I need to reschedule the ones that got postponed. You gonna be okay with ordering dinner in for a couple of nights?"

"Nope, I *insist* that you cook every single night," she teased, and giggled when he reached over to tickle her.

"Of course, honey, that's fine."

"How did you sleep?" Donny asked, his eyes shifting from playful mirth to warm concern.

"Even better than I hoped I would, to be honest," she admitted. "Being back in our own bed helped, I guess. I just *knew* I would toss and turn, but evidently not."

"I don't think either one of us moved much all night. But we both needed the rest."

She reached out her hand to clasp his.

"I would not have gotten through the last few days without you," she said earnestly, and saw the love brimming in his hazel eyes.

"You're my everything, Lizzie, so it never even occurred to me to be anywhere *other* than by your side."

The sentiment made her misty, and she leaned over to plant a big kiss on his mouth.

"You keep saying sweet stuff like that to me and I am going to want to stay here snuggled up with you all day."

He grinned.

"That would be my preference, too, but we probably ought to be the grown-ups that we are and tend to our business. Besides, I *do* know you, Liz. The sooner you are back to planning on how to best the bad guys, the better."

"Yep, you nailed it," she said with a grin, and grabbed her coffee mug. "I'm headed for the shower."

It was two minutes past five, and Lizzie had just finished off her second cup of coffee when Nathan called.

"Good morning, boss. You're up early."

"Hey there," he said. "Yeah, lots to do. I was surprised to get your message. Thought for sure you'd be in Houston for another day, at least."

"There was no reason to stay," Lizzie answered, and filled him in about Tank's parents being unable to make it down for the memorial in Texas.

"So," she said in conclusion, "Donny worked his magic and helped Renee arrange everything on the Seattle end. They all flew out late yesterday afternoon."

"I see," Nathan replied, and paused.

"What have I missed?" Lizzie asked.

"I'm working from home today. Come on over, and I will bring you up to speed."

"That much, huh?"

"There have been quite a few developments, yes."

"Okay, I'll see you in a bit then."

She disconnected the call and walked down the hall to their home office, where Donny sat at his keyboard typing furiously.

"I'm supposed to meet Nathan at his house. He's already up and working this morning, too – evidently, quite a lot happened while we were gone," she revealed.

Donny's eyebrows raised.

"Diving right in, huh? Have fun, baby."

She leaned down and kissed him.

"See you later."

Nathan greeted her at the door with a sincere, "It's good to see you, Liz."

She walked past him into the house, and once he had shut the front door, he startled her by giving her a hug.

"Um... okay," she said, and shrugged her shoulders before she hugged him back. "I think this might be the first time you've ever hugged me?"

"Sorry," Nathan said as he released her. "You're right, I don't usually. But with everything you went through this week I just... felt like I wasn't there enough for you."

"When things fall apart, you keep control and stay focused. It's what you do," she pointed out. "Besides, I always knew I had your support, Nathan, so we're good. Truly."

"Good. Coffee? There's lots of information to share with you."

"You know it," she replied. "No such thing as too much coffee."

They headed to the kitchen first, and then to Nathan's office. Once they had settled in, he got started.

"Let's see, where to start...on the task force side of things, we're taking one guy into custody tonight, and the raid on the garage is happening tomorrow morning."

Lizzie's eyes went wide.

"Wow. The team really *did* make some strides."

"Yeah," he agreed. "The electronics warrant got us some unbelievably valuable footage – including Agent Delgado's murder. We also know where they stashed his body afterward, and we will be retrieving it Sunday morning."

"Small world," Lizzie murmured.

Nathan's face took on a puzzled look.

"Reviewing body cam footage of the raid is how Houston PD figured out who shot Tank," she elaborated, her eyes haunted.

"Oh."

There was a poignant silence before Lizzie asked, "So, who watched the Delgado video?"

"Myers."

Lizzie winced.

"Bad luck of the draw, there."

"He insisted, actually."

"Why am I not surprised... how's he holding up?"

"He's stuffing it down and deflecting any attempts at conversation about it," came the sardonic reply. "He's a guy. It's what we do."

"Figures. But I will reach out later and check on him anyway. You have all the assignments laid out? And why are you picking up one guy tonight and not the others?"

"To answer your first question, yes, and I'd like you on the raid team tomorrow morning. And the second answer is, because Annie is a rockstar, and she realized who the weak link was in the suspect group. He asked her out for dinner tonight, and we're going to pick him up at the restaurant."

Nathan relayed the story of how things had played out for Annie the day she visited the garage, and Lizzie smiled.

"Smart move, to get him isolated somewhere else. And from what you have told me, the video we have combined with this guy's testimony should be a lock for getting some convictions."

"*If* he cooperates," Nathan pointed out.

"This guy's gonna be looking down the barrel at a charge of accessory to capital murder - one that can be proven beyond a doubt because it was recorded for posterity. If he has even a *single* functioning brain cell in his head, he will flip on the rest of his crew to avoid death row, trust me. And any counsel worth their salt will advise him to cooperate."

She took a sip of coffee.

"So how does Ben feel about Annie going on a date as part of a case?"

Nathan rubbed his hands over his face.

"Yeah... about that..."

"Uh oh," Lizzie muttered. "That doesn't sound good."

"It's not," Nathan confirmed. "Basically, she read him the riot act, and she's switching over to the night shift team after we get this operation done tonight."

"Well," Lizzie said after a thoughtful pause, "it's probably best, to be honest. Last thing anyone needs, especially Annie, is Ben's jealousy or whatever is going on there getting in the way of work – even *without* any active field ops happening. But during something like this? That is so much worse. If she is not one hundred percent focused, she could get seriously hurt."

"Exactly," Nathan concurred, "which is why I put him on the raid team, and he has *nothing* to do with what's planned for this evening. I am keeping those two as separated as possible."

"Well, they're living together, so..."

"Not anymore. At least, not for now."

"Wow," Lizzie said again. "He must really, *really* have pissed her off, then."

"I think it is safe to call that a huge understatement."

"Sounds like," Lizzie chimed in. "So, what do you need me to work on until tomorrow morning's raid?"

"I am so glad you asked - because I've also got this *other* case that I want to bring you in on. Ten people dead, suspected foul play involved, one young woman is missing, and another woman's just been put into protective custody."

"Good Lord. I was only gone three days, Nathan!"

He grinned and sighed all at once.

"Yes, this one came fast and furious. Get comfortable, it's a long story."

He walked her through all the pieces of the Sophie Drimmel case, from his first phone call with Susan all the way through to the previous night's meet and greet with Claire King and Detective Glen MacKinnon.

Nathan concluded the long narrative with, "Since there aren't any death certificates on file, and since poison was found in the bottles, we've gone ahead and submitted warrant requests so we can go in full bore out at Lighte's Landing. I *also* dug up some rather interesting background on the man in charge out there, Pastor Remiel Lighte."

"How so?"

"Among other things, that's only been his legal name for about seventeen years. Before that, he was known as Guenter Schmidtt – and he's got a criminal record."

A rap on the doorway paused their conversation. Bella entered the room and did not seem fazed at all that her husband was already up and working before seven a.m. on a Saturday.

When she saw Lizzie, Bella broke into a huge smile.

"I *thought* I heard Nathan in here talking to someone," Bella exclaimed as she gathered Lizzie up into a soft, warm hug. "It's so good to see you, Lizzie!"

"Good to see you too, Bel. You're getting around really well," Lizzie observed.

"Yep, just about ditched the walker completely these days," Nathan's wife confirmed proudly, then looked over at him.

"Charlie's awake and asking for pancakes and sausages," she said. "Sound good to you guys?"

"IZZY!!" a small voice yelled from the doorway, and Lizzie chuckled as Charlie ran full tilt toward her with a squeal of delight.

"Hey, munchkin," she said as she scooped him up and hugged him, then began to tickle his ribs. "I hear you want pancakes."

"Pan-CAKES!!" Charlie shouted and nodded vigorously.

"I'll help you, honey. Come on, Liz," Nathan said. "We can continue this over breakfast prep."

Lizzie sat at the kitchen table with Charlie on her lap as Bella and Nathan began to make the morning meal.

"Where were we?" he asked Lizzie as he sliced up sausage patties and arranged them in the skillet.

"Schmidtt has a record."

"Oh, yes. I will forward you my research so you can see what I mean when I say he is our prime suspect. Anyway, they found Sophie's car this week in Jacksboro, and when he arrived last night, Detective MacKinnon handed over four flash drives' worth of security footage of the immediate vicinity. I have not even started to look at *any* of that, or any of the lab results from their team processing her car, for that matter. You wanna take point on those pieces?"

"Absolutely. And I'd really like to be a part of the team that goes onsite out there when the time comes."

"That's a given," Nathan assured her with a grin. "I wasn't even going to make it optional for you."

"Good," Lizzie shot back playfully. "Means I don't have to be pushy, then."

"You two sound like siblings," Bella commented with a smile, and shook her head. "Between him and Faith, I'd say you've been fully assimilated into the clan, Lizzie."

Bella paused, then drawled, "You poor thing, you," which made Lizzie laugh.

"Actually, I feel pretty lucky. I think it's a pretty cool clan to be in."

Bella's eyes twinkled.

"I do, too."

When the food was ready Bella and Nathan carried it over to the table, along with plates, forks, and the butter and syrup.

As they gathered around the table Lizzie asked, "I don't suppose you've pulled up a map of the Lighte's Landing property yet, have you?"

"No," Nathan admitted as he cut up a pancake and two of the sausage patties into smaller pieces for Charlie. "But it is on my to-do list, and we really should. It's my understanding that place is about two hundred acres total."

"Really? Well, then, I think it might be advantageous to *also* bring in a good chopper pilot - and someone with experience using long-range thermal cameras, too. The more we know about the configuration before we hit the ground out there, the better. And with the right intel, we can narrow the focus more quickly and not waste time. Especially since this is a search-and-rescue mission as much as a murder investigation."

"You think she's still alive," he commented.

"I know that *you* think she is. If you didn't, you'd have said so straight out," Lizzie countered. "I think your famous gut instinct is telling you she's a *hostage*, not a murder victim."

He nodded once in acknowledgement, and Lizzie could tell by the look on his face that Nathan was playing devil's advocate when he asked his next question.

"Her car was found in Jacksboro, Lizzie, so technically she could be anywhere. What makes you think that Sophie Drimmel was taken back out to Lighte's Landing, rather than moved to a different location?"

"Because based on all the data you just shared with me, it sounds like that place is extremely self-contained, just the way our killer likes it. For example – none of the victims' deaths were reported to authorities, right? Secretive. But, they were all not only buried *on the property*, but in marked graves that everyone there knows about? Why the dichotomy? That in and of itself tells me that our suspect has control issues."

"And?"

"And, it just makes sense to me that whoever grabbed her feels much more comfortable keeping her close, so that he or she can make sure Sophie cannot rat them out. But our suspect also needs privacy, because at *least* one other person out there noticed her absence."

"Claire King."

"Yep."

Lizzie pondered it for several moments.

"If it were me, Nathan, I would stash Sophie somewhere on those two hundred acres, probably at the point farthest away from every-thing and everyone else on the property. Still accessible, but remote enough that no one else knows she's there."

Nathan broke into a wide smile.

"See? Thinking like that right there is the whole reason I asked you to leave Seattle PD and come work for me."

"Oh, please. You know as well as I do that you would have thought of all that... *eventually*," Lizzie assured him as she winked at a smirking Bella and reached for the syrup.

"Maybe, maybe not," Nathan conceded. "Which is why I'm glad you're here. Between the cartel and this case, I've had 'forest for trees' syndrome lately. Rick has been helpful from a tech standpoint, but he's not in law enforcement. I needed your input."

He stood to carry his plate over to the sink.

"I'm going to make a couple of calls this morning and line out that flyover. We don't have to have a warrant for that since it's public airspace, and hopefully, we'll get some good data."

"And I am heading over to the office. We have better tools there to review these flash drives, and besides, Donny was already in the zone in our home office when I left this morning. The last thing he needs is me in his space."

"We'll be meeting at the office at seven tomorrow morning to firm up the raid approach."

"I'll be there."

"Let me know if those flash drives contain anything useful, would you?"

"As soon as I know, you'll know."

Charlie gave her another big hug and kiss before she left.

"Bye, Izzy!"

"Bye, munchkin. Be good."

Over in Dallas, the alarm clock in Grace Womack's spare bedroom sounded, and a groggy Annie Adams hit the snooze bar, then pulled the covers over her head.

Well, today is the big day, she realized. *I get to be bait.*

Her stomach tightened at the thought.

You've got this, she told herself. *You are a strong and capable agent. Besides, Grace will be right there the whole time.*

She climbed out of bed and wandered down the hallway to the kitchen, where Grace stood at the counter waiting on the coffeepot to finish brewing.

"Morning, Annie. Cute jammies."

"Thanks."

"Excited about tonight?"

"Excited, but much more nervous," Annie admitted. "I have never been this deep in an operation before. The last time I did anything close to this I did not have to be anywhere near the guy. But this... this is smack in the middle of things."

"Yes," Grace conceded, "but it's not like you're going in alone. I will be there, and Mark, and the two DEA guys will be close, as well. Everything is going to work out, you'll see. Now, how about some coffee?"

"Yes, please," Annie said with a grateful sigh and sat at the table. "Hey, you've done this stuff before, right?"

"Gone undercover? Yes, I have, several times."

"Any pointers you can share?"

Grace grinned.

"A few – and one hilarious story."

She poured out two mugs of coffee, then joined Annie at the small square dinette table.

"Let's see now," Grace began, "there was one time when I was stationed in New Orleans, and we were trying to catch this guy that had killed thirteen men. Problem was, it was during Mardi Gras, which as you know is a whole other level of crazy. So, I am standing on Bourbon Street in the middle of this op, and I am trying to focus on the job, but this one drunk frat boy idiot keeps hitting on me as I'm trying to lure the guy we wanted over closer to me."

Grace took a sip of coffee.

"Finally, idiot guy grabs me by the shoulders, starts shaking me, and bellows, '*Don't you want some beads? Show me your tits!*' at the top of his lungs."

"He didn't!"

"He absolutely did."

Intrigued, Annie rested her hand on her chin.

"What happened?"

"I kneed him in the groin as hard as I could, and he let go of me – just in time for my suspect to knock him out cold. Turns out the serial murderer we were chasing took strong exception to the mistreatment of women in any way. Go figure."

Brody rapped on Ben's door at seven-forty-five a.m.

"Come on, buddy, let's go," he said cheerfully when Ben answered the door. "I've got it all packed and ready to go – the fishing poles, the bait, a six-pack, even some hot dogs we can throw on the grill. Let's go put that boat in the water and just enjoy a day on the lake."

"Hang on just a sec," Ben said, and moved back into his kitchen long enough to plug in and then turn off his cell phone and leave it behind on the counter.

Chapter Twenty-Six

Her car was still in the underground garage at the office, so when she left Nathan's place she drove Donny's SUV back to her house.

"I need to go into the office. Can you drive me over there?"

"Absolutely."

A half-hour later she kissed Donny goodbye, then walked through the front doors of her building and over to the bank of elevators.

Lizzie settled in for what she hoped would be a productive day. She fired up her computer, then navigated to the folder Nathan had built on the server where all the information gathered to date had been stored for the Lighte's Landing case.

Next, she opened a browser window, pulled up the Jack County Tax Assessor's website, and started a search for the relevant property records.

"I'm going to need more than two screens," she muttered under her breath, then got up to go check out the conference room.

As Nathan had mentioned previously, the extra laptop meant for her was still sitting on the side table away from its brethren. She picked it up, carried it back to her workstation, and set it up to the left of her dual monitors.

"There we go!"

"Looks good, Lizzie," a voice called out from behind her.

"Hey, Myers. How are you doing?"

"I'm all right. How about you?"

"I call BS on that but whatever. I'm good."

He took a seat at the next desk over.

"And *I* call BS on *that*, but whatever."

They gazed at one another for a long moment.

"How about this," Lizzie amended softly. "Neither one of us are okay, and we may not be for a long time, but Tank and Cruz would not want us to stop existing."

"That's much more accurate – for *both* of us. You need coffee? I was about to go get some."

"I'll come with you and get a cup, too. I have a feeling once I get started on this stuff it will be difficult to pull away."

They traveled to the breakroom and grabbed mugs from the cabinet.

"So," she said as she took her turn at the coffeepot, "what's on your agenda today?"

"Reviewing more footage to make sure they have not moved him," Hank said with a grimace. "Tomorrow cannot possibly get here soon enough for me to get him out of there."

Lizzie arched an eyebrow.

"They shoved him in the used oil tank, Liz," Hank elaborated, a dark cloud of fury marring his features.

She placed a hand on his arm.

"I'm so sorry."

He nodded once, then quipped, "So, you gonna just block the coffeepot all day, or what?"

She grinned.

"For the record, Nathan and I routinely joust over who gets to get their refill first."

"No need to joust, I can just pick you up and move you."

Her eyes narrowed.

"Very funny. Surely you didn't forget what happened the last time you messed with me."

"I'll never forget it, actually," he said, then asked a question that threw her for a loop.

"Are you happy?"

"Beg pardon?"

"I hear you're married now. Are you happy?"

"Yes. Very happy," Lizzie answered, and tilted her head as she witnessed a confusing swirl of emotion appear in Hank's eyes.

Why does he look like he wants to tell me something?

"Good. That's... good," he finally said. "Well, I guess I had better get my coffee and get myself to the conference room."

He stepped around her, filled his mug, and walked out of the room.

Huh. What was that about?

Lizzie pondered it for a moment, then shrugged and headed back to her desk to dive into the Lighte's Landing case.

As she had expected, once she started her research it was difficult to stop. By lunchtime she had thoroughly reviewed Nathan's notes and the existing case evidence. She ordered in a sandwich at one p.m. and then turned her attention to scrutinizing the detailed property map.

"Would you look at that," Lizzie muttered to herself as she zoomed in on the far west property boundary. "Some sort of structure?"

She opened another browser window and entered the property's coordinates, then selected satellite view and moved her mouse around to select the area she wanted to see more closely.

"I'll be damned," she said, and took several screenshots, then started a new email and copied her results in.

Nathan – make sure the pilot focuses on these coordinates, she typed, then included the latitude and longitude connected to the specific quarter-acre of Lighte's Landing property displayed in the screenshots.

Not five minutes later he responded.

Excellent work! Flyover happening tonight at ten. Pilot says we will get much better results with the infrared at night than during the day.

Thanks! she wrote back. *I'm going to switch gears now and start reviewing the flash drives.*

She stood for a moment to stretch her legs, then picked up her empty coffee cup and headed back to the breakroom for another round of caffeine.

That accomplished, Lizzie sat down again and shifted her focus to the first flash drive she had already connected into the laptop via USB port.

Unfortunately, since none of the flash drives – *or* their contents - were labeled in a way that was easy to navigate, Lizzie found herself staring at video time-stamped just twenty-six hours earlier – well *after* Sophie Drimmel's disappearance.

She growled as she stopped the video and removed that flash drive, labeled it 'number four' with a permanent marker, and set it aside.

"Okay, let's try.... *this* one," she said, and randomly selected one of the three remaining to review.

By five p.m. the second flash drive she was reviewing had yielded no fruit, and she was beginning to yawn. Lizzie packed up the laptop and all four flash drives to take them home with her, determined to continue her work after dinner.

Annie's mood had shifted from nerves to a steely determination.

Together, she and Grace had selected the perfect outfit. Annie applied her makeup then artfully arranged her dark hair under the platinum blond wig.

"You look beautiful. Now we just need to head to the office to get you wired up and back in that junker car," Grace announced at six p.m.

"I wonder if Ben's here," Annie murmured when they parked in the underground garage fourteen minutes later.

"I doubt it," Grace said. "Something tells me he was instructed to do anything else but be hanging around here today."

Annie blew out a relieved sigh.

"Good. I don't need to deal with him along with all of this."

They parted ways when the elevator doors opened on the eighth floor.

"Okay, I need to find Wilford. We will see you over there. You will do fine, Annie. Believe in yourself," Grace admonished before she turned left and headed down the hallway.

Annie smiled and pressed the elevator button to take her one floor down to the lab.

"Hey, Adams! You look good!" the tech exclaimed. "Ready for this?"

"As much as I am going to be," she replied. "So, who's putting the wire on me?"

A nervous Ramon Gutierrez arrived at the restaurant a full half-hour early and sat at the bar to wait for the woman he knew as Bianca.

Twenty minutes and two shots later, he ordered himself a double rum and Coke and his expected date a Blue Hawaiian, then allowed the host to lead him to the table that Javier had recommended he call ahead and reserve.

At seven-thirty-two, he glanced toward the host station and smiled broadly.

Bianca had arrived.

As Annie walked toward a beaming Ramon, the earpiece that had just passed a comms check in the car crackled with static, and she held back a wince.

There is some sort of interference in here, she realized. *Great, just what we need.*

But outwardly, she kept the bright smile pasted firmly in place as she approached the table - and fought off the urge to slap him when Ramon stood, put both hands at her waist, and leaned in to kiss her cheek.

"You look gorgeous," he murmured silkily as he held her chair for her, then took advantage of his proximity to trace his hand across her bare shoulder before he retreated to his side of the table and sat down.

"Thank you," Annie said breathily, and arranged the cloth napkin in her lap.

Please dear God let this all move quickly.

Across the restaurant, Agent Wilford scowled, then muttered to Grace Womack, "She does not look comfortable, at all."

"She will be just fine," Grace murmured back as she looked at her menu. "We will just have to keep a closer watch since our comms are on the fritz."

"Speaking of, I just checked. Whatever is causing that static is *also* affecting cell phone signal," he revealed. "We are cut off completely while we are in here."

Grace raised an eyebrow.

"You don't say? That's not good."

Thirty miles away a bored Hank Myers had opted to queue up the current day's garage footage and was fighting off a yawn as he watched another typical boring Saturday filled with oil changes and tire rotations.

"Enough, already," he muttered, and hit 'fast forward' to skip ahead to the end of the working day, then pressed 'play' again.

What the video revealed at five-eighteen p.m. had Hank sprinting for the elevators with his cell phone up to his ear.

At Ramon's insistence, Annie finally tried the Blue Hawaiian he had ordered for her.

"Trust me, it is really good," he said more than once, and to shut him up she finally picked up the glass and sipped daintily through the small straw.

"That *is* pretty good," she conceded, and took another, much larger sip.

"Now, what kind of appetizers do you like?" he asked, and the look on his face made it clear to her that he sincerely hoped 'Bianca' would be his dessert later.

It was not long before her drink was empty, so Ramon ordered her another one, and by the time she finished it twenty minutes later, Annie did not feel quite right. Everything was beginning to swim at the edge of her vision, and her limbs felt loose and lazy.

She shook her head to try to clear the cobwebs that had taken over, but it was no use, and her head slumped toward her chest.

"Don't... feel... right..." she slurred as she felt Ramon's hands lifting her out of her chair.

He pulled her close against him, her back against his chest, one arm wrapped around her waist, and Annie tried to struggle but found that her arms simply would not cooperate.

"Come on, beautiful. Let's go somewhere more... *private*, shall we?" he murmured in her ear before he kissed her earlobe.

———

Grace watched the activity at Annie's table and rose to her feet in alarm.

"Something's wrong," she told Wilford. "Go outside and call for backup."

"What are you going to do?"

"Get her away from him, whatever it takes."

Wilford rushed toward the front door as Grace made her way quickly through the throng of tables separating her from her fellow agent and friend.

———

Ramon began to half guide and half carry his stumbling date toward the restaurant's exit but found his path blocked.

"Bianca is that you?" the caramel-skinned woman in her mid-forties who was standing in the way called out. "Honey, did you take your insulin today?"

A weak, "Grace.... what...." was all that Ramon's companion could manage.

"You need to turn her loose," Ramon's unwanted visitor declared as she glared at him. "I work with her, and I know that when she hasn't taken her insulin like she should, this is the result."

The woman turned her attention back to the female Ramon held in his arms.

"Come on, baby girl, I got you," she crooned as she muscled Ramon's obviously impaired prize away from him.

Ramon started to protest but his words trailed off as a huge, menacing-looking, blond-haired blue-eyed man strode up.

"Bianca," the newcomer said, and scooped the barely conscious woman up and into his arms.

"And just who are you?" an indignant Ramon sputtered.

"Her brother," the man growled. "Now back off."

Undeterred, Ramon followed the meddlesome pair outside.

Hank Myers stormed out of the restaurant with Annie in his arms, and only the fact that he was carrying her limp body stopped him from causing Ramon Gutierrez severe bodily harm.

"Put him into submission and get him out of here," he snarled to a stunned Evans, Wilford, and Mark Calloway, then jerked his head back to indicate Ramon.

"Grace, you're with me. We're taking her to the emergency room."

Grace rushed ahead to open the back door of her car, and Hank climbed in, still holding Annie in his arms. Grace hopped behind the wheel and sped away.

"How did you get here so quickly?" Grace asked as she met his eyes in the rear-view mirror.

"I was already coming this way. I was watching this afternoon's footage, and I saw Miguel give Ramon a small vial of something to use on her tonight. He laughed and told Ramon it would make her more *receptive*," Hank growled.

"Son of a bitch *roofied her?*"

"Yeah," Hank said grimly, then looked down and patted Annie's deathly pale cheek, gently at first, then more insistently.

"Come on, darlin, I need you to open your eyes for me. Annie, open your eyes."

When he did not get a response, he barked, "Hurry, Grace. Hurry. I don't know what the hell he gave her, but I can't get her to wake up."

Outside the restaurant, the tail that none of the agents had noticed took pictures of each of them and then watched with interest as a handcuffed Ramon Gutierrez landed in the back seat of an unmarked sedan.

He pulled out his phone, dialed, and waited.

"We've got issues," he said the moment his boss answered. "Ramon Gutierrez just went and got himself arrested."

"Locally? Because I have contacts –"

"No, the men who just grabbed him are *federal* agents," he interrupted.

"Are you certain?"

"Positive."

A long pause, then, "I don't care what you have to do. Make it happen."

"I'm on it."

He hung up the phone and watched the three men that had captured Ramon confer briefly among themselves, then part company. Two got into the car with Ramon while the third man walked away and out of sight around the side of the building.

Chapter Twenty-Seven

Mere minutes later, the car screeched to a stop, and Grace scrambled to open the back door for him. Hank worked his way out of the vehicle quickly, never losing his hold on Annie.

"Call Nathan," he told Grace before he ran through the automatic double doors still carrying Annie bridal-style.

"I need some help over here," he called out the moment he crossed the threshold into the emergency room's lobby. "She's been drugged."

Two of the triage staff launched quickly into action, but Hank could not help but notice that three others were more nonchalant.

Furious, he stood at his full height and announced in his most authoritative voice that Annie was a federal agent and that if she died he would hold those in attendance personally responsible.

It caused him no small amount of satisfaction that they took his threat seriously - the three who until that point barely looked like they cared immediately began to work to help stabilize her. In an instant they had Annie loaded onto a gurney and whisked her past the intake desk and into a triage bay.

"Nathan's on his way," Grace said as she came to stand by Hank's side at the intake desk. "And Calloway is too. Ramon still had the vial on him; they found it in his jacket pocket when they patted him down. Calloway's bringing it in so they can run tests on it and try to figure out what he gave her."

"I tried to call you guys, several times," Hank revealed, and rubbed a hand over his face. "But the calls wouldn't go through."

"Not just cell phones. We lost comms in there, too," Grace shared. "Something about the structure shorted it all out."

They fell silent.

"Is she going to be okay?" Grace asked.

"I hope so," Hank said, his face lined with worry. "I really hope so."

"Got here as quickly as I could," Mark Calloway announced as he walked up to join them, holding up a small, clear bag with a small, clear vial in it. "Who do I need to give this to?"

The man charged with surveilling Ramon started his own car's engine and pulled out behind the vehicle transporting Ramon, making sure he kept enough distance between the two to avoid detection. He followed them all the way to a tall building in downtown Dallas.

When the car he had been trailing disappeared into a restricted access underground parking garage, he circled the block then pulled over to the curb and parked.

A quick search on his phone confirmed his hunch about the occupants of the building.

He will be in there for hours, he realized. *It will take them a while to interrogate him before they move him anywhere else.*

"And now we wait," he muttered, and with a couple of keystrokes on his cell phone's app he made sure that the tiny tracker he had slipped into the lining of Ramon's favorite jacket earlier in the week was still operating as designed.

Then he put his car in drive and peeled away smoothly from the curb, confident that he had at least six hours to rest and prepare for the next step.

Meanwhile, Nathan Thomas's wrath surged through the waiting room like a Category Five hurricane making landfall.

"What the hell happened tonight?" he thundered as he closed the distance to where three members of his task force sat huddled together in chairs in the far corner of the space.

"He drugged her. My best guess is that he used rohypnol," Myers muttered.

"Why are you even here? You weren't supposed to be involved in tonight's op."

"No, I wasn't. I was at the office watching playback and I stumbled across a disturbing conversation between Miguel and Ramon from this afternoon. Miguel handed him a vial of something and said Ramon would have more fun on this date if he gave it to her. As soon as I saw that footage, I hauled ass this direction. But I was not fast enough. I know in my gut that Ramon spiked her drink with it, Nathan. I *feel* it."

"No one saw him add this stuff to her glass?"

"He was already at the restaurant when Agent Wilford and I got there, Nathan," Grace confirmed. "He showed up God only knows how early. I noticed him in the bar area as we were walking up to the host station. So, there is no telling for sure when he added it to her drink."

"I want the restaurant's security footage from tonight seized," Nathan growled. "*All* of it. As soon as possible."

"I'll go," Calloway volunteered. "I'll take care of it, boss."

He hurried out the door.

"How is she?" Nathan asked as he dropped wearily into the seat Calloway had vacated.

"No word yet. But when we took him down, we found the vial in his pocket," Hank shared. "Calloway brought it up here and they are running analysis on it now."

"And Ramon?"

"Wilford and Evans took him into custody and they're driving him to the office."

The physician on call walking over to them disrupted all conversation.

"For Agent Adams?" she asked, and when all three nodded, she pulled up a chair to join them.

"First of all, she's going to be fine," she reassured them. "But her blood and urine results did come back positive for a heavy dose of rohypnol, and the vial you provided also showed traces of the same drug."

"How heavy a dose?" Hank asked.

Nathan raised an eyebrow.

"Why does that matter?"

"I think he gave her way too much, which is why her condition went downhill so quickly," Hank explained, then turned to the ER doctor for confirmation.

"I agree," she chimed in, "because her levels showed an exposure of around three milligrams – *three times* the dose we typically see in assault victims. Not overdose levels, but close. *Too* close."

Hank's face turned red with anger.

"That idiot could have killed her."

"If you guys hadn't brought her over here quickly it is very possible she would not have survived," the doctor informed them. "Because among other things, rohypnol impacts the victim's ability to breathe normally, and it also bottoms out their blood pressure. Agent Adams is incredibly lucky that you got her here as fast as you did."

Nathan cleared his throat.

"When can we see her?"

"I can take you back now, if you like, but we'll need to keep the visit short so she can rest."

All three agents got to their feet and followed her.

"I'm going to keep her overnight for observation because of the high dose she was given," the doctor said as they walked, "but it is purely precautionary. She should be able to go home once we are certain all traces of rohypnol have left her system. But I will warn you now, she will have one hell of a hangover. She will need to take it easy the next few days."

The doctor paused outside bay fourteen.

"Ten minutes, okay, folks? I'll be back."

"Thanks, doc," Nathan said sincerely.

"No problem."

He looked at Hank and Grace, took a deep breath, then led the way past the curtain.

The staff had removed Annie's wig during her assessment to reveal her naturally dark hair, and she looked peaceful as she slept, an I.V. tucked into the crook of her left arm delivering the medication needed to help banish the rohypnol from her system.

Grace moved to the left side of the bed and gently stroked her face.

"Hey, kiddo," she murmured. "Can you hear me?"

Annie opened bleary eyes.

"We get him?" she slurred in an unsteady voice.

"Yes, ma'am. We got him," Grace assured her.

"Good," Annie mumbled, then managed, "tell Nathan no more Mardi Gras," before she drifted back to sleep.

Grace chuckled softly when she looked over to see Nathan and Hank both sporting matching puzzled expressions.

"I told her about an op I was on once. Long story," Grace explained. "And based on that statement, she is going to be fine. If they let me, I will stay up here with her until they discharge her, then take her back to my place and put her to bed. If not, I will go home and get some sleep and then come back for her."

"Why don't you go rest and come back?" Hank offered. "I can stay and keep watch."

"You and I both need to be fresh and ready to go at seven a.m. – and we still have a suspect to go talk to," Nathan reminded him. "Why don't we ask first if they will even let any of us stay before we make our plans? Otherwise, the point may well be moot."

"Agreed," Hank said. "One question, though. Should we call Ben and fill him in?"

"Crap," Nathan muttered, and ran his hands through his hair. "I am not sure, to be honest... if I do, but Annie would not want him to know, she will be mad at me. And if I do not tell him, *he* will be mad at me. I can't win either way."

"Ask her," Grace chimed in. "Because it is *Annie's* decision to make, not ours. It might be different if she was in critical condition or unable to answer for herself, but that is not the case here."

Nathan stepped over.

"Annie, can you open your eyes for me?"

Reluctantly, she obeyed.

"Hey, boss," she whispered.

"Hey there. Do you want me to call Ben?"

The swirl of emotions across her face ended on a hard scowl.

"*No*," she said in a firm, clear voice, and was out again.

"I'd say that was a pretty clear answer as to what she wants," Hank remarked, his lips twitching as he fought to keep from smiling at Annie's surprisingly feisty tone.

"I would, too. And it *is* her decision, so, I have my instructions," Nathan replied. "And if Ben gets mad, well..."

He shrugged.

"Let's go talk next steps with the doctor, shall we?"

The subject of Annie's emphatic response arrived home worn out after an entire day of fishing and fresh air, and Ben immediately retrieved his phone and turned it on, hoping to see a message from her.

But nothing appeared.

"Fine," he muttered under his breath, and went to take a shower.

Once they had confirmed that *none* of them could stay overnight with Annie, the three walked back outside to the parking lot.

"I'll be back up here at six to take her home," Grace assured them before she headed over to her car for the drive home to get some sleep.

"My car's still at the restaurant," Hank told Nathan.

"Climb in, I'll take you over to pick it up."

Nathan's phone rang as they left the lot.

"Hey, boss," Calloway said. "The restaurant owner is *furious* that a female patron was drugged in his establishment. He said whatever footage we need we are welcome to take."

"Great. Get it and bring it to the office."

"I already have a disc in my hand."

"Well in that case, meet us outside in about five minutes. I'm bringing Hank back to get his car."

"Sure. See you soon."

A half-hour later Nathan and Hank parked side-by-side in the subterranean garage in Dallas, each eager to begin the interrogation of Ramon Gutierrez.

"How do you want to play this?" Hank asked as they walked toward the elevator.

"He drugged my agent, with the intention of kidnapping and assaulting her. No quarter," Nathan retorted in response as he punched the button to travel to the eighth floor.

"Good answer. That was my thought exactly."

"I'm sorry if I was a bit... intense when I first got to the ER," Nathan said as he stared straight ahead.

"No worries. I would have been, too."

"Thanks," Nathan replied before his tone turned to steel. "Now. Let's go nail this sleazebag to the wall."

As Hank relived the feel of Annie's slender body, limp and unresponsive, in his arms, a whole new wave of anger rushed to the surface in response.

"*Gladly*. After you," Hank offered when the doors opened.

They stalked side-by-side down the hall, Hank's height and bulkier build a stark contrast to Nathan's more compact frame, but both equally intimidating.

When they got to the door that Agent Wilford was guarding, Nathan snapped, "Has he been Mirandized?"

"Yes, sir, as we were cuffing him."

"Has he asked for counsel?"

"He hasn't said a single word, to be honest."

"Where's Evans?"

Wilford tilted his head toward the door.

"Very well," Nathan said, and handed him the disc. "Please review this and find the footage of him spiking her drink. Once you have it, knock once."

"Yes, sir. One question. Annie... is she okay?"

Nathan's all-business demeanor softened for just a moment when he answered, "Yes, thank God. She's going to make a full recovery."

"Glad to hear that," the DEA man answered, his relief evident.

Wilford opened the door for them, and once they had entered the room, he closed it again and walked away to go look at the restaurant's video feed.

Any attempt on Ramon's part to look self-assured and smug evaporated the moment he laid eyes on the two men that had just entered the room.

They approached the table quietly, ominously, their expressions still and unreadable, like granite statues.

"Shall I stay?" the man that had been keeping him company inquired.

The man Ramon had not ever seen before waved a hand, and his keeper nodded and left the room.

The dark-haired stranger sat down across the table from him, pinning him with a stark stare, while the man he had met earlier – the one who had said he was Bianca's brother - leaned against the wall, beefy arms folded over his chest, and glowered at him.

Ramon cleared his throat.

"Evidently, I was on a date with someone you're involved with?" he offered as he looked at the man across from him. "If so, I apologize, I did not realize she was spoken for."

"Not involved," the man snarled. "She's a federal agent, just like I am, and you almost killed her tonight, you complete waste of space."

He leaned forward.

"But we already have you dead to rights on an accessory to capital murder charge, Mister Gutierrez. Aggravated assault on *another* federal officer is just icing on the cake."

Ramon started to leap to his feet to protest his innocence when the big blond man shocked him by swiftly closing the distance and shoving him back down roughly into his seat.

"Cruz Delgado," the man growled as he towered over Ramon, and Ramon's eyes went wide.

"I want a lawyer," he babbled.

The dark-haired man rose from his chair and motioned to the bigger man to follow before he looked back at Ramon and sneered, "You are going to need one, because you are looking at death row. And I hope you enjoyed your dinner earlier tonight, because it's the last one you will ever have as a free man."

They slammed the door behind them on their way out, leaving a terrified Ramon to ponder his fate.

Once they were out of the room again, Nathan grimaced.

"Dammit. Evans," he called out.

"Yo."

"Run a phone in there please. Our suspect is lawyering up."

"Yes, sir."

Frustrated, Nathan ran his hands through his hair.

"Now we get to wait until his counsel shows up."

"Come on, let's go find Wilford," Hank said. "Maybe he has zeroed in on the restaurant footage we need already. Besides, I want to queue up the murder video to show the defense attorney - you and I both know Ramon's lawyer will demand proof to support why he has been detained."

Forty-five minutes later, the defense attorney retained by Ramon Gutierrez arrived onsite. Nathan escorted the guest to interview room one where his client was waiting.

"Give us a moment, please, gentlemen," he said, and went in to talk to Ramon.

"We have everything queued up and ready?" Nathan asked.

"And then some," Hank confirmed.

After ten minutes, the attorney opened the door, stuck his head out into the hallway, and motioned to Nathan.

"Here we go," Nathan murmured to Hank, who followed behind him carrying the laptop with the videos already paused at the appropriate places.

The two agents situated themselves across the table from Ramon and his lawyer.

"Gentlemen, I suppose it goes without saying that I'd like to know exactly why my client is in custody," the lawyer began.

Nathan handed him a folder.

"That's the arrest warrant," he explained. "Feel free to look it over."

The attorney did, and his eyebrows raised as he skimmed the document.

"And you have evidence of this?"

Nathan smiled.

"Irrefutable. Would you like to see it?"

A brief nod answered his question, and Nathan looked over at Hank.

Hank swiveled the laptop and arranged it in front of the lawyer.

"Just press play," he instructed before he leaned back and folded his arms across his chest.

The video sprang into life at the exact moment that showed Ramon holding a gun to Cruz's head while Javier chained his feet to the floor, and it continued all the way through Ramon helping to dispose of Cruz's body into the used oil tank.

The lawyer reached out with a trembling hand to stop the playback as Ramon leaned forward and rested his forehead on the table in utter defeat.

"Keep going, there's another one to back up the additional charges he is now facing," Hank urged.

Reluctantly, the lawyer played the second offering – this one of Ramon clearly pulling a vial from his pocket and dumping its entire contents into a tall glass filled with blue liquid as he sat in the restaurant's bar.

That video then showed Ramon carrying the glass to the table and placing it opposite his seat. It continued to roll all the way through Annie ingesting the drink over the course of fifteen minutes, and later, Hank rushing into the frame to scoop up an unconscious Annie and move swiftly out of frame again.

"I've seen enough," the lawyer murmured, his face so pale it was almost translucent. "I need to speak to Mr. Gutierrez privately, please."

"I figured you might," Nathan drawled, and Hank solemnly retrieved the laptop before they left the obviously shaken counselor alone with his obviously guilty client.

<hr>

Nathan Thomas arrived home at twelve-thirty in the morning after a lengthy initial interview with Ramon Gutierrez.

Following his lawyer's strongly worded advice, Ramon had stopped any pretense of resisting cooperation and had agreed to tell Nathan and Hank everything he knew about the Cortinas cartel's activities. In exchange, there would be a recommendation for a reduction in his sentence from death row to life in prison, to begin after his testimony at trial.

The suspect provided an extremely detailed statement of facts concerning the murder of undercover DEA agent Cruz Delgado, and a disturbing conversation with Estoban Cortinas that pertained directly to Nathan Thomas and members of his team.

He also made a full confession, on record, to plying undercover agent Annie Adams with rohypnol with the intent of subduing and sexually assaulting her.

Everything Ramon spoke of on the FBI-focused part of the situation was verifiable by video clips from the garage's security system. But Ramon's biggest value was that he would be able to provide *other* data pertinent to the separate case led by the DEA – for example, the specific schedule by which drug-hauling vehicles passed through the shop, and where they traveled when they left the south Fort Worth location.

After he briefed both agency directors, Nathan reluctantly agreed to place Ramon in protective custody until the trial and arranged to transport Ramon to a safe house once the raid on the garage, the recovery of Cruz Delgado's remains, and his statement to the DEA team was complete.

Mentally exhausted, Nathan crept as silently as possible into his bedroom, undressed in the dark, and climbed into bed beside a sleeping Bella. The last thing he did before he drifted into sleep himself was set his alarm for five a.m.

Chapter Twenty-Eight

At six-thirty a.m. Nathan was in his office in Dallas taking care of unread emails before he met the raid team to brief and head to the site. One email stood out, and he opened it the moment he noticed it.

We captured excellent footage for you, the sender said. *I will be sending it over via encrypted file as it is too big to attach here.*

Nathan smiled as he headed to the breakroom for another cup of coffee and met Lizzie coming out into the hall.

"Heard back from the tech," he told her. "Evidently the flyover returned some useful data. He's going to send it over."

"Great! I look forward to seeing it once we get back from the raid," she answered, then asked, "Did you sleep all right, Nathan? You look tired."

"Long day yesterday," he began, but noticed Ben had walked into the breakroom. "I will fill you in later."

"Sure. Hey, I reviewed three of the four flash drives that MacKinnon gave you," she revealed. "I found absolutely nothing that we can use. I called it a night around eleven. But I'll get into that last one when we get back."

"Works for me," Nathan said. "Morning, Ben."

"Morning," Ben replied, and poured his own mug of coffee. "So… how did last night go?"

"I'll update everyone at once before we cover today's plan," Nathan answered briskly, and walked out of the breakroom.

Ben cast a questioning glance over at Lizzie, who shrugged.

Nathan hurried back to his office and called Grace Womack's cell phone.

"Are you with Annie?" he asked when she answered.

"Yep," Grace said. "They just discharged her, and we are getting in the car to head to my place."

"Can I speak with her?"

"Sure, hang on just a moment."

There was a rustling, then a weary, "Hi, boss."

"How are you feeling?"

"Like I got run over by a Mack truck."

"I'm sorry. The doctor said you should be back to one hundred percent in a few days."

"Yeah, she told me that too."

"Listen," Nathan said, then hesitated.

"What?"

"I need to know if I have your permission to share last night's events with the rest of the team."

"Sure. Why wouldn't you? Oh, wait… Ben… you asked if you needed to call him last night and I told you no, didn't I?"

"Yes, you did."

She sighed.

"It's fine, share whatever you think they need to know. He will be mad that no one told him right away, but he will just have to get over it."

"Just wanted to check with you first, Annie."

"I get that, and I appreciate it. My head really hurts, so here's Grace."

When Grace came back on the line, Nathan asked, "She all right?"

"She's good," Grace assured him. "Nothing that some food and some more restful sleep won't solve."

"Let me know if she needs anything," Nathan instructed.

"Roger that. Tell the team I said be safe and kick some butt." Nathan chuckled.

"I will pass that along."

At six-fifty-five the raid team assembled in the conference room, and Nathan stood up and moved to the end of the table.

"Before we go over today's plan, I wanted to update everyone on our operation last night," he announced. "Although there was a hiccup, we arrested Ramon Gutierrez last night as planned, and he's agreed to turn state's evidence against the cartel. He gave us an involved and detailed statement about Agent Delgado's murder and is now talking with the DEA regarding the cartel's activities. Once they are done with him, Gutierrez will be transported to a safe house until the trial."

"What was the hiccup?" an innocent Agent Baker asked, completely unaware of the situation's volatility, and Nathan cursed inwardly, although his expression stayed neutral.

"Well," Nathan answered carefully, "Agent Adams suffered what turned out to be minor injuries."

"What precisely do you mean by *minor injuries?*" Ben pressed, his voice deceptively soft, but his body posture broadcasting the fact that he was building up to an explosive level.

Nathan glanced over at Hank.

"Someone spiked her drink," Hank said flatly. "Fortunately, we intervened in time."

There was a thunderous *bang* as Ben slammed both fists down on the tabletop as hard as he could, then shoved his chair back and stormed out of the room.

"Hank, take over the briefing," Nathan barked, and followed his enraged agent out into the hallway.

"Listen," Nathan began, but a snarling Ben cut him off.

"*No*. This time *I* talk, and *you* listen. Someone hurt Annie last night, and it never occurred to you to let me know? I *love* her, remember? How could you do that? How could you keep something like that from me?"

"It was her choice to make, Ben. I asked her if she wanted me to call you, and she said no. It's as simple as that."

"You know what? I am done with this. *All of it*. I am done with her, and I am sure as hell done with *you*. Consider this my one-week notice, Agent Thomas," Ben informed him in a clipped, icy tone. "In seven days, I'm gone."

And he stepped around Nathan to re-enter the conference room.

When the briefing ended, Lizzie approached Ben.

"Are you okay?"

"Why the hell do you care?"

Lizzie put her hands up and narrowed her eyes.

"Okay, you need to stop with the freaking attitude. Whatever you are upset about, I am not the cause of it. I'm just checking on you."

"Don't bother, I won't be here much longer," Ben growled, and left the room to go put on his body armor for the raid.

Lizzie fisted her hands on her hips and looked over at Nathan.

"What the hell has gotten into him?"

"He is angry that Annie did not want him notified last night. She said he probably would be."

"So, he's just going to stomp around and be a prick to the rest of us all day? You cannot be serious about keeping him on the raid team, Nathan. As out of control as he is right now, he's going to get one of us killed."

"She isn't wrong," Hank said gently from across the table. "Right now, Ben is a huge liability."

"It's more than just today," Nathan revealed with a bleak look. "He's quitting altogether. He gave me his one-week notice just now."

"That's enough of this crap," Lizzie blurted out. "I will deal with this."

And she marched out of the room to seek out Ben.

"What has gotten into you? And before you tell me it is about not being on speed dial when stuff went down last night, save it. I know that is *not* it, or at least, not all of it," Lizzie commanded when she found him in the locker room.

Ben turned to face her, and the raw pain shining in his eyes took her breath away.

"I lost her, Lizzie. I chased away the woman of my dreams because I was too stupid to keep from smothering her," he confessed. "Hearing that she got hurt last night was bad enough. Finding out that she did not want me to even know about it? That crushed me."

She sat down next to him on the bench.

"Did she move *all* of her stuff out?"

"No, just her clothes and bathroom stuff."

"Okay, so, look past the emotion and think this through, Ben. If she were truly one hundred percent done with you, don't you think she would have made sure she took *all* her things?"

"Well, I had not thought about that, but you are right," he admitted. "When Annie makes up her mind about something she moves very quickly, and she is totally committed."

"And did she actually *say* that the two of you were completely over? Because again, knowing Annie, she would have made no bones about it if that were the case."

Ben closed his eyes and frowned as he recalled their conversation in the hallway that day.

"No," he said. "She said that we were going to spend some time apart, because she needed some space, and that I needed to get my act together."

"And do *you* think stomping around snapping at people and quitting your job is the best way of getting said act together? Because *I'm* thinking it isn't."

"You might have a point there."

"I do have a point. And it is simply this – the world has not ended. Annie has not dumped you. She needs space, is all. So, suck it up, give it to her, and stop being a jackass. We need you on this team, Ben, but we also need every single member to be completely focused on what we are doing, or someone will get hurt today."

She leaned over and flung her arm around his shoulders.

"And I do not know about you, but I have already buried one friend lately due to an op that went south. I do not want to lose any more. *Ever*, if I can help it, but *especially* not today. All right?"

Ben leaned his head over to rest on her shoulder.

"Thanks, Liz. Give me a couple of minutes. I'll get it together, I promise."

"Good. See you in the garage in ten," she said, and gave him a friendly one-armed hug before she stood and left the locker room.

<hr>

Ten minutes later, as he promised he would, Ben joined the rest of the raid team in the garage. He immediately approached Nathan.

"A moment, please?" he asked, and Nathan nodded and led him away from the group.

"I'd like to rescind my resignation," Ben said softly. "And also offer an apology for earlier."

"Glad to hear that, Ben, and apology accepted. We can talk more later if you like, once we get this morning's tasks done. Is that acceptable?"

"It is."

"Okay, then," Nathan said, and clapped him on the shoulder. "Let's get back in the game. Lots to do here shortly."

They walked back over to join the rest, and Nathan clapped his hands twice.

"All right. Is everyone wearing their body armor? Good. I got confirmation from Rick about ten minutes ago that he has subbed out the garage's live feed for a playback loop. Get loaded up and let's get moving. ETA to site is about a half-hour. Crime scene and Tarrant County coroner staff will meet us onsite once the place is secured."

As Ben climbed into the first panel van, his cell phone pinged. He looked at the incoming message and smiled.

Please be safe today – Annie.

<hr>

By three p.m., it was all over but the shouting.

The raid that Nathan and Hank had planned so diligently went off without a hitch; the only troublesome aspect was that Miguel Salazar was the only suspect apprehended – Javier was in the wind, and Estoban Cortinas was safely out of reach in Mexico.

A belligerent Miguel cussed a blue streak when they handcuffed him and not so gently placed him into the back seat of one of the unmarked sedans for his complimentary trip to the FBI's Dallas office.

Then, the search began in earnest.

DEA agents concentrated on documenting, cataloging, and

collecting package after package of tightly bundled cocaine, while the FBI team combed the facility for physical evidence of Cruz's murder.

Once they had confirmed that bringing Cruz out of the tank the same way he went in was not feasible, three strategic phone calls resulted in an innovative approach.

First, a waste oil truck arrived to drain the tank. Next, a backhoe broke up and removed the concrete covering the top of the tank. After that, welders waded into the fray and removed an eight-by-eight-foot section of the outer hull.

The coroner himself, along with three members of his team, donned waders and climbed down into the tank with flashlights to examine and then bag the body and maneuver it onto a backboard. Using two slings and the ceiling hoist, the team lifted the backboard out of the tank through the large hole the welders had cut, and then lowered it onto a gurney.

All other activity in the garage stopped the moment Cruz's body was out of the tank. Every person present stood in respectful silence as his remains were slowly wheeled past them out into the sunshine and loaded into the coroner's van for transport.

Everyone, that is, except Hank Myers.

As he watched the coroner's team roll the gurney past his position, Hank, unable to hold back the surge of emotion any longer, dropped to his knees in the middle of the garage floor and wept.

His task force teammates surrounded him immediately and shielded him from view, to allow him to grieve as privately as possible.

Chapter Twenty-Nine

ANNIE, Grace, and the other agents who participated in the arrest of Ramon Gutierrez were waiting for them when the raid team returned to the office.

Both the FBI and DEA directors were in attendance, as well, and made it a point to shake the hand of every task force member.

"Debrief in the conference room in ten minutes," the FBI director announced, then continued, "and, good work, people. Very well done."

Once the debrief completed, the FBI director turned to Nathan.

"A word, please," he said.

"Sure. One moment, sir," Nathan answered, and said to the group, "Everyone hang tight for just a moment, we have one more thing to line out. I will be right back."

Then he followed his boss out of the conference room and down the hall to the director's office.

"One down, one to go. I will keep this short because you need to rest up," the man said, and handed him a folder. "Full search warrant for the Lighte's Landing property. You can head out there whenever you're ready."

"Lizzie and I will build a team and get out there within the next twenty-four hours," Nathan assured him. "I take it you escalated our getting these?"

The director smiled.

"I happen to have connections that come in handy sometimes, yes. Go home, Agent Thomas."

"I can't. Not yet. I have to interview Miguel Salazar."

"It's been handled. He is refusing to cooperate, so, we're bringing the original charge of accessory to capital murder forward for him. Which means Ramon Gutierrez just became our star witness. Make sure he's kept safe."

"Yes, sir."

When Nathan returned to the conference room, he noticed Ben and Annie talking quietly in a corner.

"Is that good, or bad?" he murmured to Lizzie.

"I'd say good, since neither are yelling," she quipped.

"We got the warrants for Lighte's Landing," he told her.

"When do you want to go?"

"I'm thinking head out early in the morning. Around seven."

"And who do you want on the team?"

"I'm open. Let's ask them."

He turned and addressed the group.

"Couple of things that need to happen," he announced. "First, Ramon Gutierrez is now giving detailed statements to the DEA to help build *their* case. Once they are done with him, I need someone to pair up with their agent to transport him to the safe house."

Ben raised his hand.

"I can handle transport."

"Okay, good. You will need to coordinate with the DEA. I don't envision that they will be done with him until sometime late tonight or early tomorrow morning. Nail that timeframe down - and get some rest in the meantime if you can."

Nathan then turned his attention to the latest order of business.

"Second, we just got the warrants we were waiting on to move forward with the Lighte's Landing case out in Jack County. I need volunteers for that team. We will be leaving to head out there somewhere around seven tomorrow morning and coordinating with local law enforcement onsite. Who's in?"

"I'll go," Annie said, and Grace Womack and Mark Calloway indicated their involvement, as well.

"You could use the help," Hank Myers said, his typically tightly controlled emotions now firmly back in check. "I'm in. Technically, I'm on leave now for the next week anyway, and I'd rather come with you guys than sit around bored."

"You sure?" Nathan asked, and the DEA man grinned.

"If I wasn't, I would not have volunteered."

"Fair enough, Hank. Fair enough."

Nathan looked around the room.

"Great work the last few days, everybody. If you're not involved in the Jack County plans, you're free to go. Lighte's Landing team, please stay. We have some security footage to look at, as well as the flyover results. Lizzie, please bring that flash drive so we can get started – and ask Diane to order in some food, please."

As Lizzie left the conference room to retrieve the final flash drive and Nathan pulled down the overhead screen to project the infrared video for the group, Ben leaned over and whispered to Annie.

"Would you please have dinner with me tomorrow night? And maybe we can talk some more?"

"I'd like that," she whispered back.

He beamed.

"Okay, cool. Call me when you guys get back from Jack County, and we can meet wherever you want."

He stood.

"I'll head up to the tenth floor now and see how far along they are," he told Nathan, who nodded.

Ben winked at Annie as he left the room.

The team reviewed the flyover coverage first and made detailed notes.

"Based on this, we really need to split into two teams, Nathan," Hank recommended, "and attack this from both sides. One to take the main area of the place, and another to drop in via helicopter directly to that other location of interest."

"I believe you're right. We need to bring in the hostage extraction team," Nathan said, and dialed the director's extension from the conference room's phone.

"Sir, I have something you need to see."

When the director joined him and saw what they had been looking at, he nodded his head.

"I'm on it, Agent Thomas. I'll take over running that piece personally. Let me make a call and line out the personnel we need."

"Thank you, sir."

Diane brought in the sandwiches she'd ordered for them, then asked, "Anything else you need before I leave, Nathan?"

"Nope. And thanks for coming in on a Sunday. I appreciate you, Diane."

She smiled.

"We're a team, it's what we do."

"See you tomorrow."

A small break was called so that the group could grab their food, and when everyone was seated again, Nathan said, "Okay, the security footage from Jacksboro's town square is next. Lizzie, queue it up."

She navigated the laptop's layout so that it was connecting into the overhead projector and pressed 'play.'

Three hours later, Nathan was scrambling to get Detective Glen MacKinnon on the phone.

"Are you still with Claire King?"

"Yes. Why?"

"I need you to bring her to the office. We've found something, and I need her help."

"What's going on?"

"At this point, it is much easier to show you both, rather than try to explain."

"Okay, sure. We will be there shortly."

"Thanks, see you in a bit."

As he hung up the phone he noticed Lizzie's puzzled expression.

"What's wrong?" she asked.

"*That* is what is wrong," he said, and pointed at the oversized screen. "We need to know who that man is as soon as possible – because I am almost positive that is *not* Remiel Lighte."

MacKinnon and King arrived fifteen minutes later, and when Claire King walked into the room, she froze the moment she glanced over at the screen.

"Do you know him?"

She nodded.

"Is that Remiel Lighte?"

"No, it's not. But the note that Sophie got specifically mentioned overhearing a conversation. Which means at least two people are involved in all this, right?"

"I would think so," Nathan confirmed.

A couple more questions, and Claire and MacKinnon were free to leave.

"I will call you when it's safe," Nathan assured them as he walked them both to the elevator.

Upon his return to the group, he strode over to the laptop, captured a still image of the man on video, and called down to the lab.

"I am about to send you a picture and a name," he directed. "Find out everything you can about him. *Quickly*."

***

By nine p.m. Nathan's favorite lab tech had provided a list of aliases and a disturbing criminal record on the man in the picture, and Nathan stopped the group's activities for the night.

"Get some sleep, everyone. We leave at seven a.m. sharp."

Chapter Thirty

His alarm sounded at five-thirty a.m. and roused him from a solid sleep. The first thing he checked was his phone, to make sure that Ramon's location had remained unchanged overnight.

Satisfied that Ramon was still being held in the tall building, he hustled to the shower in the tiny motel room he had rented to clean up before leaving to start another day of surveillance.

In Pantego, Nathan Thomas eased out of bed and got his own shower, then dressed and poured coffee into a travel mug for the drive to the office.

He arrived at six-twenty and waded through emails until six-forty-five, at which time he strode down the hall to meet his team and head to the garage.

They departed for Jack County promptly at seven a.m. as scheduled, a three-vehicle caravan with a total of ten agents besides Nathan – the director had thought it prudent to beef up the ranks. This group would be approaching the property via the front gate.

The director had already made plans for the FBI's crack hostage extraction team to function unseen and hopefully unheard at the far end of the property, where Lizzie had first noticed the small outbuilding on the satellite-view map.

By the time Nathan's group met up with Jack County Sheriff's Office personnel at eight-thirty, the DEA was finally done with Ramon Gutierrez, and he was handed over to Ben and DEA Agent Baker for transport.

The trio rode the elevator in silence down to the garage, where Ramon was bundled, still handcuffed, into the back of one of the DEA's fleet cars. Baker climbed behind the wheel and Ben opted to ride shotgun in the front passenger seat.

"How far out is it?" Baker asked.

"About two hours."

"Better get rolling, then."

With that, Baker grinned, started the car, and backed out of the space.

When he reached the parking garage exit, he asked, "Which way?"

"Take a right and head down two blocks to Akard Street, then take a left. We need to get on Interstate 30 heading west."

"You got it."

Neither agent noticed the black pickup truck whose occupant watched them exit the garage, then pull away from the curb and fall in behind them eleven cars back.

"Morning, Agent Thomas," Sheriff Bill Miller drawled, and extended his hand in greeting.

"Morning, Sheriff, it's nice to meet you."

"Likewise. Glen MacKinnon read me in a little bit when he called me," Miller said. "Anything you need from us, you got it. I've interacted with Pastor Lighte a few times over the years. Always pleasant and willing to help. I don't believe you'll get any resistance today."

"Well, perhaps not from *him*," Nathan quipped, and pulled Miller off to the side to reveal some data.

"Well, now, that changes things," Miller admitted. "That one always did come across as a little too smooth for my taste."

"I don't suppose there's any way to know if he's on the property currently."

"Nope," the sheriff sighed. "We'll just have to get out there and hope for the best. I'll take point on the drive in, and you all hang back. If that one is manning the controls, he will be more likely to open the gate if he thinks it's just me paying a visit."

"We'll follow your lead, Sheriff."

Twenty minutes later, Sheriff Miller pulled up to the gated entrance to Lighte's Landing and pressed the button.

"Good morning, Sheriff Miller. How are you?"

"Doing well, Pastor Lighte, doing well. Listen, I've got some people with me, and we really need to come in and talk with you. Can you please open the gate?"

"Absolutely, Sheriff. I'll meet you all out in front of the main building."

"Thanks, Pastor," Sheriff Miller said, and stuck his arm out the window and waved the cars following him forward as he drove through the gate.

When they'd parked and exited their vehicles, a tall, blond man with kind green eyes walked over with his hand extended to greet the sheriff.

"Nice to see you again, Sheriff," he said sincerely, then looked at the others.

"Good morning, everyone, I'm Remiel Lighte. Welcome to Lighte's Landing. I must say, this almost looks like a military action," he remarked as he took in Nathan's group, all armed.

"I'm going to speak frankly with you, Pastor Lighte. There has been evidence uncovered out here that needs a closer look," Nathan said as he walked up. "I'm Agent Thomas. I'm with the FBI, and I have warrants to search Lighte's Landing."

All color left the pastor's face.

"Warrants? What for?" Remiel asked, and Nathan could tell the man's shock and confusion was genuine.

"Let's head inside and sit down, Pastor," Miller said gently. "It's not really a short story to tell."

"Oh, my. Yes, let's. Please, right this way."

They followed Remiel into the building, where he led them to a conference room and closed the door.

"What's going on, and how can I help?"

Meanwhile, a helicopter with four of the FBI's best tactical unit members onboard spotted the small, tin-roofed structure barely visible beneath the trees on the far western border of Lighte's Landing.

"The canopy's too thick to rappel through," the team leader told the pilot. "Put us in fifty yards south in that small clearing."

"You got it," the pilot replied, and maneuvered his machine into place, then hovered while three of the hostage rescue unit descended to the clearing a hundred feet below via ropes.

The member remaining onboard kept a watch over the surrounding area while the three on the ground sprinted toward the tiny wooden building.

"Door locked. Breaching," the team lead said, and kicked it in.

Forty seconds later the personnel on the chopper heard, "Send down the basket. Got one in pretty rough shape."

Nathan took point in explaining the reason for the visit, and as he did, Remiel gasped with surprise.

"Now, sir, I have to ask you," Nathan said gently. "What was the reason you changed your name?"

Remiel closed his eyes.

"Sometimes our sins still haunt us, despite our best efforts," he muttered, and sighed before he opened his eyes again and leveled a direct, honest gaze at Nathan.

"I was born Guenter Schmidtt, and as Guenter I was... not a nice person," Remiel admitted with a shake of his head. "I was maligned, angry at the world. I had some bad breaks throughout my childhood, and instead of overcoming them I used them as excuses to do harm to others. I cheated, and I lied, and I stole. And then one night, about eighteen years ago, I hit rock bottom. I got to the point that it was either take my own life, or, turn my life around."

He sighed again.

"Luckily for me, I happened across a man named Abel, who had the peace I wanted and had been searching so desperately for, and long story short, he saved my life and put me on a different path. I became a new person. A different person. *Whole* again. And with that, came a new name. Did you know that Remiel was one of the seven archangels, and that several faiths refer to him as the 'angel of hope'? *That's* what I wanted to be to others. To pay forward that kindness – that light of hope - that had been shown to me. Hence, Remiel Lighte."

He smiled warmly at his guests for a moment, then turned solemn, and his green eyes darkened with anger.

"And now, you're telling me that Lighte's Landing is overrun with evil. With *murder*. I won't stand for it. Agent Thomas, you and your team have carte blanche to roam every square inch of this property if it helps bring the truth out into the light. I understand that you have a warrant that already allows this. I am just telling you, up front, that I want this solved as much as you do."

Nathan leaned forward and said, "I am looking for one individual in particular. We have compelling evidence that he is directly involved in all this."

When he heard the name, Remiel's eyes went wide.

"Surely not."

"I am afraid it has been one hundred percent verified. Now, you mentioned a man named Abel. Was his last name MacKensie?"

"Yes, it was. Why?"

"And he is buried here on the property, correct?"

"Yes, he passed quite unexpectedly about five years ago..."

Remiel's words trailed off as the truth hit home.

"Are you saying that he also killed *Abel*? He murdered my mentor, the one that saved me from myself?"

"Yes, I believe he did - and he *will* pay for that, Pastor, rest assured. Where is he now?"

"At this time of day, he could be anywhere on the property, Agent Thomas. But I have a very good idea of where to start looking first."

Four doors down from Remiel's office the two conspirators had locked themselves in, panic threatening to overwhelm them. The ringleader had overheard part of Remiel's conversation with his visitors and had immediately gone in search of his accomplice.

"But how could they possibly know?" his partner in crime hissed. "Unless... it was Sophie, wasn't it? I *told* you she was trouble. I *knew* I should have killed her when I had the chance... but *no*. You had to be such a freaking bigshot."

"You know what? I'm tired of your whining," he said as he pulled his silenced pistol from his pocket and fired once into the middle of his now former conspirator's forehead.

I need to get Sophie and get the hell out of here. Cut my losses. I can always start over somewhere else.

He eased open the door and risked a quick peek down the hallway. Seeing no one, he hustled out the building's back door, crept around the side to where one of the golf carts was parked, and headed toward the cabins.

When he reached his, he hurried inside and grabbed the bag that he always kept packed for emergencies, then hustled outside again to his SUV.

He drove as calmly as he could through that part of the property, waving casually at other residents, and took the turn leading down to the lakeshore.

And about four hundred yards after the narrow road he was on curved around out of sight of the cabins, he veered off onto a much older - and until recently barely noticeable – unpaved trail. He typically used the golf cart to navigate it, so that his activity would not be as obvious.

But the time for subtlety was over. He barreled down the bumpy route as fast as possible, his sole thought to escape with his prize.

His tires skidded to a stop in front of the cabin, and he was shocked to see the door standing wide open.

No, not open, he realized once he got out of the vehicle and got close enough. *Broken. She got out! But how?*

In Remiel's office, Nathan's phone chirped twice.

"Excuse me a moment, Pastor," and glanced at his phone. It was two texts from his boss.

They found Sophie Drimmel alive. They're flying her to Harris Methodist Hospital in Fort Worth.

They also saw a black SUV driving in the direction of the cabin where they found her.

"Remiel," Nathan prompted, "there's an old cabin at the far end of the property. Do you know how to get to it?"

"Yes, I do. Why?"

"That's where he was holding Sophie. I believe that he has gone to collect her and then he's going to try to run. We have to get out there."

"Let's go," the pastor replied, and jumped to his feet.

"Hank, Lizzie, with me," Nathan shouted to them before he, Remiel, and Miller piled into the sheriff's car and took off like a bullet.

"Annie, get the team moving on this building," Lizzie barked, and Annie nodded as she watched her teammate and Hank go flying after Miller.

"Turn up there," Remiel pointed to the right after they had blown past the cabins. "And then once the road curves, there will be an old path off to the left. That will lead us right to it. You guys might want to buckle up. It's going to be bumpy."

Miller took the detour from paved to unpaved with a massive amount of horsepower, and the back of the car fishtailed a bit, but he wrestled it back into submission and floored it once more.

The trail twisted and turned, and as they navigated a blind curve Miller cursed, then jerked the wheel hard to the right to keep from hitting the oncoming SUV head on.

Lizzie and Hank's sedan skidded to a stop several car lengths back. They got out, weapons drawn, and aimed at the suspect vehicle coming toward them.

"Tires," Lizzie shouted, and they both opened fire.

Hank's fourth round found its mark, and the driver's side front tire erupted, pulling the SUV into a dangerous lurch to the left. The driver panicked and overcorrected, causing the SUV to flip several times before coming to rest on its roof roughly thirty yards off the path.

They were almost to the tiny town of Cresson, Texas when Ben realized they had company.

"Baker," Ben muttered as he glanced out at the side mirror again, "that truck's been following us for a while now."

"You sure?"

"Yeah," he confirmed. "I have a bad feeling about this."

"Only one way to know for sure, right? So, let's test it out. Hang on, this could get a little bumpy," Baker quipped with a lopsided grin. "We clear to the right?"

"One car about seven lengths back," Ben confirmed, then clutched the door handle as Baker abruptly took a hard right turn from the left-hand lane.

The little coupe he had just cut off honked its horn and the driver flipped them the bird, but Baker either did not notice or did not care. His focus was split equally between the unobstructed pavement in front of him and the truck five car lengths back that had just accelerated to try to close the distance.

"Oh, yeah, definite tail," he muttered. "Need to get up on the highway."

"There *is* no highway through here besides the road we were just on," Ben told him.

"Seriously? That just won't do at all."

He abruptly made two more right-hand turns to get them back to the main road, and then Baker gunned the motor.

"They're still back there," Ben murmured calmly. "And gaining on us. What next?"

"Working on it," Baker grumbled as they flew through Cresson and back into acres of open countryside flanking the twisting, winding stretch of US Highway 377 South.

"The next big town is Granbury," Ben pointed out. "About ten minutes away. Let's get there and get to the police station."

Baker pressed the accelerator all the way to the floor as Ben glanced back at a frightened Ramon and growled, "Keep your head down."

"Radio ahead, Ben, let them know we've got a problem," Baker suggested, and Ben had just pulled out his cell phone to make contact when their car jolted violently – the truck had not only caught up to them, it had rammed them.

"Get down!" Ben yelled when he heard the first shot fired, but Ramon Gutierrez did not heed the warning; the second shot directed at them pierced the back of his skull.

Several more shots rang out, and Baker yelped as a round went through his left shoulder, shattering the socket and rendering his arm useless. He lost control of the car and veered off the road, slamming hard into a small grove of trees.

The truck that had accosted them drove past, slowed down enough to make a U-turn, then headed back toward Dallas, its driver not even bothering to take a second look at the carnage he had created. Instead, he made a call letting Estoban Cortinas know that the singing bird had been silenced.

It was several minutes before the next vehicle happened by. A farmer on his way into town pulled over, approached the car, looked inside, and called emergency services from his cell phone.

Seventy-seven miles to the north, the man Remiel had known for the past six years as Andreas had been taken by ambulance to the hospital in Jacksboro.

Nathan's team struck evidentiary gold when they searched the man's office and stumbled across the secret enhancements to the property's security system – and all the recordings from them.

Down the hall they also found Joanna, the resident healthcare professional, dead in her clinic from a gunshot wound to the center of her forehead. But once they began to dig into her files, it became evident that not only health records were kept in her locked cabinets

– and that she was not quite the victim her death scene made her out to be.

Nathan had just given further directions to his team regarding Joanna's dubious documentation when his phone rang, and he wandered out into the lobby area to take the call.

"Nathan," his director said solemnly. "I've got some news."

Lizzie sensed something was not right, so she followed him out to the lobby, and she slowly approached him as Nathan sat down abruptly, a look of sheer and utter shock stealing the color from his face.

"When?" he rasped and listened some more, reaching out blindly for Lizzie's hand.

"What's wrong?" Remiel Lighte whispered.

"I don't know," she whispered back, and winced at the way Nathan clutched her fingers so tightly that she could hardly feel them.

"Yes, sir," he said. "We're on our way."

He hung up the phone in a daze.

"Nathan, what's going on? What's happened?"

He slowly lifted his gaze to hers.

"Baker and Ben were ambushed," he managed. "Baker took a round in the shoulder, and Ramon Gutierrez was pronounced dead at the scene."

"What about Ben?"

He didn't answer.

"Nathan," Lizzie demanded, and wrested her hand free of his so that she could take him by the shoulders and shake him.

"What about Ben?"

Nathan slowly shook his head from side to side.

"No," Lizzie exclaimed. "Oh, God, Nathan. *No.*"

"We have to tell Annie," he murmured, trying his best not to break down. "How are we going to tell Annie?"

"Would you like me to gather your team?" Remiel asked softly, and Nathan nodded.

Nathan closed his eyes and hung his head, Lizzie's hands tightening on his shoulders, as Hank, Grace, Mark Calloway, and Annie entered the room and walked over to join them.

"What's going on?" Hank asked warily, reading the thick tension in the air.

"I don't even know where to..." Nathan trailed off, swallowed hard, ran his hands through his hair, and forced it out.

"The director just called me. Agent Baker and Ben were transporting Ramon Gutierrez earlier this morning, and someone ambushed them. Ramon was dead at the scene and Baker took a round through his shoulder. And Ben... Ben..."

"Don't say it," Annie cried out. "Don't you *dare* say that to me. He's fine, do you hear me? Ben's hurt, maybe, but he's going to be fine. We're having dinner tonight, and..."

"I'm so sorry, Annie," Nathan choked out before his tears overwhelmed him.

"*No!*" Annie shouted, then turned and fled, and a concerned Hank raced after her.

She sprinted outside into the sunshine, her body already racked with sobs, and turned her face up to unleash a primal, wounded scream at the bright blue sky and white fluffy clouds that seemed to mock her heartbreak.

Time slowed to a crawl as Annie finally collapsed under the weight of her grief. Hank caught her, then cradled her as she wept.

Chapter Thirty-One

Nathan and his core team left Lighte's Landing immediately after the fateful phone call to return to Dallas. The other FBI agents onsite, along with Sheriff Miller and his deputies, assumed the role of evidence collection.

The chopper team relayed news that led to the discovery of a shallow grave roughly one hundred yards from the cabin that Sophie Drimmel had been imprisoned in. DNA testing done the following afternoon would confirm its occupant to be eighteen-year-old Brittany.

A sample taken from Sophie Drimmel during her intake evaluation at Harris Methodist Hospital for comparison would later cement what most involved in the case already suspected. The same man who had held her captive and assaulted her repeatedly had assaulted Brittany, as well. Further proof - videos of those horrific acts, and of Brittany's murder - would be discovered among the ten full file boxes of items seized out at Lighte's Landing.

Sophie, who in addition to her physical injuries was severely dehydrated, was reunited in her hospital room with both her sister Susan and her friend Claire.

Her attending physician estimated Sophie's physical recovery would be complete in seven to ten days.

Her psychological recovery would take much, much longer.

After the initial surge of overwhelming, soul-searing, shattering pain, Annie Adams had gone blissfully numb. The drive back to Dallas had been a blur, as had the next two days.

On the morning of the third day, Annie rose at seven-forty, showered, and then slipped into the dress that Ben had always said was his favorite. She sat on her bed in Grace's spare room and brushed out her hair almost as an afterthought.

A light rap on the doorframe made her blink, and she slowly turned her head.

"Hi, Grace."

"Hey there, honey."

Grace came over and sat beside her on the bed.

"Everybody's been by to see you, you know."

"I know," Annie whispered. "I just... wasn't ready."

Grace carefully wrapped an arm around her and squeezed gently.

"I know. And they do too."

Annie laid her head on her friend's shoulder.

"I don't know if I can stay, Grace," she announced. "I think I want to go home, spend some time with Mom and Dad up in Tulsa for a while. Figure some things out."

"That's understandable."

Annie closed her eyes and sighed.

"How much time do we have?"

"It's scheduled to start in about a half-hour."

Annie swallowed hard.

"Okay," she managed, a single tear tracing down her cheek. "Okay."

"Come on, baby girl. I'll be right there with you the whole time."

The church was standing room only, but the team had saved the two of them seats, and Annie took her place among them, with Grace on one side of her and Hank on the other.

As the pastor walked to the front of the overcrowded chapel to begin the memorial service, Ben's work family linked hands, all the way down their row.

And when the pastor began with, "Our world is much less bright this morning. Those of us privileged enough to know him knew that Benjamin Allen Tinsing was a kind, loving, brave, and fiercely loyal soul," his teammates bowed their heads and mourned him.

"I think it's a good idea if I take a leave of absence," Annie murmured to Nathan later as they and the rest of the Dallas office gathered at Ben's favorite restaurant for his wake. "I need some time away to sort things out."

"I understand completely," he told her, and squeezed her hand. "Just know that we are always here for you, no matter what."

"I know, and I appreciate you all," she said. "It's just... too fresh. I need some distance."

"When do you plan to leave?"

"I plan to pack up my stuff at Grace's and head out within the next few days. I haven't spent much time with my parents in the last two years. Now seems like a good time to remedy that."

Ben's friend Brody strolled over to join them and wrapped her up in a hug.

"Rough day," he murmured, and she nodded.

"I need a favor, Brody. I was going to try to go over to the apartment, but I just can't seem to work up the nerve. And I know it's probably not the right time..."

"Annie, whatever you need, just tell me. I'll do what I can to help."

"Would you be willing to help me pack up my things that are still over there and put them in storage?"

"Sure, I would be glad to. When?"

"Sunday, around nine?"

"I will meet you there."

Two days later Nathan, Lizzie, Hank, Grace, and Mark sat around the conference table in the Dallas office, sifting through box after box of evidence and piecing together the exact timeline of events out at Lighte's Landing to forward on to the U.S. District Attorney's office.

Andreas, whose real name was John Fredericks, was prominently featured throughout the notes and files recovered from the onsite clinic. Joanna's real identity of Jill Youngblood came to light by way of fingerprint analysis.

Deeper research also revealed that Jill and John were first cousins – and that the duo had been implicated in several con artist schemes in a three-state area, but they had always managed to elude authorities.

Another suspect surfaced and was arrested based on the meticulous records kept – Lucas Dinsmore, who had been masquerading as crematorium director Filip Smith, and who had been brought into their scheme when he began dating Jill.

All told, the trio had committed fourteen murders over a six-year period. Only those victims with no living relatives had been returned to Lighte's Landing for burial. For the others, the residents of the property – including Remiel – were told that the individuals had recovered enough from their ailments to go home to their loved ones.

But none of the fourteen had ever even made it to the hospital, much less home.

The compulsive need to document that Jill Youngblood possessed resulted in a crystal clear and undeniable trail – selecting victims based upon possible financial gain, then making each target sick enough to warrant transport away from the property.

In each instance, John and Jill were the ones 'helping' their target by purportedly taking them to get medical attention.

But what was really happening, according to Jill's notes, was that instead each victim was taken to Lucas's crematorium, tricked into signing documents that named the trio's shell company as sole beneficiaries of their estate, and then killed, usually with an injection of succinylcholine, before being cremated to negate any chance of an autopsy.

With no death reported to authorities, each victim's revenue streams – social security, retirement pensions, and other means of income - continued to flow uninterrupted and was diverted into the bogus company's coffers.

Preliminary estimates of the trio's total take over the previous six years would come in at around two million dollars. Later, at John Fredericks' and Lucas Dinsmore's trials, the actual verified number read into the record was much closer to seven million.

By two p.m. Sunday every item belonging to her had been transported to the storage unit except for the few pieces Annie had decided to take with her to Tulsa. Those she shoved into the trunk and backseat of her car.

But she did take one thing that did not belong to her – Ben's favorite sweatshirt that he'd owned for years. The moment she'd seen it in the closet she had burst into tears, pulled it off the hanger, and hugged it to her chest.

Once she'd composed herself, Annie removed the apartment key from her keychain and handed it over to Brody.

"What's going to happen to the rest of his things?" she asked softly.

"He told me once when we were on our second tour in Afghanistan that if anything happened to him to take what I wanted from his CD collection and get rid of the rest," Brody answered with a pained smile. "Never in a million years thought I'd have to do it this soon."

"I'm so sorry. I know this is hard on you, too."

"Yes, it is," Brody replied softly. "But that is not your fault, Annie. And if you ever need anything, you know how to reach me."

"I do. Thank you, Brody. You're a good friend."

She tiptoed to kiss his cheek, and he watched her wipe away more tears as she got into her car and drove away.

Then he went back into the apartment and into the bedroom. Brody walked slowly to the far side of the bed and opened the drawer of Ben's nightstand.

"I kept my promise to you, my man," he murmured, his voice hoarse with unshed tears as he picked up and opened the ring box that a nervous and excited Ben had shown to him three weeks before. "You swore me to secrecy, so I didn't tell Annie about your surprise."

Click here to preorder End of Secrets – the seventh installment in the Vital Secrets Series – will be released in Fall 2022. Read the 'blurb' below!

Sometimes reunions aren't happy…

Still reeling from an unexpected loss, FBI profiler Nathan Thomas finds himself embroiled in war on two fronts – against a cartel that's declared open season on his team, and a shrewd serial killer desperate for Nathan's undivided attention.

Want 'Wall of Secrets', the Prequel to the Vital Secrets Series, *Free?* Visit my website.

Join my newsletter and receive 'Cast of Characters', a supplement to the series, Free!

One of the best things an author can receive is honest feedback about their work.

If you could take just a moment or two and leave a review on my book on BookBub, Goodreads, and other similar places, it would mean the world to me.

I appreciate your support!

Also by D.F. Hart

Vital Secrets

Mystery, Suspense and Thriller written as D.F. Hart

Book of Secrets

List of Secrets

Web of Secrets

Path of Secrets

Carnival of Secrets

House of Secrets

End of Secrets

Vital Secrets, Volume 1-3

Vital Secrets, Volume 4-6

Raven's Path - Coming in 2023

Mystery, Suspense and Thriller written as D.F. Hart

Raven's Rise

Raven's Attack

One Last Gift – An Anthology by James N. Richardson (D.F. Hart, Editor & Publisher)

Love's Defender Series

Steamy romantic suspense written as Faith Hart

Saving Brielle

Minding Mari

Protecting Andria

Another Try Novellas

Contemporary romance written as Faith Hart

Never Say Sorry

Save Me a Dance

Falling into Place

Love Notes

Read My Lips

Out of the Blue

One Last Try

The Another Try Collection

About the Author

D.F. Hart resides in Texas. Her favorite authors include Frederick Forsyth, Ken Follett, and J.D. Robb. Other interests include hidden object and puzzle games -she loves a good mystery storyline!

Of writing, she says: "It's a lot of work, but also an escape. A lot of tears and sweat go into a story, building believable characters, shaping the plot so that the reader can't wait to turn the page. Sometimes I'll wake up at 3 a.m. with that perfect line that escaped me earlier in the day running through my head. But it's worth it. And the brilliant part is, you get to create a little universe of your own. Anything can happen; there are no limits."

She happily pens mysteries and thrillers under D.F. Hart, and contemporary and suspenseful romance as Faith Hart.